Slowly they conve... looked a lot like a ma... see that, human or n... lot of desert between them, but Busk wouldn't be able to miss a detail like that. The intruder was unarmed, and Wilcox and he each had a rifle.

At four hundred yards range, Wilcox slowed. Busk stopped.

"Halt!" Wilcox bellowed. His voice reverted to a soft, clipped Maine accent, and the one word came in two syllables.

The running man came on. He had no hair. He had no nipples. His skin was gray and shiny.

Space aliens? Busk wondered as he aimed his rifle.

"This is a restricted zone," Wilcox shouted, sounding utterly innane.

"Halt or we shoot, damn it!"

Busk smiled grimly. Shooting wasn't in their orders unless people were inside the wall and trying to destroy materiel.

Wilcox raised his rifle and fired into the air.

The running man held out his arm.

Wilcox *melted.* . . .

Other TSR™ Books

Warsprite

Jefferson P. Swycaffer

Cover Art
JEFF EASLEY

TSR, Inc.
PRODUCTS OF YOUR IMAGINATION™

WARSPRITE

Distributed to the book trade in the United States by Random House, Inc. and in Canada by Random House of Canada, Ltd.

Distributed in the United Kingdom by TSR UK Ltd.

Distributed to the toy and hobby trade by regional distributors.

ADVANCED DUNGEONS AND DRAGONS, AD&D, and DRAGONLANCE are registered trademarks owned by TSR, Inc.
FORGOTTEN REALMS, PRODUCTS OF YOUR IMAGINATION, and the TSR logo are trademarks owned by TSR, Inc. ™ designates other trademarks owned by TSR, Inc.

First Printing, March, 1990
Printed in the United States of America.
Library of Congress Catalog Card Number: 89-52092

9 8 7 6 5 4 3 2 1

ISBN: 0-88038-915-X

TSR, Inc.
P.O. Box 756
Lake Geneva, WI 53147
U.S.A.

TSR Ltd.
120 Church End, Cherry Hinton
Cambridge CB1 3LB
United Kingdom

This book is for L. Jefferson Swycaffer, my father,
an accomplished man of many skills,
notably the stringing of barbed-wire fence,
who taught me to ride, shoot, drive, and wire dynamite.

My Thanks to Andy P. McQuiddy,
for giving me a by-mail tour of San Antonio.

PROLOGUE

No one has ever claimed full success in defining humanity.

Jettisoned from a future war of galactic scale and epochal duration, two robots fell to earth. Their missions had no relevance to the world they now stood upon. They were nothing more than castoffs, afterthoughts, tools used once and then discarded.

Like land mines buried and forgotten, these two machines remained dangerous, all the more so because their original purpose had been lost. The brutal warring cultures that had built them had few similarities to the humanity they might once have been; the dimensions across which they fought had little resemblance to Earth. Perhaps something essential in their human makeup had been lost. Perhaps it was remembered, but only dimly.

The two robots were like humans in as many ways as they were inhuman. One pursued; one fled. One dreamed; one fought. One showed the worthiness of humanity.

Afterthoughts sometimes have lives of their own.

CHAPTER ONE

Delta wandered naked through the snow-blanketed forest in bewilderment. All about her, huge shaggy-barked boles of thick trees shot up from the uneven, hummocky ground. A light snow was falling, without any wind. The flakes fell straight whenever an opening in the canopy of the treetops allowed them to; elsewhere, they accumulated on the bare boughs overhead. Periodically a branch would become overloaded with its burden of snow, and the cold white pile, still only loosely packed, would fall to the ground with a quiet rustling noise.

All about Delta, this soft noise pattered, an accompaniment to her own soft footfalls as she trudged over the rough forest floor.

The colors were unrelieved black and white. Trees, dark and cold, thrust up through soft banks of powder snow. There were no leaves on the trees, nor on the bare twigs of the undergrowth that clung here and there to the tops of steep banks. Trees and skeletal bushes waited with chill patience.

There was one other color in the forest: silver. Delta reached up and brushed a loose powdering of snow from her cold silver shoulders. Snow puffed up when she lifted her bare silver feet and crunched down again beneath her next step. Her nude silver body reflected the forbidding trees. It also reflected the gleaming white of the snow. Silver, shining, made of softly rounded plates and sections of a stiff, hard metal, Delta's body was in the form of a human woman, tall, slender, yet muscular and firm. Her thighs were thick and strong; her hands long, yet powerful. Her stomach was flat, sweeping up into high, arching breasts. Her neck was slender, supporting her long, high head.

She walked, not knowing where her next steps would take her. The woods climbed to her left, up into a pattern of hills, but that wasn't her path. Every now and again, to her right, gaps in the trees would show her glimpses of the world beyond. What she saw was not reassuring: rolling hillsides and the lower halves of stark mountains, their tops cut off by the dirty gray clouds. She walked on, and the trees closed back in. Her world was black and white.

She walked, and thought.

Fifteen minutes ago, I did not exist. Now I do. This world is so different. . . .

Different?

Fifteen minutes ago, I did not exist. What have I known? Where is Chroma? Where is Chrona? Where is Luma? I do not recognize Erga, Veloca, or Therma.

But . . .

Fifteen minutes ago, I did not exist. Who has bequeathed me this mind, these memories? I seem to know so much, but I feel I know so little.

I am following another: That is my purpose. All else is subsidiary. Knowledge and thought must serve this sole task. I am following another. He is ahead of me. I can feel him.

And when I find him . . .

What then? Will I know what to do?

He is mightier than I am. He has power. He is ahead of me . . . that direction . . .

I am following another.

Fifteen minutes ago, I did not exist.

Her face was long and high and oval. She had two silver lips, behind which silver teeth could barely be seen. She had a small, delicate mouth, above a diminutive chin. Above that, her face was a blank silver surface, without eyes, without a nose, without any features. Flat, bare, unrelieved silver swept from nape to scalp and down her smooth reflective face.

Her feet had five flexible metal toes each. Her long, sensitive fingers had two joints, and her thumbs one. Her hips were broad, and her shoulders wide and round. She had no genitals or anus, and her breath did not smoke in the cold air as she walked.

She walked, and thought.

Nowhere are there straight lines here. Every surface is a fractal, and every visual edge is also. I see only crooked, jagged lines. The heavy structures about me rise in broad, vertical, irregular shafts, then branch. The branches branch again. And again. No two of these structures are the same, but they all obey the same geometry. The angle of branching is preserved. Overall branch diameter is conserved. These things have grown here, rising up and taking form, like . . .

Like what? Crystals precipitating out of solution? Instructions diverging from a central coordinating unit? Or minds, branching in genealogical descent, growing down through time, through thought? . . .

This white matter, moving downward, falling . . . Why? The motes of it are fractals as well: involute, recursive . . . symmetries of great beauty. Randomly formed, yet flowing from a static center, molded by firm probabalistic constraints . . .

I am following another.

She walked on, and the afternoon slowly faded into an icy evening. A breeze began to pick up. With it, the snow fell more steadily, the flakes fatter, flying with greater force. Delta continued to walk, naked, through the storm and the gloom, wondering if Luma, the world's light, were fading away forever. Through the darkness, she walked, steadily, uncomplaining. The texture of the ground changed beneath her feet, from snow-covered forest humus to jagged rocky outcrops. Ahead, a faint roaring sound grew moment by moment louder. Delta, never having known fear, walked steadily toward it until it seemed directly before her and slightly below. The air thundered with the force of the sound, and the rocks beneath her feet trembled faintly.

Ahead of her, darkness opened away: a chasm. She had come, unawares, to the edge of a cliff, and below her was nothing but a drop to a watercourse rushing with hurrying snowmelt. So far, in her brief walk through the woods, she had never chanced to stumble or to fall. The thoughts were as alien to her as the world was. She continued forward; her foot came down on emptiness, pitching her forward, tumbling her for a long, heartsick moment through space. She fell heavily on her back, sprawled over the sharp, flinty stones by the water's verge. The pain of the impact was astonishing, but by luck, she failed to take damage.

A fine mist descended upon her flat, featureless face. She felt it and wondered. Beside her, the rushing and roaring continued unabated, very loud now for being so close at hand.

She got to her feet, listened for a long time to the sounds. The vague outlines of the canyon rim above her could be discerned in the quickly dying light. Before her, within arm's reach, unceasing motion rushed from left to right, sluicing noisily downhill, until the rocks resounded from the crashing force.

Slowly, carefully, Delta walked along the edge of the water, picking her way in thickening darkness over spray-slicked boulders. To ease her passage, she increased the coefficient of friction on the surface of her hands and feet, an ability made possible by the alien metal of her skin, and planned each move before making it.

A short while ago, I did not exist.

I am following another.

I am following Omicron.

* * * * *

Just how far ahead of Delta he was, although in the same darkness, the mind of Omicron didn't know. He knew she was after him, and he knew he must flee . . . but where, in what direction?

Equally uncertain to him was the nature of this place. Less prepared even than Delta had been when she first stood in a snowy forest, Omicron was also not equipped with the kind of keen, analytic mind that Delta enjoyed.

Flame blossomed, and sharp, actinic lights blazed out in swathing, devastating beams where Omicron found himself. Timber burst in loud, rolling explosions as water and winter-slow sap superheated. Flaming gases and liquids jetted from Omicron's hands; incendiary beams of coherent light swept the clearing.

Finding himself unattacked, Omicron paused . . . then opened up again with his weaponry at the slow-moving cloud of steam that expanded to engulf him. None of his weapons could dissipate it; Omicron took to the air in desperate flight.

Eventually, flying blind, he plowed into the solid granite face of a low mountainside. He flailed at the stone cliffs, even while sliding downward among rattling fragments of stone. At the last, he toppled over a ledge and fell into a narrow space behind a two-story wooden house, near the center of the small town of Ramshorn.

The town consisted of six buildings clustered beneath the cliff, built on a small level space before the mountain dropped away again below. Omicron knew nothing of the small towns of men; he saw only threats. Rising, he lashed out again in fury, squandering energy against rocks and trees, against the buildings and their inhabitants, unable to discern the features of the terrain from his imagined foes. His weapons were terrible. The eleven people who lived in Ramshorn died in instants; some never even awakened from their sleep.

Trembling in a brittle wrath that was only a minor step removed from fear, Omicron released new destructive energies into the evening, not knowing that any who might have opposed him were already dead. An unseen, cold light seeped from his outstretched hands, and where it passed, things died. Tall, winter-dormant trees writhed and slumped, their cells dying, bursting and liquefying noisily. Black, steaming sap flowed for a while, then refroze; the limp, naked trees twitched, moving slowly in the murk like freshly killed snakes. Omicron's rampage lasted for only a few moments. Then, spent, he stood alone in the darkness.

Robotic, like Delta, Omicron was in every other respect as unlike Delta as the two were each unlike the snowy wilderness in which they had landed. Omicron stood manlike, although too tall, too broad in the shoulders and hips. His limbs and body were covered with skin, but it was a thick, gray hide more like leather than like human skin. His legs and arms bulged with musculature; his belly was flat and corded. Like Delta, he was hairless; unlike her, he had been given a face. On a human, his face would have been handsome, even appealing, deep-featured and thoughtful. His eyes were a dark, slatey gray—observant eyes, intellectual eyes. His obvious physical power lent a sinister aspect to his searching expression. More ominously, he seemed frightened. He looked about himself, searching for the pursuit he knew could not be far behind.

Standing in the fading light, he paused and thought. He knew himself hunted. He knew himself helpless. Only flight could save him. Flight to a place of safety.

Only . . . He looked up into the dark sky. There was no place of safety. He blinked in sudden fear. Had he waited in this one place too long already?

Nothing he saw here made any sense. He sought to understand before his fear drove him to flee again. He tried to draw conclusions about this utterly alien terrain. He ran his hands over his body, knowing that it, as well as his mind, had not existed even as recently as twenty minutes ago. His intellect was not equal to the task. Trying to analyze his own mind, he again failed.

Planting his huge feet firmly, he tried to reason. And yet all was confusion. He stood in uncertainty, thinking about the antigravity engines encased beneath the armor of his skin and frame, yet afraid to take to the air.

Seen as a unit, he seemed more humanlike and incomparably more powerful than Delta, his pursuer, but certain trade-offs had been made. His intellect was not the equal of hers. His body was slightly more fitted to this world, although it could never easily pass in human society. His mind was substantially more alien. These were the choices that had been made in their creation.

While he paused, the twisting, writhing trees slain by his wanton use of his weaponry slowed and became still. Their branches and twigs were knotted, curled into fantastic, tortured shapes. Inside the shattered houses of Ramshorn, the cindered remnants of human bodies lay strewn about, equally twisted.

You're after me, my foe, Omicron thought, fear clutching at him. He knew that he didn't dare wait to meet her.

Come, then, he thought. *Come follow me. I cannot evade you forever, but I can find a battleground that fa-*

vors me. He was totally unaware of the enormity of his crime in having devastated Ramshorn village. It wouldn't have mattered to him if he did understand.

Activating his flight engines, he soared into the sky, this time understanding a little of the nature of "up" and of "down," yet still unaware why these directions should be different from any others. His scientific intellect could not compete with Delta's; his tactical and strategic intellect, however, had been well formed.

Flight was necessary.

Fear was also. He knew he could not run forever. He knew he would someday need to stop and face his enemy. He would fight . . . on his terms, in a time and place that he had prepared in advance, under conditions that favored him. He would fight, but no sooner than he must.

Evening gave way to midnight, then to the darkest part of the night, and finally to a snowstorm-filled, wind-howling paleness that passed for morning. Omicron had put almost a hundred miles between himself and Delta. However, he didn't know where Delta was. She, linked to him by a sympathy more subtle than any gross means of mechanical detection, knew his exact distance and bearing. She knew him, and could never be unaware of him. They were paired, pursuer and tremulous prey.

Robots.

CHAPTER TWO

Sam Taramasco—"The Trapper"—licked his lips and looked about the crowded terminal of the San Antonio airport. Outside, in the cloud-dimmed daylight, a small jet shot off, up into the warm, humid air. Everywhere he looked, he saw people—young people, students jetting in or out now that the colleges had let out for the winter break.

He looked at the students, seeking for the difference in detail that set them apart from him. Was it his age? He was only a year or two older than most of them. He smiled thinly. He also wasn't much wiser. They were callow and noisy, dressed in their rigorously casual winter attire. Sam, in his dark brown business suit, carrying a thin leather briefcase, looked and felt foolish. He was too small to wear a suit, and too young. He kept moving, avoiding confrontations. He dreaded the moment when a helpful tourist or airport official would look down at him, smile, and offer to help him find his folks.

He knew himself to be the moral and intellectual superior of this crowd of rushing students. Deep inside, however, he felt very much like one of them.

Look at them, he thought to himself, his face twisted with bitter emotion. He knew he was jealous, yet all he could do was accept it. Around him was the best of the new generation. Surgeons and research attorneys in the making . . . or bag ladies and street people and guys who'd never amount to a damned thing. He saw two young women, girls really, blondes, chatty and boisterous. "Californians," he sighed with deep disdain.

He strode on, trying to look as if he was above the level of this rabble and knowing that he was really just another of them, with one important difference. They could still succeed in their ambitions, but he had already failed. *God, how hard it is to hide my jealousy, to bottle up my hatred.*

His jet-black hair hinted at his mixed ancestry: Italian and what the census bureau euphemized as Native American. What had his great-grandfather been? Comanche? Sioux? Apache? Aztec, for god's sake? The family lore told of an abduction and a rape, and a child growing up in shame. Sam, smiling thinly, knew that the "Native Americans" hadn't had many opportunities for rape. He wondered where the shame really lay.

High cheekbones and a ruddy, brownish complexion hinted at his ancestry, although he knew it spoke more of his grandfather's Italo-Turkish origin than of the rumored American Indian abductor. He was quite short, which added to his youthful appearance.

Chromosomes from all over the wide world crawled,

swam, or flew, coming thousands of miles in order to merge. He shook his head, smiling. *And all they got out of it was me.*

He was dawdling. He had a job to get done, and it was best done quickly. Still he lingered, people-watching.

Big, tanned Dallas businessmen lifted their nose at what they saw as the provincial little San Antonio airport, seeing all the Mexicans waiting behind counters and driving trucks. Lanky, towheaded, red-necked farm boys craned their necks and gawked, clutching their tickets the way a lottery winner would clutch his, lest it be torn from his grasp. A nun shepherded a stiff coterie of young schoolchildren, each as like the other as brass parts stamped out in a mill. Another nun, identical to the first, guarded the rear of the procession.

It's no damned fair! Sam raged behind his flat, impassive face. *Everybody's just like somebody else. . . .* He clamped the thought off, choked it away, denied it. It passed, as quickly gone as all his thoughts of loneliness.

Most people don't know why they aren't rich, he mused, comforting himself with an old, familiar ache, replacing the deeper, sadder pain of loneliness. *But not me. I'm not rich, and I know exactly why.*

He shrugged and began to walk a little faster toward the boarding gate. He fell in at the end of a line of people waiting to be processed through the security metal detector.

Most people aren't rich because they haven't dared to try new, crazy things. Their imaginations aren't up to their potential. And that's sad, damn it! He looked once more about him at the colorful throng of people, caught in the hurry-up-and-wait of the airport.

It's sad, because every one of these people has infinite potential. I do, too, but I'm daring to live up to a bit of mine.

Two security guards stood by. One sat behind the X ray, glancing over the interiors of carry-on bags. The other leaned against the black plastic frame of the metal-detecting gate. Sam saw them as gray people, sexless. Then he shook his head and looked again. There was no such thing as a cardboard cutout of a man or woman. These two, both men, were as individual as Sam was. . . . No, he refused to go quite *that* far. . . . They were men, one with a mustache, one without, their ubiquitous Texas tans slightly paled from their indoor duty. The man who was standing rested his hand on the butt of his revolver in an unconsciously lazy posture that looked dire and threatening at first glance. The other, scanning the screen, had a faraway glazed look, not unusual for someone watching a display screen for the whole of his shift.

Sam tossed his briefcase onto the conveyor belt and watched it disappear beneath the curtained recess where the X ray would violate it. He paused for a fraction of a second, then passed through the doorway frame of the metal detector.

The detector buzzed. Although it was a soft sound, Sam stopped short, a blush darkening his already dark skin. The guard straightened casually and appraised him.

"Pull all your keys and coins out of your pockets," he said, his expression simultaneously relaxed yet alert.

"Uh . . . okay . . ." Sam stuttered. It bothered him that he he didn't know, just then, whether he was playacting or was really embarrassed. He placed his huge ring of keys and a meager handful of change into a small plastic tray that the guard held forth.

"Lotta keys."

"What?"

The guard smiled at him. "Lotta keys."

Sam smiled sheepishly. "Yeah." He glanced at the bundle. There couldn't have been fewer than fifty keys on that ring.

"Go on back through the gate. Just the way you came." The guard guided him gently with a nudge. "Okay, now walk back on through."

No buzzer sounded.

"Go on ahead, then," he said. "And don't forget your briefcase."

The flat leather case had emerged from the X-ray machine and had come to rest on a platform at the end of the small conveyor belt.

"Oh," Sam said. "Right." He scooped up the case and walked on down the hall on unsteady legs.

The X ray had failed to detect his bomb or his gun.

Most people don't know why they're not rich, but me, I know. He saw three men ahead of him, waiting. And they were obviously waiting for him.

I'm not rich because every time I build a better mousetrap, I go and get my pecker caught in it.

He walked up to the three men. They were airport officials, not just security men but security and administration staff. Their expressions were serious and displeased.

"Are you 'The Trapper?' "

"The Trapper, sirs, at your beck and call." He forced his voice to sound sprightly and fey.

"You got through?"

"No problem."

The heaviest of the men, overweight and balding and pale because he spent *all* of his time indoors, shook his head in disgust. "Damn it!" He looked at Sam as if suddenly suspecting a trap. "Open the case."

"Here?" Sam said, his eyes wide and astonished. "In the hallway?"

"Come along," said one of the others, a tall, slim, tanned, and exercised man whose hair was graying. He wore his thick gray business suit as if he had been born to it. He was obviously an airport administrator; by a process of elimination, Sam determined that the third man had to be the FBI agent.

Two of them led the way, while the portly airport security chief fell in behind. His eyes never left the briefcase. The administrator, in the lead, unlocked a door and let them all into a small office. He flipped on the lights, and a fan started running, just like in a bathroom.

"Open it."

Sam smiled and let the case drop open. There, for them all to see, was a flat wad of pink, puttylike explosives, with a detonator that looked like a wad of chewing gum stuck into it. There were no wires, and even the batteries were no more than globs of sticky chemicals.

He opened the divider between the two halves of the case, and the gun was revealed.

The security director ran his hand through the few hairs remaining atop his round head and squinted at the ungainly weapon. The airport administrator looked at it, seemingly without comprehension. The FBI man glanced once at Sam for permission, then reached down and lifted the gun from the case. He held it near his face.

The gun looked like a vaguely gun-shaped biscuit, a croissant baked of some unusually porous dough. It was small and lumpy, unpleasantly irregular. A crooked, stubby trigger protruded from beneath it. The FBI agent was a gun expert, deeply appreciative of the mechanical beauty of firearms engineering. His expression now reflected a mixture of disdain, disgust, and unwilling appreciation.

"One shot?" he asked.

"Yep." Sam raised an eyebrow, giving his face a humorous cast. "The thing flies into powder in your hand." He laughed uneasily. "Hurts like the devil. It's like getting your hand slapped . . . hard."

"Range?"

"Five, maybe seven feet."

The agent shot him a glance.

Sam shrugged. "Aboard an airplane . . ."

"Hell," the security man breathed. "You could fill a suitcase with forty or fifty of these. . . ." He shook his head.

"Is this one loaded?" the agent asked, as if oblivious to the security official's idea.

"Of course," Sam said blithely. "Otherwise the test wouldn't have been—"

"Right."

"I've got the formula here—" Sam patted his jacket pocket—"if you guys want to look it over."

"Jeez." The security man reached for the gun. The FBI agent held on to it for a moment longer than necessary, then released it to him. "Jeez." He held it up and sighted along the pitted upper surface.

"Just mix the ingredients together, then bake at a low temperature."

"How low?" the FBI man demanded.

"Low enough so that the ammunition round inside doesn't detonate." Sam looked at him coolly.

"Detonator?"

"Pyrophoric chemicals. You break the airtight seal. That's what the trigger does. That's *all* that the trigger does." He reached inside his jacket and brought out an envelope. He waved it in the air for a moment, then let it fall to the desktop.

The FBI agent nodded. "We'll be mailing you your money."

Sam stared at him for a moment. "Mailing me my . . . Hey!" He forced back his anger. "You promised me my consultant's fee on delivery!"

The agent swallowed. "But you're not a consultant yet. You've never signed on, officially. We can't—"

"Can't what? What do you want me to sign? A goddamn loyalty oath?"

"The law requires—"

"I don't give a damn what the law requires!"

"That's the problem," the agent said, not loudly.

"I've worked with you guys before. C'mon." A thought came to him. "You're not mad at me because I'm so damned good at making bombs, are you?"

The agent said nothing.

"Damn it, this is good stuff! It passes your X-ray machines. And the pistols . . . it took me a hell of a long time to come up with that formula. Hey, it isn't my fault your detection systems aren't as good as they ought to be. I'm just trying to help you make America safer."

The agent lifted his head sharply, then relaxed and smiled. "Sure, kid. But, you see—"

"You know," Sam continued, his face hot, "I'll bet there are people out there who'd pay plenty for it. You'd rather I go to the Arabs?"

The agent took a deep breath. "No. I'd really rather you not do that." He controlled himself with an effort. Sam, seeing the strength that the man held in check, realized that he really didn't want to mess with him. Then the agent's expression changed, and he looked at Sam quizzically. "Kid, you're good. You're diligent, and you're honest. But here's the kick: We'd have to deputize you in order to hire you as a consultant. We have to *know* you won't go to the Arabs. Or anybody else. Look, we've learned a lot from you, and we'd like to continue working with you. We can get you lab equipment, machinery, and if you keep producing results, we can get you a real consultant's job."

"Like a kept man. A goddamn company man putting in his ten to four." Sam's voice grew louder and louder. The airport security boss and the administrator both looked acutely embarrassed. "A stooge just like you!"

The agent tried to smile but only managed to look coldly angry. "Look, I meant what I said, kid. You're pretty bright. I'm glad you had the sense to come to us with your inventions. A really dumb fellow might have tried going the blackmail or bomb-threat route. You're not like that. I'd like to help you. I'd like to hire you. But you're going to have to give us some of the things we need."

"Like what?"

"Your full name."

"You already know that." Sam laughed. "You've run a thousand checks on me by now."

"I want to hear your name from you. You've been playing 'secret agent' games with us. You call us and tell us to meet you at the airport. The first time you tried that, we had to decide whether or not to shut the place down."

"I explained that!" Sam protested. "It's a test! A demonstration! I didn't misrepresent myself, and I didn't say anything ambiguous."

The agent waited for a moment. "We asked you your name. You said, 'I'm the Trapper.' "

"I know. And you had marksmen waiting for me, too."

The agent's smile wilted a bit. "I never told you that part."

"I spotted them."

"You're good, kid. What can I tell you?"

"I'm not going to sign any damned security documents!"

The airport security man bulled forward and faced Sam closely. "He's not asking you to, dummy."

"Hey, back off. Leave the kid be." The FBI agent sighed. "You antagonize people, Trapper."

"You're a real stinkard, you know that?"

The agent shook his head. "The money's on the way. Give some thought to what I've said. We'd like to have you. Stay cool."

"Yeah." Sam left the office and made his way back through the airport to the parking lot. For mid-December, the San Antonio sun was unpleasantly hot, even when dimmed by a thick, high layer of clouds.

The money's on its way. Great! They'd promised him a thousand dollars. He wondered when it would arrive at the post office box he held under a false name. He wondered, too, if an agent would be there to watch him get it.

This is just wonderful. Sixty percent of everything I get goes straight into Mr. Cook's collection account, and I get to try to live on the other two-fifths for the next month. He took a deep, unhappy breath. The hot air dried his throat. *And I still owe the rental fee on this damned suit.*

Sam Taramasco, "The Trapper," had made an expensive mistake a year or so ago. He'd slandered the president of Cook Chemical Industries. The lawsuit had drained his resources, and he'd lost badly. Cook, wealthier than Sam could ever become, now earned sixty percent of everything Sam took in.

He also saw to it that Sam was unemployable.

Most people don't know why they aren't rich, Sam sighed to himself. *But I know why I'm not. I've got a big mouth.*

He walked across the parking lot and headed for the streets.

CHAPTER THREE

The darkness had become absolute, impenetrable. Delta plodded along by the side of the river. The roaring water vibrated, sending small tremors through the solid stone. Delta felt this trembling and tried to learn from it. The rocks seemed so hard; she had no way of measuring their internal resonance and thus discovering anything useful about them.

She went slowly and carefully, but stumbled anyway. Her foot, stretching out, feeling for a toehold, was seized and pulled by the cold, swift water. She lost her balance and toppled bodily into the whirling stream.

For the next few seconds, Delta flew down the center stream of the cold-water rapids, fetching up against deep-anchored stones, then flying loose again, propelled by the stream. The water forced her deep, and she ground along sharp river-bottom gravel. She slammed against sheer rock walls to her left and right, then bounced again into the swiftest part of the river.

She struggled to break free but found the current impossible to fight. The river thrust her along, grating her mercilessly against stones and unclimbable rock banks.

She discovered pain; she learned some of the limits of her body's flexibility. She learned that cold granite rocks that had been whetted for centuries by this icy river were even harder than her hard metal skin. Her surface was dented, scraped, scarred, torn. . . .

Once she passed roughly over the jagged teeth of a rock wall, where the water heaped and hissed. Her body cleared it, but her right foot became caught in a gap between two stones. The magnitude of the sensation of pain stunned her. Her foot bent, held, then was dragged on through the notch. Its internal joints and workings, the servomechanical drives that simulated the functions of muscles and tendons, were crushed and twisted. Her foot hung, numb and limp, as she flipped and crashed over the driving rapids.

She learned even as she suffered. She paid attention to the environment, studying it carefully. In only a few moments, she had divined the essential nature of water: fluid, noncompressible, massive, constrained to move in laminar-flow patterns, gravitationally driven. Of the nature of solid and immovable stone, she learned more painfully. Stone was hard, highly massive, and inert. Her mind extrapolated the forces and energies and envisioned a flow of stone. She imagined an avalanche of great and small rocks, rushing down a broad canyon and gathering speed. . . .

She tumbled into a deeper pool, where the water flowed momentarily slower. Delta caught her wits and dove, swimming down and back until she found a place where the forces were small enough for her to counter. The darkness was inky, silken. . . .

Her hands could reach out and brush the huge underwater sides of boulders. With her good foot, she stirred up the pool's gravel-littered floor. Cold water poured into the pool some eight feet over her head, swirled around and about, and flooded out again ahead of her. She bent down and caught up a handful of gravel. The rough grains made a tiny gritting noise when she squeezed them together in her fist. She squeezed more tightly and understood that these fragments of stone were not infinitely hard. They had been broken away from their parent boulders and were destined to become fine sand. She knew, then, why the river boulders were smooth and rounded, yet the rocks of the cliff face had been jagged.

She felt with her hands at the places where her metal skin had been dented or torn. The dents broke her surface symmetry, but they had ceased to ache. She tried to wriggle her damaged foot. It responded sluggishly, awkwardly. She could sense that it was not utterly ruined; she hoped it would bear her weight.

I can control my skin, she thought. With an effort of will, she caused her surface to become frictionless. The water that had tugged at her as it moved now glided effortlessly over her, around her. She stretched out her hand and was surprised to feel how little resistance the water gave against the motion. *Is this all?* she wondered. She knew, instinctively, that it was not. Her skin was now harder than it had been. She touched the surface of the boulders behind her, then scraped at them with her fingertips. She could feel the stone grating under the pressure. Running her hand carefully over the surface, she felt the lines of parallel grooves.

My ankle is ruined. And it had no need to be. She shrugged in an almost human gesture of resignation. *Now I know.*

She waited patiently in this comforting pool, in a quiet underwater corner where the currents were playful and gentle. Before very long, a glimmer of light penetrated the corner. She found that she could see the outlines of the individual stones and the pale, flat floor of the pool.

The light grew stronger. Delta carefully swam upward to meet it.

Climbing out of the pool and onto the rocks, she got her first view of the hurrying water. For several minutes she watched it, entranced by the endless random variations of ripple and swirl and by the way the water foamed where it broke against the rocks.

She had room to climb to a rough natural pathway just out of reach of the water's sucking grasp. She was forced to favor her damaged ankle. It had stopped hurting, but it still failed to function properly. Overhead, the sky continued overcast, a glowering mass of swift-moving gray clouds. No snow fell, and Delta saw the way the snow already on the ground melted, forming slow-moving rivulets that snaked across the frozen soil and thence down the rocks to feed the river.

She thought for a few moments and smiled. In her mind, she considered the high mountains, branching rivercourses (very like the branches of a tree), and snowfalls that melted into larger and larger rivers. What then? She failed to imagine a worldwide watersink; she couldn't dream of the ocean.

Omicron was over two hundred miles away, still roughly ahead of her, at a lower altitude.

The knowledge of his location gave her pause. She knew, without seeing him, without hearing him, exactly where he was. Omicron was in *that* direction, at *that* distance. Something linked him to her, some echo or signal or unknown sense. It was as if he made a noise she could hear at any distance. The knowledge was also discouraging to her, for he was so very, very far away, and widening the distance at a rate that was faster than she could walk.

She would have to be patient, then. Limping slightly, Delta continued resolutely across the cold waste.

*   *   *   *   *

Omicron, flying high through the clouds and into the sunlight, saw the world with a different perspective. He dove, then climbed, then dove again, flying low over snowfields and greenswards. A cloud of small birds, alarmed by his approach, shot out of a stand of bare trees. Omicron crashed through them, radiating his deadly energies. The birds, shrieking in pain and distress, fell to the ground, writhed, then melted into the snow. The snow softened a little, surrounding the small pools of thick red liquid, then quickly cooled. Had Omicron stayed behind to look, he would have seen a pattern of red spots in the glistening snow, as if the trees had, by some arcane alchemy, been bleeding from the tips of their branches.

He flew high, shooting up into the fringes of the

atmosphere. He paused, gazing blankly at the curved limb of the world. Fatigue caught at him. He needed energy.

Slowly he spiraled back down to the high mountains.

*   *   *   *   *

It was nearly noon when Delta noticed two white snow hares nuzzling the snow aside, digging with their front paws. At almost the same moment, she first became aware of the sun as the source of the day's light. She moved to examine the two rabbits, but they raised their heads at her approach and quickly took flight. Delta cocked her head to one side in puzzlement.

Later, she left the stream behind and walked in a direction more nearly toward her distant quarry. She climbed hills and descended them on their far sides, always moving more and more downward. Her damaged foot slowed her, especially when climbing, and she learned exactly how much of her weight it would bear. She watched the sun, although its gleam was visible only as a bright patch of light behind the high masses of dense clouds. The light swelled and faded as the clouds moved with the wind; Delta watched, and tried to learn. Once she saw a high-circling hawk, its wings extended but motionless. Delta marveled, her eyeless face raised in an expressionless salute to the bird's rare beauty.

Before long, she saw a thing that was, in this world, unlike anything she had seen before—a straight line.

It was still far away. She picked up her pace and moved toward it. As she neared it, she perceived more and more details. A line had been drawn along the hillsides, climbing and dipping, but perfectly straight in its plan. The sun was fading toward the western hills when she finally reached it. She stopped, put out her hand, and gently touched the top strand of barbed wire in the five-strand fence.

The fenceposts were narrow steel stakes, driven into the hard ground. Delta touched the metal and thought of herself. Other posts were spaced regularly. Delta lay her cheek next to the wire and sighted along the fence. It ran straight down one slope and up the next, which it topped, and then was lost.

At the wire itself, Delta gave only the most cursory of glances. Two wires twined, and sharp barbs protruded in a four-spined threat. The wire was made of cold, hard metal. Just like her.

That the fence was a barrier seemed obvious. Unwilling at this point to defy the purpose of anything she found, she turned to her right and followed it.

Less than eight miles beyond, she found another sure sign of intelligent design—a gravel road.

It had become nearly dark when she stepped down off a low bank and onto the road's surface. She could see enough to understand the purpose of the road, to see how the gravel had been spread smoothly over the packed and flattened dirt beneath. She looked to her right. The road curved smoothly away and disappeared around the brow of a hill. Ahead of her, the road straightened, running parallel to the fence, which continued straight ahead, as if haughtily unaware of the road that had swung in from nowhere to join it. It was the fence that defined the lines across the territory, and the road must perforce adhere to that definition.

Delta walked ahead, her metal feet crunching with a limping, uneven rhythm over the gravel. What manner of beings had built the fence and graded the road? Delta didn't know.

It soon became quite dark. In the darkness, then, she walked more slowly, feeling for possible irregularities in the road's surface.

The night's darkness deepened to utter blackness. The wind, which had been dying down throughout the day, picked up again, a brisk, keening breeze that sighed over the snowfields and sang a strange low moaning song as it caused the tight-stretched strands of wire to hum. Small bits of wood or straw, even the smallest pieces of gravel, flew up in the wind, to be flung against the back of Delta's metal legs.

A cold, bleak daylight found her still walking. Omicron was farther away than ever. Delta wondered if the chase would ever end, or if she was a being destined to walk forever in the direction of her enemy, never closing the widening gap between them.

In the meantime, the puzzle of the world she was now a part of kept her mind busy and almost happy. Sometime during the night, the loose, sliding gravel of the road had been replaced by a hard, compact surface.

More and more evidence of intelligent design came to be visible in the growing light of dawn. She saw roadside reflectors and traffic signs. She saw plowed fields. She paid particular interest to a cement culvert under the road, through which a stream gurgled noisily. And she saw, and sighed contentedly, that the marching fence had kept pace with her throughout the night, and that it accompanied her still. Its music had comforted her when the breeze blew the hardest; now, in a silent, slightly misty dawn, the fence ran beside her without noise.

From behind a hillock in the middle distance, away to her right, on the unfenced side of the road, a tall plume of gray smoke rose. She saw it and understood that it was shaped by the same kinds of forces that shape clouds. Ignoring it, she walked on.

Trees, growing in regular order and at regular intervals, closed in on both sides of the road, making it a shaded avenue. And the fence stopped, or, rather, metamorphosed. The five regular strands of barbed wire and the steel-stake fenceposts came to an abrupt halt, and the function of the fence was taken up by another kind of barrier. It was a fence of white-painted wooden slats, nailed to uniform square wooden uprights, also painted a crisp white.

Delta smiled wryly. The fence had been a reassuring note of constancy in a world whose conditions seemed to vary wildly. With a foolish emotional tug, she approached the last of the fenceposts and rested her hand momentarily on it. She touched the wire in what was almost a caress.

Then she went back to the center of the road and continued to walk.

* * * * *

Five miles farther on, she encountered two men who were walking in the opposite direction.

At some distance, perhaps a mile, she could see them, although indistinctly. They looked enough like her for her to assume they were like her in most ways. That thought reassured her; she was not utterly alien to this world. She watched the two as they walked, and she saw that they walked as she did, legs pumping, arms swinging, shoulders swinging, torso swaying slightly to balance the stresses. Neither of them had a limp, but she doubted somehow that either of them had spent the night tumbling down a watercourse.

They saw her, too, at perhaps half a mile. One nudged the other and pointed. The other pulled off his cap, shaded his eyes, and made an unusual gesture with his free hand. They kept walking.

At a quarter-mile, the two men stopped. Delta, not knowing why, continued toward them.

When Delta was some three hundred yards from them, they began to talk, and their speech grew louder and louder. They gestured at one another, and they gestured at Delta, but what they did most was talk. They seemed agitated, and Delta wondered why.

When at two hundred yards, Delta suddenly realized what she should have understood earlier: If she was like them, then they had the right to expect her to be like them. There were two of them, and only one of her. They had halted and she had not. And she was walking in the opposite direction along the road. Apparently these lapses were deviations from the proper use of the road, and these people were as confused as she was, they by her impropriety, and she by their reaction to it. She halted.

The range was close enough for her to discern other differences. But how important were they? What were the parameters? What dimensions of differences existed? They wore clothing from head to foot, while she was naked. They bore loose wisps of hair on their heads, which drifted from beneath their caps, while she was hairless, her head smooth and round. Their faces had deep contours, with large noses in the center and with two wide, mobile eyes beneath puzzled brows. Her face was like theirs in the construction of the chin and mouth, but above that, her face was smooth and blank.

They were pale, and she was silver.

"Who the hell are you?" one of them shouted at her. She didn't understand the words, couldn't sense the fear that the anger covered up, and she had no answer.

She couldn't just stand and do nothing, however. In a tone of voice as much like the man's as possible, she responded, "Who the hell are you?" She had never spoken before, and it surprised her to hear her voice. It was higher, softer, and slightly more musical than his had been.

The two men looked at one another, a quick, nervous glance. Then, their eyes fixed on Delta, they began to confer, their voices low. Delta saw that the two men were not identical, either in dress or in formation. Their faces seemed to present the easiest way to differentiate between them, but other differences showed also. One was taller and slimmer than the other. One's hair was brown, while the other had shorter gray hair. Their proportions differed—the lengths of their limbs, the width and angle of their shoulders, the size of their boots, which implied a difference in the size of their feet.

They patted and prodded each other for a moment, then began to walk very slowly toward Delta. Delta, in tremendous uncertainty, mimicked their pace, approaching them slowly and gradually.

The humans came within one hundred yards of the robot. They slowed their steps, but continued to edge forward. Delta slowed also. She wondered if she should move just the way they did, with faltering footsteps, with arms moving loosely and held a little apart from the body, one foot moving forward and the other foot drawn up to it in a gait totally unlike their earlier normal stride. She compromised by adopting that shuffling gait but kept her arms hanging straight by her sides, her back stiff, and her neck vertical.

At fifty yards, the two men stopped again, and so, perforce, did Delta.

"Is it a man in a suit?" one of them said. Delta could hear the words, which made no sense to her.

"Ain't a *man* at all. Look at the knockers." The other's voice was different from the first's. Delta wondered at the broad variation of their voices and their bodies. The data points provided too small a sample for any meaningful statistical measures, but she still found it intriguing in her naivete.

"You know what I mean. A guy—gal?—in a suit?"

"It's a gal's voice."

"Y'think?"

"Um-hm."

"No face, Pop."

"I noticed that."

"And where'd her nose go? Her face's too flat."

"Um-hm. I don't like this. I don't like it at all."

"Who the hell are you?" the first one, the shorter, wider one with the brown hair, shouted again at Delta.

She held perfectly still, trying to guess how to make a reply. She thought about answering, "Is it a man in a suit?''—the first man's first comment to his companion. She smiled to herself. It was too risky, no matter how much it appealed to her. "Who the hell are you?" she responded.

"Where you from?"

"Where you from?" Delta echoed him.

"Gettin' nowhere, Son. Hang it up."

"Pop, this is . . . well, I dunno, but it's gotta be . . . well, important, wouldn't you say?"

"Nope. Not important. Dangerous."

"What're we gonna do?"

"There's a phone back at Winkler's."

"The FBI?"

"Nope. Sheriff DeSoto."

"Yeah . . ."

They turned away and walked at a goodly speed along the road. As they walked, one or the other of them always kept his head turned, keeping an eye on Delta. She stood motionless, in silence, until they had passed out of the range of her vision.

I don't know what just happened, but it isn't my purpose to understand. I have a different purpose.

I am following another.

Shaken, but necessarily resilient, she began walking once more.

CHAPTER FOUR

The morning air still hung fresh and cool and motion-less over the lonesome paved road. Delta followed it, marveling at the richness of the countryside's textures. The parallel rows of trees flanking the road stood silently and patiently. Tall and thick, yet naked, their leaves having long since fallen away, the trees parodied Delta's nudity. Their branches were reflected in her mirrored surface as she trudged, limping, down the center of the road.

Beyond the trees, visible between their thick boles, she could see the light frosting of snow that still covered the ground. It was little more than a layer of damp slush and would melt away in perhaps a few hours. For now, though, it was a clean white sheet from which trees, bare bushes, and fenceposts sprung. The horizon was still closed in by the thin morning mist, limiting visibility to a range of about two miles.

In this cold, unmoving air, sounds carried farther. Delta heard the faint distant noises of morning, without knowing their import. A horse whinnied and was answered by another in a neighboring paddock. The sound was a high, breathy tremolo, lent power by deep undertones. Dogs barked, repeating from quarter to quarter their shrill reports. Far, far away, the river roared on, flowing over the spillway lip of a concrete dam.

And Delta smelled the smells, which were more subtle than the smells of the forest. The faint chemical traces of leaf mold and winter-still sap in the trees drifted slowly through the silent air, along with the fresh rain scent of the melting snow. The macadam surface of the road had a peculiar odor, pungent and sour.

As she walked, she saw driveways rolling off from the road, always to the unfenced right. It seemed unfortunate to her that the regular spacing of the trees had to be sacrificed to make room for these. She considered following one, but quickly discarded the notion. The pattern of the world seemed to favor travel forward and down, in the direction of increasing complexity.

Even as she thought about it, she heard a new noise. It was as different from the random animal noises about her as the straight man-made fence had been different from the dispersed pattern of the forest's trees. It was a low mechanical throbbing, a humming or roaring sound; the surface of the road trembled, very slightly, beneath Delta's feet.

Not knowing fear, she continued on, wondering in what form the sound would manifest itself.

The sound grew in intensity. In only a few minutes, she saw the black and white sheriff's car appear, growing more and more solid as it materialized out of the mist. She looked at it and slowed her pace. Its headlights blazed, and Delta gazed raptly at the color of the lights. Atop the car, the red emergency light was unlit, but Delta saw the bright red of the dome and was obscurely pleased. Colors—chroma—meant that the world featured something, at least, that she understood.

She stopped. The car sped on toward her, then braked to a swift, smooth halt. Delta, seeing the operation of the car, instantly grasped the concept of the rolling wheel and understood why the road had been flattened and hardened, and why the grade had always been limited. She saw the plume of hot exhaust fumes jetting from the rear of the car, and she smelled the raw, rancid smell. She heard the uneven idling of the engine. These things she did not understand and thus ignored.

Most importantly, she had not failed to observe the clear glass windows and windshield and the three men inside the car. She waited patiently while three doors opened, letting the men out.

Two of them were the ones she had seen before. The third was very much like them: pale of skin, bearing deep facial features, and wearing clothes. Unlike them, he had a thick red beard and mustache and wore a star of shining metal on his chest. At his hip hung a large revolver in its black leather holster.

"Owe you two an apology, seems," the third figure said softly, his eyes fixed on Delta's unmoving form.

"Never mind that," said one of the others. "What the hell *is* it?"

The sheriff pushed his broad hat back up on his head. "Dunno."

"We tried talkin' to it," one of them said. "Nothin' happened."

"Did too," the other snapped. "She repeated you."

"How's that?" the sheriff asked, his eyes never leaving Delta's blank, featureless face.

"I said, 'Who the hell are you?' an' that's what she said right back."

"Um-hm." The sheriff shrugged. "Might's well give it a try." He raised his voice. "Who the hell are you?"

Delta waited for a moment, then repeated the meaningless words. "Who the hell are you?"

"Told you."

"And she walks with a limp. What's that mean?"

"Naked as a jay, and just as shameless. Pretty."

"Pretty *big*," the sheriff muttered. "Six-foot-six, unless I miss my guess."

"What're you gonna do about it?"

The sheriff crossed his arms across his chest. "I don't have the faintest idea." He shook his head. "Maybe I can get her in the car. Not good to let her just parade around out here like this."

"How you gonna get her in the car, Sheriff?"

"Open the fourth door, will you?"

One of the two men shrugged and went to the car. He reached inside, unlocked the door, and tugged it open.

"Okay, now go around the other side and get in. You, too."

"Hey, I ain't ridin' back there with . . . with . . ."

The sheriff never looked away. "Keep your voice down and do just as I say. You get in the back, and you—" he shrugged his shoulder to indicate the other man—"get in the front. And not another word out of you."

Sullenly the two men obeyed.

The sheriff raised his hand and beckoned slowly to Delta. Then he backed away, one step at a time, moving toward the car.

Although there was much that Delta still did not understand, several important elements had become clear. The men communicated complex ideas through their speech, by a complex arrangement of pitch and tone and other sounds made by rasping and slapping their lips and teeth and tongues. She could mimic the sounds but had yet to learn the meanings. But there was more: She began to get the vaguest glimmer of the workings of authority. These two men had seen her and had brought the third with his car. Now he disposed the men's actions and sought to direct Delta's movement as well.

Because she had no reason to resist, she obeyed, following him and climbing lithely into the car. The sheriff closed the door after her, at which point the other two men somewhat reluctantly closed theirs. Finally the sheriff got in, slammed his own door, and, turning the car about, drove at some speed back along the road the way he had come.

Delta bore the ride in silence, watching the men. The sheriff alternated between watching the road and eyeing her in the rear-view mirror. The man in the front passenger seat held his neck stiffly at an angle, facing just ahead of the sheriff, but staring sidelong at Delta. The man to her right jammed himself up against the door, trying to keep as far from her as he could. He watched her with wide, trembling eyes.

They're afraid of me! Delta realized with a start. Although she had seen little of the world, and less of men, she understood pain. She thought of her foot, torn in the cold-water rapids, and she remembered the flight of the two rabbits that had been startled by her approach. She slowly began to gain a faint, imperfect knowledge of danger and of avoidance.

She studied the men, but she also kept a watch on the landscape. The road, straight for so long, curved sharply and began to descend. The row of trees gave way to an open, hilly countryside, and as the mist began to burn off with the faint warmth of the sun, the horizon opened out. Green fields appeared, sheltered by neighboring hills. Delta was astonished by the beauty.

Huddled in a tiny valley, the small town that they came to next seemed little more than eight or nine buildings clumped together astride the road. Trees, bare and stark, were everywhere; a tongue of the forest filled the valley, and the houses were nestled among the boles. The buildings had been painted bright, gay colors, which winter's force had faded slightly over the years. But Delta saw the bright blue, white, and red of the gasoline station, the brilliant green and yellow of the motor hotel, and the deep brown of the general store, and she was fulfilled. Even the pristine white of the church, its steeple rising to a sharp point above the town, seemed colorful; the shape of the building caught and held her attention.

Sheriff DeSoto slid the car to a brisk halt before his sheriff's substation and leaped out of his seat in a rush. The two farmers were almost as quick to flee the car, and indeed almost fled the scene entirely. Curiosity overcame their fear, however, as did an element of shame. They stood back, their heads upturned, looking at Delta.

"Okay, you fellas stay there and wait till I get her inside." The sheriff looked around a moment and saw two or three people coming out of the roadside diner, onlookers brought out by the way he'd thrown gravel from his car's tires when the car slid to a stop. He pushed his hat back on his head, rubbed his bushy beard, and drew a deep breath.

Delta quietly let herself out of the car, although it took her a moment to fathom the workings of the inside release. Since the sheriff and the others had left their doors ajar, she did also. As the sheriff stood by in uncertainty, the onlookers saw the shiny alien robot and stopped abruptly, as if they had stepped into an electrified fence in the middle of the highway.

"You go explain this to them," he snapped, and the two farmers, looking back over their shoulders, hastened off to join the spectators.

"You, get inside," he said to Delta. The words meant nothing to her, but she understood, barely, what he meant by the gestures he made with his arms and hands. She preceded him up the concrete steps onto the substation porch, walking carefully, favoring her right foot.

The sheriff had his pistol out now, and the expression on his face was cold and businesslike. He edged ahead of Delta to open the door for her. She entered.

The inside of the jailhouse was the warmest place Delta had ever known. A kerosene heater in one corner threw out an almost tangible blast of heat. The air held the faint smell of the burning oil, as well as a strangely fragrant hot metal scent. The scents of the sheriff and his leather and his guns also filled the small office. Incandescent lights hung from the ceiling, and an uncovered lamp sat on the corner of the desk.

What most struck Delta, however, was the way the room was cluttered. Papers littered the desk and had fallen onto the chair behind it. A small trash can had been crammed to overflowing with papers, soda pop cans, pencil shavings, and orange peels. A rack of rifles stood against one wall, the guns secured by a chain and closed in behind glass. Files had been shoved every which way into shoe boxes, cartridges for the guns had been poured into coffee cans, and a vast crowd of photographed faces had been pinned to a bulletin board.

Delta would have examined those more closely. Even at a glance, she could tell that the faces were all human faces, like those of the sheriff and his friends. No two were alike. But the sheriff had gone before her and continued making his slow, careful "come hither" gestures. Delta shrugged and followed him.

He opened the barred gate to his one-cell jail and gestured for Delta to go in. She went partway in, then froze, her mind working faster than it ever had before.

The cell had no exit. The door was barred, as was the window. She saw, and ignored, the details of the bunk, the shielded light fixture in the ceiling, and the glistening stainless steel toilet. She saw the bars.

They were just like the strands of wire in the fence that she had followed for so long only yesterday. And like the fence, the door of the cell had a function.

Containment.

Everything in the office was contained. Bullets in cans. Papers in boxes. The kerosene-flame heat inside the stove, and the heat from the stove inside the building. Guns behind glass in a case on the wall. Rubbish in the can on the floor.

And Delta inside a cage. She shook her head and backed out quickly. She looked at the sheriff, who had gone quite pale. He frowned, gestured for her to go back inside. His other hand was clamped close to his side, and the pistol jutted out from his white-knuckled grip.

No. No. No. Delta wished she knew how the humans communicated with one another; she sought to explain, with gestures of her own, why she could not allow herself to be contained.

The sheriff put his free hand roughly on her shoulder and shoved her toward the cell. Delta staggered, caught herself by the edge of the iron door frame, and pushed herself slowly out into the room. The sheriff had backed away. He stood in the center of the room, seeking to use his body as a barrier. Delta recognized that he was trying to contain her with himself, that he was ready to serve as a door, a fence, himself.

She walked forward, toward him, and when she moved toward one side, he moved with her, blocking her. She sidled the other way, and he followed, always standing between her and the door.

"Listen, little gal," he said, the words meaningless to Delta. "Neither of us wants any trouble. . . ."

She touched him, the metal of her breasts pressing against his shirt front. He was softer than she. He shoved at her shoulders, but this time she would not be moved, and she was much stronger than he was. Moving slowly yet inexorably, she bulldozed him out of her way, never thinking to use her arms for extra leverage. He tried to trip her in a judo throw; the action staggered her, but her superior dexterity allowed her to recover her balance almost instantly.

She moved past him, going for the door. He dropped on her from behind and linked his arms around her in a bear hug.

He has me contained! Delta thought in momentary panic. With a quick, frightened effort of will, she caused her metal surface to become frictionless and superlatively hard. She flexed her shoulders, and the sheriff's grip slid loose.

In a last attempt to stop her, he kicked out, aiming a low, vicious strike at her injured ankle. For the second time in her existence, Delta experienced pain. She fell to one knee, which, being frictionless, slipped from beneath her. She had to change the consistency of her skin before she could brace herself with her hands. The sheriff moved closer, then shook his head and backed away. Delta stood slowly, backed up, and opened the door.

"Who the hell are you, lady?" he asked plaintively, dropping his pistol back into its holster.

She turned to face him one last time. "Who the hell are you?" she said, and was gone.

*   *   *   *   *

Sheriff DeSoto might or might not have given pursuit. Chasing robots wasn't in his usual line of business. But while he shook his head and wondered, his telephone rang. Abstractedly, he answered it.

A deputy of his had discovered the ruin of the small town of Ramshorn. Eleven men and women had died. The buildings had been razed. The trees had been destroyed. The sheriff's eyes narrowed. The deputy at the other end of the line described the twisted, half-melted trees, the fire-blackened rocks, and the charred bodies of the citizens of Ramshorn. "It wasn't natural," he kept repeating. "It just wasn't natural!"

"Too many unnatural things going on around here," the sheriff said softly. He rubbed at his nose. Getting that robot lady back had suddenly become his first priority.

She was involved, one way or another. It only stood to reason. He put his hat and coat back on and went out into the morning street.

* * * * *

Delta soon realized that the sheriff's plan to contain her was not to be so easily thwarted. She had only run a little way along the road when his car roared up behind her. Trying to outrun it only put an intolerable strain on her ankle. The car overtook her easily. She dodged aside, and the car swerved to follow. At the last moment, she dived off the road completely, tumbling down a low bank to splash into a snow-melt bog in a ditch. Leaping up, she clambered out of the ditch on the side away from the road. A narrow space had been cleared, beyond which the trees gathered, nearly as thick as they had been in the forest she had first seen.

The car, as she had surmised, was contained by the road. She hurried away, moving deeper and deeper into the wood until she no longer heard any sound of pursuit.

She looked down at herself. Mud and grime dulled the shiny hue of her silver skin. She reduced her surface coefficient of friction, letting the mud drop away. Once again she gleamed.

Several times during the day she saw humans, and every time they saw her. She found that she could run faster than they could, and hurriedly escaped their shouts and frantic gestures. Before long, she was surrounded by a cordon of men advancing in a tight line. She was forced to dash between two of them. They closed to cut her off. She collided harshly with them, wrestled free of their embraces, and darted away into the forest.

By nightfall, she had traveled only a short distance, in absolute terms, from the village, but had traversed nearly forty miles in her flight. She had learned how to double back, how to use rough terrain to her advantage, and how to move silently when men were nearby.

She didn't perceive until late at night that the men followed her by her footprints, which were distinctive enough. No one else would be abroad barefoot in the dead of winter, and no human footprint would sink quite so deep into mud or damp leaf mold. She only caught on in the pitiless darkness of the night, when she saw men crisscrossing the forest floor, bending to examine her trail with their lanterns and hand flashes. From that point on, she took care to leave fewer clues of her passage.

Shortly before dawn, the sky split from side to side with a gigantic bolt of lightning. The ground-shaking cannonade of thunder followed so closely after that there was no perceivable interval. Moments later, a heavy rain began to fall, the drops huge and fat, pummeling Delta joltingly and drumming with a musical metallic clatter upon her head and shoulders. She saw how the drops splattered mud when they hit, and she realized that her trail was being obliterated for her.

Lightning flashed again and again. She was puzzled by the varying length of time between flash and subsequent crack of thunder. The rain flowed off her smooth surface, and she marched slowly from tree to tree in the darkness. To her surprise, when the morning came, she saw no sign of her pursuers.

Am I not contained? she wondered. She had never known freedom before, but now she found that she enjoyed the sensation.

* * * * *

Mrs. Lucy Gessenby, an elderly recluse, was known by several nicknames to the locals. She was "Missus Gessenby," "Widow Gessenby," or, most unkindly, "Old Widow Jeeby." Her husband was gone, her children grown, and her only companionship the imaginary company brought to her home by the television.

It was a fine television, her only joy: a huge twenty-five-inch color set, with remote control and no less than twenty-three different channels to switch between. The dish antenna in her backyard connected her, by satellite relay, to programming from all over the globe, but that meant nothing to her. She was content to sit back in her overstuffed chair, lift her feet up onto her hassock, clutch a warm blanket around her, and take in the colors and voices through her blank, staring eyes and delicate, nearly deaf ears. So deaf was she, in fact, that although she kept the volume turned most of the way up, only the faintest whisper of sound penetrated to her. Many television programs, fortunately, came with closed-caption signals, so that people who had special decoders could read the subtitles at the bottom of their screens. That, too, meant little to her.

Once every week, her oldest daughter drove out to visit her, to collect the bills and other mail, pay the payments, sit and converse for a time in sign language, and then drive away. To Mrs. Gessenby, these visits were only a little more real than the visits she received regularly from movie stars, big-city detectives, foreign spies, and hospital doctors.

She never knew that she had another visitor, a gleaming silver robot in the shape of a naked woman, who stood motionlessly atop a wooden box outside her window. Had she known, it likely would have meant nothing to her.

Delta watched Mrs. Gessenby's television, understanding only a little of what she saw and heard—at first. Her mind was active, alert, and efficient, however. She organized the images and sounds into statistical columns, broke them down by structure, and reassembled them, over time, into a language: English. Spoken and written.

The words, blaring overly loud from the television set, puzzled her the most. She listened for long weeks, filing the information away and reconstructing it again and again. Every word seemed to refer to another; every word depended on all the others. They modified themselves in unusual ways, warping themselves around a cycle of crooked syntax and twisted semantics until sometimes Delta thought she must go mad from the illogic of it all.

"Who the hell are you?" the farmers and the sheriff had asked her, and she had answered in kind. But the words, the insane words . . . "Who" was a placeholder, a vacant variable, a box or can like those in the sheriff's office, for containing a man, woman, animal, or robot. "The" was a pointing finger, like the sheriff's last gesture at her. It indicated things, but as with a pointing finger, it meant nothing until one followed it to see what it was aimed at. "Hell" was the word someone used the same way Mrs. Gessenby used the volume knob on her television: It made the other words louder. "Are" was a road, and it linked one place with another. Some words had roads between them, and she knew that she could say that some of them "are" the others. Dogs "are" critters. Men "are" handsome. The Russians "are" coming. And "you"—"you" was Delta, Delta herself, a thing that fingers pointed at, that roads led to, and that containers gaped for. Delta was the "you" that "was" "the hell"—who?

Why am I different from the humans? she wondered. She had seen the young starlets in their bathing suits and very quickly—television being what it was—understood the difference between the sexes. But no one *ever* appeared nude, and no one had shiny silver skin.

Three times during the month she spent outside Mrs. Gessenby's house, the sheriff came around. He entered without an invitation and spoke loudly to the elderly woman. He never realized that he could have whispered just as well as shouted. She was reading his lips.

No, she hadn't seen a strange woman, she said in her odd, squeaking voice. Yes, she would keep an eye out for her. Yes, she knew his phone number.

The sheriff went outside, walked slowly around the house a few times, and then drove away. Mrs. Gessenby was already back in her chair, intimately linked with the television.

* * * * *

Every night, after the old woman had turned off her tired television set and hobbled slowly into her back room to sleep, Delta looked for Omicron. Simply by standing still and feeling, reaching out with her mind into the darkness, she could tell where he was. The link between them was similar, she guessed, to the link between the television set and the people whose images appeared on its screen. Most days Omicron was farther away than he had been the day before, but not always. Often, he was to the southwest, and at a lower altitude. Some days he didn't move at all. Other times he made long trips. He seemed to stay between five hundred and one thousand miles away, and he never passed to either the north or the east of Delta's position.

She knew where he was.

She wondered if her contact with the sheriff had been providential, for she knew, deep within her being, that her purpose was to arrange the containment of Omicron.

"I am following you," she said softly under the winter trees. She didn't want to wake Mrs. Gessenby.

CHAPTER FIVE

Heat haze gave the distant blue mountains a warped, wavering, surreal appearance. Flat desert sands, strewn with a sharp litter of rocks, stretched away in the distance, fading in and out of focus. Desert plants pointed their spiny limbs upward at odd angles, twisting and writhing in the superheated air.

Private First Class Edward "Buster" Busk, not long out of his basic training at Fort Dix and his advanced training at Fort Gordon, slowly walked his rounds, the loose sand sliding beneath his boots. When he had dressed this morning, his clothes had felt fresh, crisp, and clean. Now they sagged and felt limp, and wetness showed through under his arms and across his chest and his back, dampening his collar. He knew the sweatband of his cap was moist and oily as well, and his socks stank.

His clothes were wilted, but Busk wasn't. He sighed deeply, inhaling the hot, dry, furnace air, and kept his eyes open. He was alert. He even managed to keep a bit of spring in his step.

"Mister-One-Hundred-and-Ten-Per-Cent," they'd called him. He'd been overweight and out of shape when he enlisted, and his life had seemed to be less at a crossroads than at a dead end. The army gave him something to push for: It set goals in front of him. He rose to the challenges.

Little by little, the weight had come off. One and two at a time, he increased his quota of push-ups. They'd made him healthy, physically fit, strong enough to patrol. Nor had they slain his inner spirit, but in the way of the army, had refined that, too. He'd been an indolent, spoiled youth, a freethinker without discipline. The army had whipped the unconscious nihilism out of him and given him jingoism in its place. He cooperated gladly, being intelligent enough to see the rewards that endurance would offer him.

He never stopped trying, and eventually he always succeeded. He helped the men in his platoon to win the softball championship at Fort Dix. He fired his rifle with grim accuracy. He choked down his nausea and passed the tear-gas test. He plugged away and never gave up.

At 1600 today there would be an underground test of a nuclear device. Busk was on the desert line, patrolling alongside a long, barbed-wire-topped length of chain-link fence. His squad had been warned of protesters and picketers and told to walk the perimeter.

Busk shrugged. He wished they were still doing aboveground tests. He'd have rather liked to see the fireball, especially in the night sky. An explosion was just an explosion. As a boy, he'd made fireballs in the sand with a mixture of gasoline, alcohol, and black powder. He shook his head and looked out into the desert. If the Department of Energy wanted to make bigger explosions way out in the middle of the desert, that was fine with him. Why should it draw protesters?

Sixteen men and women had been arrested at the front gate only yesterday. They'd demanded that the test be canceled. Upon receiving no response, they spread out and blocked the access road. The guards, men with whom Busk had bunked and trained, moved out and arrested them.

Now another group was moving out across the desert, trying to sneak into the test range and force the cancellation that way.

They wouldn't be so brave if we were still doing aboveground tests, Busk thought.

He sipped a little water from his canteen and spat it out again. The air was magnificently hot. Busk's uniform wilted a little further, but Busk did not.

On the horizon of the sand, just where the mountains flattened out into the desert, a figure moved. Busk shaded his eyes and looked carefully. A man, roughly three miles out.

Okay, Busk thought. *That's why I'm here.*

The figure walked on, his pace unusually swift. Busk frowned. He glanced at his watch and counted the man's paces. The heat haze distorted the figure, who seemed almost to be swimming through the blazing air. The man was forced-marching, twenty-six paces in fifteen seconds.

He must be a real iron man, Busk thought. *He won't be here for a while, though.*

He lifted his radio. "Sentry Five to guard."

"Busk?" The corporal's voice was tired. Busk tried not to smile, but couldn't help himself. Wilcox was from Maine, and he hated this desert with all the Yankee hatred he could muster.

"Someone out there. Coming in from the northeast." He waited while Wilcox fished out his binoculars. Doubtless he had to set down a cold beer first. Busk looked in the direction of the guardpost, six hundred yards behind him, down the line of the fence. It looked black and boxy and uninteresting.

"Got him. Keep your eyes open for more."

"Yep."

Busk thought about unshipping his own binoculars but decided against it. Wilcox would radio in the report, and a jeep would soon hurtle over the treacherous, rocky ground. One more protester would find himself in a Nevada state jail, awaiting prosecution.

That man was certainly marching fast.

Busk smiled. A man rushes headlong to his imprisonment.

Minutes passed. The man came on, his legs flashing. The sun shifted slowly, falling behind Busk, shining on the front of the strange, hurrying man.

No one can keep up that kind of pace in this heat. A small thrill of alarm passed along Busk's spine. From the south, a plume of dust moved—a jeep on an intercept course. To Busk's eye, the jeep was moving no faster than the swift-pacing man.

He continued his patrol—to the bend in the fence, another four hundred yards, then turn and come slowly back. The jeep seemed to take forever to come near the man. Busk stopped, shaded his eyes against the sun with both hands, and watched. The jeep drew up alongside the man. The man refused to stop. The jeep swerved to cut him off. Busk's eyes narrowed. The man was outpacing the jeep.

A sudden cloud of dust erupted. Busk waited for a long, long minute, then heard the faint popping of semiautomatic weapons. He squinted. A blazingly bright light flashed, a bar of light that seemed to hover in midair. Busk blinked several times to make the light go away.

The dust cleared. The jeep moved on, with no one in it, creeping at idle speed over the desert floor. The man jogged on, coming nearer. No soldiers could be seen.

Busk thumbed his radio. "Sentry Five to guard." There was no response from Wilcox.

Despite the heat, a chill flew down Busk's back. He ran the six hundred yards to the guardhouse. Wilcox waited, pushing uselessly at the keys of his dead radio. He looked up at Busk.

"Can't get anyone."

Busk swallowed. His hand gripped his rifle more tightly.

Wilcox straightened. "Looks like it's you and me." His face had tanned quickly in the desert, but his New England skin tone still somehow showed. His blond hair, sweat-dampened, snaked over his forehead.

The two men, rifles hanging from their hands, ran along the fence for six hundred yards, then paused to catch their breath. The marching man continued toward them, seemingly unaware of their presence.

"Big one," Wilcox muttered.

Busk squinted. "Six-foot-six. More. Three-fifty.

Marching at more than eight miles an hour."

Wilcox looked at Busk. "How do you figure that, Busk?"

"I've been watching him against the ocotillo."

Wilcox's fatigue almost led him to ask what the difference was between "ocotillo" and ordinary damned cactus. Everything in the desert was so dead and sharp. . . . He took a drink from his canteen.

"Let's go." Wilcox stepped off into the desert.

Busk wanted to argue. He wanted to tell Wilcox to wait here, while he went out to confront the man. *We better not leave the fence unguarded*, he thought nervously. He ground his teeth together and ran out after Wilcox. The men in the jeep would fail to report, and the army would send a follow-up team. For now, though, the job was in their hands.

Slowly they converged on the marching figure. It looked a lot like a man, but it was naked, and Busk could see that, human or not, it wasn't male. There was still a lot of desert between them, but Busk wouldn't be able to miss a detail like that. The intruder was unarmed, and Wilcox and he each had a rifle.

At four hundred yards range, Wilcox slowed. Busk stopped.

"Halt!" Wilcox bellowed. His voice reverted to a soft, clipped Maine accent, and the one word came in two syllables.

The running man came on. He had no hair. He had no nipples. His skin was gray and shiny.

Space aliens? Busk wondered as he aimed his rifle at the strange figure.

"This is a restricted zone," Wilcox said, sounding utterly inane. The running man was only two hundred yards away now.

"Halt or we shoot, goddamn it!"

Busk smiled grimly. Shooting wasn't in their orders unless people were inside the wall and trying to destroy materiel.

Wilcox raised his rifle and fired into the air.

The running man held out his arm.

Wilcox *melted*. Busk only glimpsed it, out of the corner of his eye. He thought he saw a flash of deep purple light; he turned and thought he saw it envelop Wilcox. He was never sure. It was a swift death. Wilcox was dead before he had time for a last thought. His cells burst from within, and his pale flesh turned bright blood-red and seeped into the thirsty sand.

Orders were clear about self-defense. Busk knelt, lifted his rifle, and emptied the clip into a tight pattern of hits, centered on the man's chest.

The man stopped, then walked slowly forward toward Busk.

Busk frowned. His body seemed to shake from the pounding of his heart. He lifted his rifle to use it as a club.

The man stepped up close and took it out of Busk's hands.

Busk tried to struggle, tried to strike the man in the face. The man's eyes were gray and shiny, the same leaden tone as his skin. The man looked at Busk, then planted his palm over the soldier's face. Busk felt his eyes close, although he never lost consciousness. He tried to move and could not; he'd been paralyzed.

The sand beneath him cushioned his fall, although a

small, sharp scrap of rock got lodged under his left knee. He lay supine, eyes closed, feeling the warmth of the sun tanning his face. He heard the footsteps of the man, running along toward the testing grounds. The sunlight came through his eyelids, red and warm. Busk wanted to sleep, to forget having seen Wilcox dying, to forget this impossible man who had slipped past them.

Distantly he heard the man rip the chain-link fence apart.

Hours passed. Busk tried to reckon the time.

Then the ground trembled, and he knew what time it was. They hadn't stopped the test. They should have. That man—or monster, or whatever he really was—had been in an unstoppable hurry to get near it.

High above, he heard an airplane circle. He thought he heard sirens, but he knew that the control center and test range were far too distant. He waited. The sun lowered itself in the sky.

Buzzards, Busk thought irreverently. *They'll be along soon, and I can't move a muscle!*

Footsteps crunched through the sand. A hand gripped the front of his uniform and dragged him up. The man had come back. He threw Busk crudely over his rockhard shoulder. Busk's eyes stayed closed. The man jogged on, maintaining his impossible one hundred paces per minute. His shoulder was painfully hot, unnaturally hot, not so much as if the man burned in a fever but as if he were made of heated metal.

Oh, god! He's probably radioactive, too! Busk groaned inwardly. He smelled smoke and didn't know whether it was the front of his shirt or his own skin.

Soon he passed into unconsciousness.

*   *   *   *   *

Omicron's timing had been exact. Clawing with his hands, he had driven a tunnel down through the stone and into the test chamber, where a forty-eight-kiloton nuclear weapon waited to be detonated. The fireball that should have been contained by nearly a quarter-mile of rock had an escape route, although for the flaming gases to jet free, they first had to get by Omicron. Thirsty for energy, he inhaled the nuclear fire and absorbed it through his skin.

Replenished, he returned the way he had come. On the way, a small human figure teased at his curiosity. He picked it up and carried it with him, the way a man might pick up an odd bit of metal from the street and hold on to it for no particularly important reason.

*   *   *   *   *

Busk awakened on the damp floor of a cavern. Solid blackness, the darkness of night or of the grave, hung before his eyes. It was evening over the desert: it was night within the cave.

The man who had captured him stood before him.

"God," Busk muttered. The man was as tall as he'd guessed him to be, and as bulky. His skin glowed, a cool, unpleasant fluorescence. His body was still hot.

"God," the man said, mimicking Busk almost perfectly. To Busk's surprise, the same word—"god"—echoed out of his radio, still clipped to his hip.

Busk clambered carefully to his feet. He looked about,

trying to see details by the faint light that his captor gave off. The cavern was a wide, open one, probably high in the mountains. He wouldn't be able to climb out, not with that monster watching him.

Busk shook his head, pointed his thumb at his chest, and said, quietly, "Busk."

The man's eyes narrowed, then he pointed his thumb at his chest in the same matter-of-fact gesture that Busk had used.

"Omicron."

The voice was harsh and flat. Once again it came over Busk's radio at the same time he heard it with his ears.

My radio! Busk thought. He grabbed at it and keyed it to transmit. "Mayday! Mayday! All posts! This is Private Busk. All posts. Help!" There was no answer.

"Omicron," his captor repeated loudly, angrily. He shook his head oddly, as if annoyed to hear Busk's radioed voice rattling in his head. Busk stared, wide-eyed. The voice echoed oddly, coming from the monster and from his radio. There was no other radio traffic. His captor was both transmitter and receiver of radio signals, but otherwise Busk was very much alone.

Busk held his hand out, palm forward, feeling the heat radiated by Omicron's skin. It probably was more than just heat, Busk realized. *He went in there and he exposed himself to that blast. Damn!* He sighed. *I'll know how much exposure I've taken when my hair starts falling out, I guess.*

Omicron held out his own hand, palm forward. Busk touched it gingerly. It burned, but not badly. Busk guessed it to be between two hundred and three hundred degrees.

Here we go, then. . . . . Beginning with the list of obvious nouns—man, rock, light, dark, Busk, Omicron— he stepped the strange being through his first language lesson.

CHAPTER SIX

The Quentin Corey Museum of Nature and Antiquities had, as two of its more interesting antiquities, its curator, Madeline Lenoir Schenk, and the caretaker, Grant H. Alexander. Although they were museum staff and not exhibits—not per se, anyway—the two elderly gentlefolk served subtly as a reminder of a bygone era. Their day had been a polite one, but a bloody one as well. The war that had seen the introduction of poison gas had also begun with Germany's formal application to Belgium for permission to invade. Madeline enjoyed reminding people of that, in hopes of demonstrating the innocence and innocence lost, the *sans souci* and worldwide misery that had come into being in so short a period.

"They would go calling us their 'lost generation,'" she once said, in her fractured English. "I am lose? *Zut!* In San Antonio, United States of America, at desk, have pen in hand. No lose." That, then, settled that.

Outside, the heat had grown steadily; within the museum's thick stone walls, the temperature remained a cool sixty-two degrees. The building, officially closed, stood darkened, and only a lone, wan circle of light shone from the high ceiling skylight. Three sounds could be heard: first, the sloshing of Grant's mop along the smooth tiles of the floor; second, the faint, faint rustling of pages being turned as Madeline wrote in her journals; third, the soft, insistent beeping of an electronic alarm.

Madeline's office was no more than a niche on the main exhibit floor of the museum. The backs of display cases left room for her desk, for her wheelchair, and for very little else. A high cabinet contained most of her personal belongings. Her wastepaper basket was clean and empty.

"Maddy?" Grant's voice, although enfeebled by age, still held a querulous, stubborn note.

"It is what, Grant, that you are want?" Madeline asked, not looking up. Her voice was soft and mellifluous, although her accent was murderously thick. She was hunched well forward in the antique three-wheeled wheelchair she favored.

"When will that lad return to silence his equipment? I mistrust the sound of that beeping."

"It reminds you of something, *non?*" Madeline put her pen aside and spun the chair about. Behind thick eyeglasses, her eyes were alert and saucy.

"Tanganyika, nineteen eleven." Grant straightened, holding his mop upright. "The insects made a noise just like that." His eyes narrowed. "A small, repetitious sound, perhaps easily overlooked. We lived with it and we slept with it. One day, it stopped suddenly. . . ." He hefted his mop, tucked it under his arm and sighted

along the stick. "What a whopping big rogue hippopot-
amus! A bull, lust-crazed in the mating season. It took
all three of us to bring him down—Fenton with his car-
bine, Dexter with his small-bore, and me with my seven-
fifty express."

Madeline smiled at him. "Was this over your Lake
Rukwa exposition, or when you hithered upstream for
Lake Victoria?"

"Expedition," he corrected her. "Lake Rukwa. I'll
never forget . . ."

The plaintive beeping of the electronic alarm ceased
abruptly. Grant whirled, aimed his mop, and grimaced,
the feral bloodlust hot in his aged face.

"Don't shoot, Grant." A figure materialized out of
the cloaking darkness. "It's only me. Sam."

"Sam?" Madeline wheeled herself forward to meet
him. When she was near him, she stood up from her
wheelchair and walked a bit. "You are looking up in the
dumps."

Smiling, Sam Taramasco acknowledged her effort at
sympathy. "Yes. And down in the mouth. Sorry. The FBI
wasn't interested in my bombs."

"Faddle!" Grant snorted. "Bombs in airplanes. Bad
form. Bad form." He ran his hand over his seamed face.
His short-trimmed white hair gleamed in the near-
darkness. "I don't think much of this action-at-a-
remove warfare, if you ask me. When I was a lad, war
had an element of chivalry left in it. Hunting, too, for
that matter."

Sam, attentive and polite, nodded. "Big-game hunting?" he asked, deferring to one of Grant's favorite topics. "I agree completely. No one could feel anything but

disdain for modern poachers with automatic weapons."

"Very right!" Grant leaned his mop against the wall and launched into a thunderous retelling of one of his tumultuous African safaris.

Sam winked at Madeline, then settled down to listen. Madeline walked slowly and stiffly about the office, then reluctantly returned to her chair. Grant H. Alexander, as stuffy as he was, served Sam as a bracing yet soothing mental balm. But when he truly needed comforting, he knew that he would still be able to turn to Madeline.

Grant's blustering story buffeted Sam, and he paid close attention. But his eyes were drawn again and again to the back of Madeline's wheelchair. She was not completely paralyzed in her legs, he knew. He had seen her walk several long city blocks without any sign of weakness or pain. But her steps were always unsure, and she always came back to her chair. Unlike Grant, she told her stories only reluctantly. Her injury had come to her on September 9, 1914, when she participated in the famed French taxicab race to reinforce the front at the First Battle of the Marne. Her taxicab had been struck by a howitzer shell. The soldiers in her charge had died. She had been sixteen years old at the time, and although she remembered the entire incident with a peculiar, ageless clarity, she had only once spoken of it to Sam.

"Did you know," she had said, her voice low, her eyes troubled, yet the humor in her soul as irrepressible as ever, "we kept running our meters? Patriots, but taxi drivers also always." She had smiled wanly and shaken her head. "French honor wins this war for us, you may be insured."

Sam knew her true secret. She could speak English as

well as an Oxonian professor of literature, sans accent, with an utterly clear inflection and intonation. She merely chose not to, and her twisted malapropisms were an affectation. So, at times, was her wheelchair, although at other times, she would find herself in deep pain.

She let Sam keep his electronic equipment in an unused room at the museum, when otherwise he would have had to sell it. She let him live here as well. The museum, of which she was the chief curator, housed antiquuities and artifacts, both natural and man-made, from the distant past. One small niche, however, was crammed with the most up-to-date electronics equipment available. That was also where Sam kept his bedroll and a small satchel of clothing.

Grant's tale wound down eventually, as Grant's tales always did. He lost the thread of his narrative, not through forgetfulness but from his habit of constantly following new trails of associations in his mind. After people had listened to Grant for any length of time, unless they were blessed with unusual patience, the phrase, "Ah, but that reminds me . . ." on his lips would fill them with a dull, hopeless ennui. Sam, although not patient at all in his normal life, never grew tired of the old man and delighted in whatever he might be reminded of.

Nor were Grant's tales apocryphal: Many of the exhibits in the museum were prizes he had brought back, and zoos throughout the world maintained breeding stock directly descended from the animals he had captured alive.

". . . that being when I ran with Chief Tommy Wildhorse in Utah," Grant said, his voice sonorous, resounding in the great hall. The echoes reverberated from the high, domed ceiling and from the long colonnades. Grant had come back home, in his narrative, from Africa to America by way of the Punjab; the trenches of the Great War; the Amazon and the Andes; St. Louis, Missouri; and finally Salt Lake City.

Sam shook his head in wonder. He would have gladly listened to more, but Grant had run down. He now sat heavily atop a packing crate, his hands and feet shadowed in the darkness of the museum floor.

Madeline looked up, smiling wanly. "You are talking the floor polished?"

Grant leaped up and whipped his mop into the air with a flourish. "No, *ma'am!*" With an elaborate wink at Sam, he plunged the mop into the bucket, spraying suds left and right.

"Oh," he said, pausing for a moment. "Might you be so kind as to inform us which one of those infernal devices of yours it was that had been beeping at us for the past two hours?"

"Just a radio-signal sensor, Grant." Sam lifted his hand, gesturing at the empty air. "The radio spectrum is as uncharted a wilderness as Africa ever was. I'm listening for . . ." He paused.

"Invading Afghanis?" Grant suggested.

"*Non, non,*" Madeline sputtered in interruption. "The Afghanis are more invaded *against* than *by*, these years." She turned about. "Science does always not know what it looks for. When you have see it, then you know what you have see. *Voila.*"

Grant snorted. Sam shrugged. Madeline turned back to her journal.

*   *   *   *   *

Sam slipped edgewise into his cramped utilities closet.
The ceiling was high, perhaps seventeen feet overhead,
with a single forty-watt light bulb screwed into a porce-
lain mount. Someday, Sam knew, that bulb would burn
out. It would be a Herculean task to replace it, in this cu-
bicle that was only four feet wide by five feet across. At
times, it seemed to Sam as if he did his best work here, in
this elevator shaft of a closet, rather than at the bright
and orderly labs at Cook Chemical Industries. His labors
then, under fluorescent lights, in an ultramodern facility
in the best industrial park in the city, had seemed dull,
hopelessly uninspired. Now, living in an alcove behind
an exhibit of cave bears, working in a closet, he found
himself on-stride and making unprecedented progress.

It was the business suit, he reasoned. *I'm sure of it. No
one should ever have to try to do chemistry while wearing a coat and tie.*

Electronic gear filled every inch of wall from floor level
to above Sam's most extended arm's reach. He'd made
the shelves himself, fitting the devices into the space
available, solving the close-packing problem with the aid
of a re-breadboarded Halcyon Model 38-B home computer and an algorithm he'd invented himself. A yoke of
wires snaked down the wall from a hole high in the back.
Sensing instruments and antennae on the roof of the
museum reported their findings to him here.

Do Maddy and Grant understand me? he wondered.
The thought came unbidden to Sam's mind. He
thought about the light bulb. It had burned warmly in
the ceiling, pumping light into the dark corners of the

closet, for as long as he had been coming here. Madeline Schenk and Grant Alexander had first welcomed him to the museum when he was a babbling child of seven.

The light bulb could not last forever. Nor could his friendship with the two people who were the whole of the museum staff. He smiled, a bit weakly. Did Madeline and Grant still see him as a child? Was it merely toleration?

No. I sense something deeper. Something real.

Madeline Schenk was driven, almost religiously, by her reverence for truth. Grant Alexander stood by her side, obviously devoted to her, yet equally driven, by forces Sam didn't yet understand. Did they love one another? The answer, obviously, was yes, although they were not lovers. Once, long ago, had they been? Sam gave up thinking about it. He would never dare ask, and neither Grant nor Madeline would open the topic on his or her own.

Let's see what kind of ghosts are roaming the spectrum, he thought happily to himself. He spun his dial quickly across the numbers, megahertz to kilohertz, hearing the comforting babble of voices and music as they slurred by. Mexican stations, and American-sponsored stations broadcasting from Mexico, dominated the frequencies, spreading wide, horribly overpowered. Between them, local stations aired music, sports, news, opinions.

The alarm had been triggered by an anomalous intrusion into the regulated bands. His indicators gave only a vague clue to its location. His fingers became gentle upon the dial. He found WSRG, a country music station in Kentucky. He slowly moved the dial and heard KNX, a fifty-thousand-watt news station in Los Angeles. The two stations' signals overlapped; both broadcast at 1070 kilohertz. Sam heard a strange, and strangely pleasing, blend of a newscaster's voice and a lonely guitar-accompanied song. Between the peaks of the two signals, *terra incognita* lurked, a narrow wasteland where a strange new signal might hide.

Sam's technology was a curious blend of the ultra-modern and the ramshackle. Instead of styling himself "The Trapper," he had toyed for a short time with the nickname "The Scavenger." Texas turkey buzzards were the first thing that word brought to his mind, however, and it took more dedication than Sam had to name himself after them. His equipment was the cast-off obsolescence of radio stations, university labs, and ham radio equipment stores. The arrangement, the cross-connections, and the redesigning he'd done made his setup uniquely his, and, paradoxically, a better setup than could be found anywhere in the state. The whole, most definitely, was greater than the sum of its parts.

What had triggered the alarm? Sam moved the dial back and forth in minute, almost microscopic adjustments. Soon, listening with his eyes closed, he found what he sought.

It was a tiny pulsating twitter, on an amazingly narrow band, broadcast at an incredibly low power. Static crashed around it, the surf of ethereal waves over the small island of meaning. Sam sighed and smiled. He took a reading and double-checked it, with his eyes squinting closely at the dial. Pleased, he entered it into his logbook.

Then, satisfied with his catch, he sat quietly and listened to it. It warbled, an almost birdlike sound, pleasant yet also somehow plaintive. The thunder of the static tried over and over to swamp it, but still it sounded.

It could have been anything. Sam had heard the roaring of Soviet radio jammers, as loud, brash, and uncompromising as the Soviet state itself. He'd heard the singsong of International Code, transmitting secrets of weather and wind and position to distant stations. He'd heard, but been unable to decode, the reports given to Earth stations from orbiting satellites. He'd heard sunspots, in their merciless roar and sputter, closing off the word from the other side of the globe.

He'd never heard a chirruping tone merrily sounding a *tremolo* in the midst of the AM radio band.

As he often did when he found a new frequency, he tried to respond. After a moment's thought, he sent out a brief, two-second inquiry on the same frequency, one octave lower, without trying to counterfeit the vibrating quality of the tone. This done, he noted the effort into his project book, breathed out a heavy sigh of satisfaction, and began to shut off the parts of his apparatus that were not continually on the alert. To his amazement, the hour was past ten.

Outside, in the museum office, Grant and Madeline were still awake. Sam let himself in and smiled a quiet greeting to the pair.

"What did you find, lad?" Grant asked, his arms akimbo and his legs spread wide, taking the attitude of a military colonel of the Great War gazing down at a messenger.

Sam smiled. "I was looking for a rhinoceros. I found a bluebird."

Grant threw back his head and laughed. He stepped forward and clapped Sam heavily on the back. Sam was amazed again, as he always was when he realized anew how strong, solid, and lively Grant was. It was hard to believe he was truly ninety-three years old; when Grant laughed, he seemed ageless. Sam looked again. Grant was very old indeed, thin and tired, kept alive by pride more than anything else.

"A bluebird? Hmph! Dangerous, boy . . . they sometimes charge when cornered!"

"You'll protect me?"

"Hm?" Grant looked at the strapping young lad, whose only weakness was naivete. "Well, I should jolly well say I shall. There are still two or three guns of mine in my quarters. Let them come, bluebird, blackbird, or crow!"

Madeline pulled her wheelchair out from her desk, spun smoothly around, and looked at the two. "Take notes, this times, Grant Alexander! If you are shooting a radio wave for these museum, you are skin and clean him, too."

Grant frowned. "Well, yes, of course, Maddy."

Sam withdrew, closed himself in his room, unrolled his bedmat, and was soon asleep.

CHAPTER SEVEN

Coldest winter snows could not chill Delta's metallic skin, nor could the sun's rays warm her. Her injured ankle did not improve; every step she took gave her a deep, jolting pain. She went on, refusing to let the pain defeat her. She looked upon the world, her eyeless face observant. The horizon-wide panorama unfolded around her, and she marveled at its beauty.

Serrated mountain peaks drew their sawteeth across the sky. Green vales dropped away, each with a signature in the bottom of skeined silver, where streams merged and drained away. Stands of trees sighed in blustering winds. Stones, from the tiniest pebbles to titanic granite monoliths, stood motionless, but still changing from hour to hour as the sun painted their surfaces with shifting shadows.

The works of man seemed in harmony with nature. Houses, containing men and their warmth, were contained by the sky and the valleys. Roads constrained traffic but flowed along natural gradients up and down the mountains. Airplanes, high above, flew in straight, silent lines, while nearer, closer to their earth, birds flew in zigzag courses from tree to fen.

But men bore guns, and the guns channeled their hatred in straight lines. A word of warning had gone out, passed from mouth to mouth throughout these high hills: A metal woman, naked and immoral, wandered lost, on some devil's errand. And a small town, Ramshorn, had been destroyed. There were eleven men and women waiting to be avenged.

On cold, ice-blown nights, when snowflakes blew in a low mist across the ground and the stars seemed like cold points of impotent hatred in the enemy sky, Delta had listened at windows. She remembered watching, peering in from the haunted darkness, while a farmer lifted his telephone and accepted the message.

He'd listened to the report. A metal woman. Shoot to kill. Keep the children indoors.

"No use in phoning the authorities," he'd agreed. "Probably laugh at us."

Laughter must be a terrible, terrible weapon, Delta thought.

"Something the air force won't tell us?" he'd asked. Delta never heard the answer, but the farmer had nodded with silent wisdom.

"Hell, if it isn't one thing, it's another. Remember the grizzly a year, three years back? Goddamned 'endangered species.' " The man laughed, showing clean, white teeth.

Delta found herself attracted to the man, this farmer

whose eyes and hands went to his gun as readily as they went to his wife. Human interactions seemed ruled by misunderstandings, and it was only a misunderstanding that made her his enemy. She knew he was not hers. She wanted to knock on his door, to explain.

"I won't hurt you. I can't hurt you. Please listen to me. . . ."

It wouldn't work. It never worked. The few times she had dared to approach people and speak soft words of peace, they had listened, nodded, and sent secretly for their sheriffs, who tried, one way or another, to imprison her.

I must not be contained, she knew. *I am seeking another.*

Day by day, step by limping step, she descended from her mountains. The weather and the climate grew warmer, dryer. Then another range of mountains lifted up before her, and she was forced to make the ascent.

She was naked, alone, and her ankle troubled her. But she was heartened by the beauty of the world and the diligence of its people. They were in opposition to her; they sought to contain her; but she knew that they were honest, industrious, and always did what was right in the end.

Omicron was ahead of her, four hundred miles to the southwest, at a lower elevation. She always knew where he was but nothing else of him.

Does he look like me? The appearances that have captured us are important in this world where appearances contain messages. She limped onward.

At the top of the chain of mountains, in the midst of a quiet downpour, she felt Omicron, as she always felt him, and at the same time she felt something else.

It was a new sensation, startling, almost frightening. She felt it first as pain, then as a disorienting and dizzying feeling, completely unlike anything she'd yet felt on Earth. It was as if her visual field had split in two and the world were double-exposed. It was as if two voices spoke at once, voices very different yet speaking the same words. The new voice was eight hundred miles away, to the south and east. For two seconds, her existence was focused along two perpendicular axes, and she didn't know which way to turn.

Then the universe returned to normal. Omicron was before her. She stepped forward, favoring her hurt foot.

* * * * *

Omicron could move faster than she could. Weeks went by, and she was forced to change the direction of her travels many times. Omicron was to the southwest, then to the south, then the southeast. For one horrible day, he was far to the north of her, and she was forced to retrace her steps. She could not despair. That was not a capacity built into her. She understood, however, that her quest was to be a difficult one. More troubling was the return, once every three or four days, of the new voice, the voice that split the world in two.

North and south, east and west, were artificial directions. She understood them but did not judge her place by them. There was only one direction: She walked toward Omicron. Whenever the new voice spoke, there were momentarily two directions. It was as bothersome as the appearance of a new spatial dimension would have been. Her mind was unable to adapt. The intervals between these visitations were long, and the effect was always brief. Delta wondered about them and thought as deeply as she could. The intruding voice came from a place that was fixed. When she traveled east, it came from a direction more and more directly south of her. When she went west, it receded to the southeast. But although she moved, she understood that it did not.

Omicron moved with a terrible freedom. The new, world-splitting voice never moved at all.

Delta made her decision: The effect must have some meaning for her, or it would not exist.

I am seeking another. But I learned language from an old woman's isolation, and I learned the way of the world from a man who bore a gun. This, then, has something new to teach me.

She went on, traveling through the high mountain ranges. Her daily progress could have been reckoned at less than twenty miles; she could have been overtaken by any trained mountaineer or high-altitude hiker. She didn't need to eat or to sleep. Both of these were concepts unnatural to her. But she learned. Rabbits sleep. Bobcats eat.

Men hunt.

Omicron was far to the east, on whatever strange mission that called him. The source of the new voice was ahead.

*   *   *   *   *

Behind her, a pair of men paced, heavily bundled against the cold air. Each bore a rifle slung over his shoulder. One squinted through his binoculars. He slowly scanned a segment of the mountain face before him. A tiny glint caught his eye. Was it water, slicking a smooth rock, reflecting the sunlight?

"Duncan?" He pulled the binoculars away from his face, looped the strap over his head from back to front, and handed the instrument to his friend.

Duncan Cantrell held the glasses to his eyes and squinted through them.

"I see it."

"Damn robot. Made up to look like a Las Vegas whore."

"My friend Andy, up Grand Junction way, couldn't find out anything about her. Someone offered to show him footprint casts, but he couldn't tell anything from looking at 'em. He thinks maybe they were fake, anyway."

"Andy always was a suspicious cuss."

The two men stood still for a moment longer, breathing out plumes of smoking air. No wind blew, and the clouds, although darkening the sky, were high and gray. The mountains stabbed, blue and dark purple, at the sky.

Together the men marched on, steadily closing the distance between them and Delta, coming toward her from behind. Their rifles weighed less heavily on their shoulders, more heavily on their minds.

The day passed. Delta found herself scrabbling up a rough scree of sliding rock. Where the rock had sunk beneath the soil, stunted, wiry brush grew. Delta had to gauge every footstep for traction, safety, and for the pain it would cost her.

Against the pale rocks and dark scrub, her bright figure was alternately hidden and revealed. She toiled upward slowly. The two men moved more swiftly, with more expertise.

"Four o'clock," Duncan said, glancing at his wristwatch. He rolled his jacket sleeve back down and tucked the cuff inside his glove.

"Yeah. Dark soon. We're getting mighty close."

"Close enough to rush her?"

"Yeah. Just about close enough to do that."

The men didn't look at each other. Their fears were hidden from each other, perhaps hidden from the men themselves. There was nothing left to be said. This was the thing that had killed eleven people at Ramshorn. It wasn't human. It was their right to kill it.

Duncan first, with Hank on his heels, the two men lumbered into a rapid jog. As they ran, they unshipped their rifles and held them out to the side as counterweights. Crashing through the brush, clambering up the rock, they moved to the attack.

Delta heard, then turned and saw.

"Stop right there, you!" Hank shouted.

Delta froze. She'd seen what guns could do before, on the television. She didn't understand what was happening, but she knew enough to stop, face the men, and raise her hands.

Puffing from their exertion, the men rushed up to her, then stopped at a distance of twenty feet.

Duncan pushed his cap back on his head, exposing strands of thick black hair. His eyes narrowed.

Hank, his face red from the cold, worked the action on his rifle, chambering a round.

No one moved or spoke for a long moment.

"Who are you?" Duncan asked, his voice softer than he'd meant it to be.

"I am Delta."

Duncan swore, one biting word of infinite frustration. Hank held his rifle steady.

"Are you a woman in there?" Duncan shook his head. *Talking robots? Kid-stuff movies.*

"Duncan," Hank said, his voice tight. "Look at her knees, her elbows. No *way* anybody's in there."

The articulation was too tight. Duncan felt the hair at the back of his neck stir, and a shiver ran along his back and arms. He swore again.

"Duncan?" Hank was near to panic.

"S'all right. Don't—don't do anything." He looked at the robot. Tall, fair of form, as attractive and unsubtly sexual as a naked department-store mannequin, she had no face, no eyes, only a mouth with metallic lips. "You're Delta?"

"I am Delta."

"Do you say anything else?"

"I am not your enemy."

"Damn it, are you a robot, or . . . or what? And why'd you kill everyone in Ramshorn, up Wyoming way? Why?" He shouted the last question at her.

Delta paused. "I don't know what you mean. Are you seeking to contain me?"

Duncan wondered if he looked as much a fool as he felt, trying to talk to this enigmatic woman. Glancing at Hank, he was obscurely relieved to see his partner still holding tight, balancing on the edge of fear.

"We're going to bring you in. That's right. Unless you

want to find out how bullet-proof you are."

"Bullet-proof?"

"Duncan," Hank hissed. "Look at her feet."

Duncan drew back a step and looked down. Delta's feet were as bare as the rest of her. They looked curiously human-like, but were still mechanical. The toes were jointed oddly. He wished Andy had been able to tell them more about that plaster cast of her footprint.

Then he saw the crumpled metal and scrape marks that deformed her right ankle. No doubt remained in his mind. No human was inside this suit. It was a machine, all the way through. Involuntarily he stepped back again.

Hank lost his nerve, then, and fired. Delta, knowing only one defense, increased the hardness of the metal of her body.

The bullet slid away, buzzing off into the evening air with a ricochet whine.

Delta fell to her buttocks, her legs splayed and her arms extended behind her. By hardening her skin, she had also rendered it frictionless. She promptly began to skid downhill, slipping and bouncing over the rocks she'd so laboriously climbed earlier.

Duncan and Hank looked at each other in astonishment. Then they jumped off after her in hot pursuit.

Delta had heard the word "dignity" and had a vague understanding of the idea of an undignified exit. Frictionless, sliding, bounding high into the air and impacting harshly over the rocks, she sped faster and faster down the hill and into the canyon below. More carefully, the two men followed. Then, with one accord, they stopped.

The sun was setting. The canyon was already deep in shadow. A crashing noise reverberated out of the depths, growing more and more distant each moment.

"Damn!" Hank muttered.

Duncan shook his head. "*God*damn."

They looked over the rocks in the failing light, looking for any scrap of metal, any metallic smear where Delta had scraped over the rough stone.

"We're gonna have something to tell old Andy," Duncan muttered.

"Let's . . . let's build a fire," Hank suggested, his voice low and unsteady. "She might come back after dark. . . ."

"I thought we ought to hike a bit first, but . . ." He swore. "What about it, Hank? Are we going to follow her some more tomorrow?"

"You asking me?"

"Yes, I'm asking you."

Hank sat on the cold stone and cradled his rifle in his arms. "Let's talk about it tomorrow."

* * * * *

With a crash, Delta slammed against a clump of boulders near the bottom of the ravine. With an effort of will, she kept her surface frictionless, fearful of a further plunge but even more afraid of the damage she might do to herself without this protection. She slid a little distance up one boulder, then settled down again, slipping little by little over the rocky ground.

Restoring her surface to a more normal condition, she tried to stand. Her damaged ankle would not support her weight.

She felt her ankle with her hands: The joint had been further damaged. Her foot now stuck out from her leg at an odd, useless angle.

In despair, she sat again. The rocks were solid against her arms. Darkness had claimed the ravine, although she could see the silhouette of the high hills against the pale sky's gray twilight.

I am chasing another. She composed her thoughts, then pulled herself into an upright sitting position. She crossed her right leg over her left thigh and grasped her ankle with both hands.

The full strength of her grip had never been tested. She bore down on her ankle with all of her might, trying to straighten it out, to force the twisted interior structures into their correct positions.

I am not my body; my body merely contains me. The pain was elemental, a force she could not ignore. It was like light and gravity, like rock and mankind. She refused to give in; she squeezed and twisted.

I will not be contained. My volition is free and boundless. I choose!

The metal of her ankle made small protesting noises. Yet if it were necessary, she knew she had the strength of will to tear her foot completely off and walk the width of the world on the stump. She would arrive where she was going if it had to be on her hands and knees.

I am chasing another. The thought defined her. It contained her.

Her ankle joint gave a loud grinding, grating noise and fell back closer to its normal form. She waited for a time, then tried to stand. Her ankle now bore her, although the pain was greater than it had been. She took a few hobbling steps.

I choose.

She chose to walk throughout the night, feeling her way carefully.

·

CHAPTER EIGHT

As Delta moved south, the air gradually grew warmer. Different plants thrust up through the cold, damp earth, and different animals scuttled for cover beneath them.

The going was more difficult, however. Erosion had twisted the hills into unusual and sharp contours. Every vista was as magnificent as the last. Delta limped along slowly, her head held high, reverently accepting the view through her flat, eyeless face. A new concept had come to her during her trek: concentricity. She played with it for a time as she played with a pine cone she had picked up along the way.

The stars at night spun overhead, making a great circle of the sky. Northern stars sunk behind her; new southern constellations appeared as she walked. No more natural conclusion was possible than that the world was round. The circle of the horizon was round also, fully visible on those rare and wondrous occasions that she stood atop a tall peak, scanning all about her to savor the beauty of the countryside. Trees were round; people were round; pine cones were round.

She walked, part of her attention fixed on the trail ahead. Pines, round and very large, leaned all to one side, braced like spears on the flank of the high mountain. A soft blanket of brown needles made walking easy, almost painless.

Far below, the sound of rushing water echoed upward, a sound Delta knew well. The black, bristly pine cone sat on the silvery metal of her hand. She relished the contrast, its roughness against her smoothness, its darkness against her light. The hill sloped steeply down to the left. She walked gingerly across it, descending more carefully.

Before long, the trees vanished, becoming smaller and smaller the lower she went. It almost seemed that they sank into the ground as she walked. The soil grew rocky and dry. Below her, she saw the river, shining silver, rippling in its proud strength. She paused. So much water; so much power. A very small stream had bent her ankle, and she was never free from the pain of it. How much damage could a larger river do to her? But she knew now what she hadn't known then: Changing the metal of her body into a frictionless surface gave her a defense against being caught. Turning her metal imperviously hard defended her against harm. If she had known that when her ankle had been snagged in the stream so many days ago . . .

Streams and rivers were lovely, but she had learned to fear their might. She continued on, moving parallel to the river, keeping always within sight of it, never approaching it more closely.

The land was changing. The metamorphosis was subtle, lovely, and endlessly surprising to Delta.

Ahead of her, cold upland desert plateaus beckoned. She walked on, her limp not terribly pronounced.

*   *   *   *   *

News of the destruction of Ramshorn had barely penetrated the popular attention of a nation daily fed with tales of small disasters. Tornadoes buzz-sawed through a trailer park in a suburb of Scranton; two small planes collided over Oakland; a section of bleachers collapsed in Baton Rouge. Ramshorn had had its day in the light of publicity and was forgotten. Other news took its place. Three soldiers had died shortly after an underground nuclear test in Nevada. That, too, caused only a momentary ripple on the surface. Then other disturbances roiled the waters, some greater, some lesser.

That was only the broadcast news. There was a middle way, a network of communication larger than the grapevine of local rumor, smaller than the sky-tainting fanfares of the national media. Men and women had died in Ramshorn, and they had surviving kin. The sheriff who had once grappled with Delta knew men farther to the south. Two hunters had taken a shot at her; the brother of one of them drove a truck. The tale had been told to the police, the marshall's office, the state troopers, even the FBI. Only those along the middle way really listened; only they knew how to listen, and what to listen for.

Sheriff DeSoto told his family as he sat with his feet up

in front of a bright, snapping fire. At school, his son tried to draw a picture of the robot, bearing down on the silver crayon until the picture was a gray smudge. One of his classmates had lost an aunt at Ramshorn. His mother called Sheriff DeSoto. The word traveled north, then south again.

In Nevada, the army, sorely alarmed by Omicron's trespass, sent messages back and forth along a middle way of its own. Investigators on the scene took measurements of the radiation leakage from the tunnel mouth. The sergeant of the guard was brought in for interviews. Every paper that had ever been filed under Edward Busk's name was retrieved. Andrew Wilcox's files drew similar scrutiny. Telexed messages flashed back and forth, standing out only with difficulty from the sheer background volume of investigative chatter the army generated.

No generals were informed. No units were mobilized. A few leaves were canceled, a few travel vouchers filled out, a few special precautions ordered. Nothing seemed to be happening that had never happened before.

* * * * *

"Okay, why'd you kill Wilcox and not me?"

Omicron faced Buster Busk in the darkness of the cave.

Several days had passed. Busk was tired, fevered, and suffered from thirst. He would have given all he owned to see the sky, to feel the sun on his face. The cave was cold and cramped, and he couldn't find any way out. To be buried alive was bad enough, but to be buried with this man-shaped thing . . .

"Wilcox wasted energy. You applied it properly."

Busk was tired of the toneless, almost careless way his captor spoke to him. He was tired of the way the voice came from his radio as well as from the darkness in front of him. He was tired of giving language lessons to a voice that might just as well have been a machine's. Omicron was a tireless pupil but didn't often give information in return.

"What do you mean? He fired a warning shot, darn it!"

"You shot to kill."

"I sure did! What'd it do, bounce off you? I got you with nine good hits."

"You applied energy efficiently."

Blast! Did he learn talk like that from me? "I might've done the same as Wilcox, and he might've done the same as me. You—" Busk swallowed—"you melted him down. Why not me?"

"I needed to learn. Your rifles can't hurt me. I can make my skin hard. Tell me what other weapons you have."

"Mister, you got in close to a nuke. That's it. We haven't got anything better than that. How close did you get, anyway? How did you get down to it? They fire those things off pretty deep down."

Omicron chose not to answer. He waited silently for a time in the cavern.

Busk scratched at his arms, which were peeling. *Feels just like a sunburn. It doesn't hurt, just itches like crazy. Am I going to die?* For a moment, a crazy thought passed through his mind, a regret that he would never be able to father a child safely. *Kids? Nuts! I'm a twenty-eight year old virgin, all awkward and homely, with no girl friend and no social life but the army. I've got worse things to worry about than whether or not my kids would be mutants.* The sorrow lingered, however.

"Who has power?"

Busk was momentarily taken aback. "The army, I guess."

"Who has most power."

"Well, the army. Strongest army on Earth. The Russians have more tanks, but ours are better."

"Who are the Russians?"

Put my foot in it that time, didn't I? Buster damned himself thoroughly. "Neighboring country. To the north." It was the first time he'd lied to Omicron. It was the first time he'd dared to.

"Do they have power?"

"Not as much as we do."

The darkness closed in on Busk, wrapping him in folds of blackness. He wanted out. He wanted to live.

"What kinds of power?"

"Guns, tanks, bombers—"

"No!" Omicron's voice was unusually loud. It was the first time he'd expressed impatience. He'd learned English quickly . . . astonishingly quickly.

Busk shivered in the darkness. "I don't know what you mean!"

Omicron stopped. In the darkness, he stood, silently trying to think. Busk shivered, then stopped himself, stock-still in the darkness. His radio was humming. It hadn't made any sounds earlier, when he'd tried, somewhat frantically, to call for help. The radio always echoed

Omicron's words, of course, and Busk had grown accustomed to ignoring that. But now, in the deep silence of the cavern, it was making soft sounds when Omicron was *not* speaking.

As quietly as he could, he pulled it loose from its belt clip and drew it up near his ear.

He could hear Omicron thinking.

Omicron thought in English, but a more primitive, coarser English than that with which he spoke. It was as if he were still accustomed to thinking in a different language, perhaps some machine language or electronic-signal code.

Heat power skin. Heat power damage skin, rifle impact harmless. Sunlight power skin. Sunlight power weak. Nuke?

The thoughts went on for some time. Busk could hear them, could barely make out the words as they flashed by at high speed. Omicron, like Busk, thought in symbols as well as in words. Busk couldn't understand all of the chirps and squeals that he heard, but he understood the words. And he, himself, could think faster than Omicron could.

Omicron spoke again, startling Busk when the words rasped loudly through his radio. "What is a 'nuke'?"

"It's what you got close to. It gives off a sudden burst of light and heat—a large amount of power, very quickly." He licked his lips. "It's sort of like a small bit of the sun, brought up close." He held his radio close to his ear and waited, scarcely breathing.

Sunlight power, nuke power. Power necessary. Follow Little Busk.

Busk smiled ironically in the dark. *"Little Busk?"* Is

that how he thinks of me? Let's try something. . . .

"Omicron?"

There was a sudden silence in the cavern, both in the air and through Busk's radio. Omicron had stopped thinking.

"You asked about power." Busk wet his lips. "I think you ought to know that there are many kinds of power. Some of them are very subtle." He moved his hands, gesturing unconsciously. But to this alien mind, the languages of arms and of stance and of facial expression, even of tone of voice, were unknown. Busk had only his words to save him. "Power comes in many forms. Some of them only a human could recognize."

For example, there is the power of persuasion, he thought, almost desperately.

The cavern remained quiet. Then slowly Omicron began to think.

Many kinds of power. Only a human can sense. Little Busk can lead.

"And I never waste power, Omicron." Busk spoke casually, as if unaware of his captor's thoughts. "I respect it too much for that."

Omicron digested this as well. *Follow Little Busk. Learn more from him. Collect power.*

From that moment on, a new balance existed between Edward "Buster" Busk and the terrible machine that had taken him. Busk never quite knew which of them was truly in command.

* * * * *

Highways and cars were not completely new to Delta. But never before had she seen long, flat stretches of road across level desert clay. The geometric flatness of this high desert amazed her. She recognized in it a hint of the perfection that the earth always strove for and could never attain.

When she made careful observations, she could even measure a tiny portion of the earth's curvature. She concluded, much to her amazement, that the planet's circumference was some seventeen million times as great as the distance from her feet to her face. Her observations, primitive in nature but correct in principle, were substantially in error. The world was actually roughly twenty-five per cent larger than she had guessed. Eratosthenes of Alexandria had made an estimate no better for being too large, two thousand years before Delta had set foot on the earth.

But as always it was the beauty of what she saw that stunned her. Small twisted scraps of plant life fought up into the sun, dogged, determined, proving the unfailing insistency of life. At night, small animals came out of hidden burrows to scratch the loose sand for seeds or to prey upon one another. Here again, Delta saw the concentricity of the world: Animals fed upon animals that fed upon seeds and stalks. Perhaps even larger animals fed upon the ones she'd seen so far as being at the top of the cycle. As trees and streams branched from one strong limb into many smaller ones, so predation branched, so that the majority of all living things both hunted and were hunted after as well.

The chain always ended. Plants hunted after no one, and Delta saw no one come to hunt the small pale foxes that prowled at night after mice. She never saw the quick, lean coyotes or learned of the mountain lions that could still be found in the woods. She knew that Omicron was her prey, and that she was man's.

Sometimes she saw tilled and tended fields and marveled at their green expanse. Sometimes she came to badlands and was forced to scramble up and down steep inclines and declivities. In the daytime, she was companioned by splashes of sunlight reflected from her own silver surface. They played over the ground, moving with the freedom that was denied her.

Sunrises filled her with a unique awe. As the night grew old and the small animals retreated to their holes, the quietest hour came, and the east began to glow a deep, dark blue. Slowly light returned to the darkened world, and the desert seemed to pause for a moment in reverent silence. The plants cast murky, ill-defined shadows until the moment the sun appeared over the distant horizon, giving birth to long, grainy blue shadows with crisp edges. Then, heat, light, and limitless flat vistas of multicolored charm took Delta's spirit and bore it up. She limped farther across the plain, sustained and nourished by the living light of day.

Cultivated fields seemed more common. So did fences, which occasionally she was forced to damage in order to cross. She still followed the intermittent beacon, the voice that was almost that of Omicron but was not quite.

Behind her, away to the west, Omicron went about his mischief, waiting for her to come to him and encounter him.

I will have you, Omicron, she vowed. But first this new voice needed to be found and to be dealt with appropriately.

One day, in glorious clear air and warm temperatures, although winter had not yet turned over into spring, Delta limped bravely into the outskirts and suburbs of San Antonio, Texas.

CHAPTER NINE

Yesterday's Monday holiday had left the city of San Antonio tired, with the out-of-sorts fatigue that remains once the joy of celebrating has passed. Spring was on its way, however. Men held their heads high, walking to their places of work. Trash blew along the streets and was collected by road crews. The deadly collisions of the night past were now only skid marks on the concrete and broken glass from liquor bottles lying shattered in the gutter.

The ugly side to mankind's celebrations could be seen by those who knew where and how to look.

Delta knew nothing of Presidents' Day; she had no way of knowing. To her, the city was a revelation. The cars that sped by were as varied in shape and color as the rocks of the mountains or the trees that clothed the hills. Buildings lined the streets, tall and stately, monuments to the ingenuity of mankind's obsession with barriers.

Walls bound the universe into two parts, indoors and outdoors, and windows in the walls gave a glimpse of the other side.

Few people so far had noticed Delta. Those who had would stop, run their hands back through their hair in astonishment, and stare after her as she went. One man cursed at her, shaking his fist from behind the fence that enclosed his lawn. A young boy stared at her in amazement and followed her for a block, until his nerve failed him and he sped home. Two teen-aged girls looked her coolly up and down, then pointedly looked away, their chins high.

So this is the home of mankind, Delta thought, stunned by the differences between one man and the next. She walked on, taking it all in. Her flat, blank face had no eyes; she could, however, gape in astonishment, her metal-lipped mouth wide. The buildings, so tall; the traffic, so fast. And the men, the women, so vivid, energetic, creative, noisy.

She remembered what she had seen of them on the television as she watched through the windows on the cold evenings in the mountains. Humans were the masters of the world. Here, among them, Delta felt their power.

She moved on through the city. Around every corner, something new startled her and forced her to think again. She saw a storefront whose silvered glass reflected her own image back to her. She had never seen herself. It took her a long moment to understand what this strange, shiny thing was, this humanlike, womanlike thing. She crossed the street and approached the window, ignoring the protests from the drivers.

This is I? She saw her image in the window, and the reflection of that image in her flat, reflective face. She reached out her hand to touch the glass. Her image reached out also.

She turned to her left and walked on. The city unfolded around her, a thing of brick, glass, metal, concrete. There were trees, too. She stopped again, a few blocks farther on. A rolling greensward stretched out between the streets—a park, with trees, bushes, even a small watercourse.

The wilderness contains the city, which contains a bit of the wilderness. Concentricity was so simple, yet so elegant. She loved all of the rules that made up the world; she loved them because they were knowable.

While crossing another street, she heard a distant siren. The sound intrigued her, and she stopped to listen. Immediately a chorus of horns began to blare as cars slowed to avoid her. The siren, louder than the horns, approached, and when it came near enough, the horns stopped, as if shamed or cowed. Delta looked at the drivers inside the cars: a man with an open coat; a balding man who leaned from his car window and shouted an obscenity at her; a young man who stared in confusion, then narrowed his eyes and wheeled his car around and past her.

The police car arrived on the scene. Two officers jumped out and ran up to her, their guns and other equipment bouncing at their belts.

"Move it, sister. Off the street." The officer who spoke to her was thin and pale and had a small, bushy mustache across his upper lip. The other man stood back and gestured for traffic to pull around them.

Delta walked the rest of the way across the street and stepped up onto the sidewalk.

"Okay. Hold it right there." The policeman stared at her.

Am I so alien? Delta thought. *I have no eyes, yet I can see. Is it my nakedness? Is it my metal surface?*

The policeman was, in fact, quite taken with her naked metal surface. Delta's breasts were high and round, her legs were shapely, her buttocks were plump.

His partner came up beside him and tilted his head to one side in concentration. He, too, was muscular and slim, with thick arms and strong hands. His hair was fair, a light sandy brown; his eyes were light blue.

"Did you see the way she limped?" he muttered.

The first officer ignored him. "Take the mask off, sister. Why did you wander into the street? What are you advertising, anyway?"

Delta wondered what to say. "I am not your enemy."

"Who said you were? Mask off. Now, sister."

"Mask?" Delta felt herself out of control of the situation, with no chance of gaining any equilibrium. Men always asked the wrong questions of her.

"Take . . . it . . . off," the officer said, not loudly but with emphatic force.

"I'm not wearing a mask. I have nothing to take off."

The second officer snorted, a derisive, sardonic sound. "I'll say."

The first officer's face flushed. "All right. Turn around, spread your legs. Up there. Against that wall." He spun Delta around by her shoulder and gave her a shove. She tried clumsily to comply.

"Wait a minute," his partner said, looking Delta up

and down. In the street, traffic moved slowly past the obstructing patrol car, and drivers slowed further to watch the spectacle of a robot being shaken down by two policemen.

The officer tried to find a fastener for Delta's armor. It had to come off. Where were the snaps?

"Chuck . . ." his partner said, his voice low and very serious.

"What?" The officer backed away a step, knowing that his partner's voice meant trouble.

"Look at the way she's put together. The knees. They have awfully narrow places. Elbows, too."

Delta turned around to face them. The men drew their revolvers.

"Please," she said, her voice soft and low and even. "I am not a threat. I cannot hurt you."

"Geez, it really is a robot!"

"Yeah." The policeman shook his head in wonder. "Look, you go radio for a backup and get the traffic moving. I'll—I'll handle things here."

"Right." The sandy-haired man walked back to the squad car, waving his hands strenuously. Traffic picked up a little.

"Who made you? Where do you belong?" the dark-eyed man asked.

"I am named Delta. I am going this way." She pointed in the direction of the strange call that had brought her here. For the moment, the voice was silent, but she knew that it would call again. She also knew—for she could never *not* know—where Omicron was: hundreds of miles away, to the west and north.

"You're not going anywhere. It's too dangerous to just

let you wander around. You'll have to come with me."

"To containment?"

The officer frowned. He felt like a fool for talking to a robot. "Detainment. To the station. For questioning. You're causing too much of a public nuisance here. Come on." He reached out for her hand.

Delta, in fright, jerked back and began to turn away, ready to run. The officer, his face growing angry, stretched for her. He grabbed her roughly by her wrist, whipped her about, and pulled her arm up behind her back. She felt no pain from the officer's hold, but her injured ankle nearly buckled beneath her. The policeman took advantage of her momentary unbalance to reach to his belt, draw forth a set of handcuffs, and clap one cuff tightly around her wrist. Before Delta could protest, her other wrist was cuffed. The policeman shoved her, not brutally but roughly, and she found herself facing him again. It seemed so difficult for her to keep her footing amidst the buffeting. She saw the barrel of the man's gun trained squarely upon her midsection.

Am I contained? she wondered, finding her arms constricted. A tiny thrill of panic shot through her.

"Donny?" the officer called back over his shoulder, his eyes never wavering. "You call for a backup? She's putting up resistance."

"Backup on the way." The other man came back from having moved the car. Delta looked at the car, recognizing it as being basically similar to the sheriff's car back in the mountains. The lights on top seemed unmistakably definitive.

"What the hell kind of machine is this, anyway?"

"Has to be some kind of high-tech marvel," Donny

said, his voice unimpressed. "There's just no room for anyone inside there." He had his own gun out but held it pointed down. "Nobody could fit in there."

"Yeah. I see what you mean."

Delta stood in motionless anguish. Why was there nothing she could say to bypass these men's enmity?

"I am a friend. I mean no one any harm."

"You'll get to explain that to the detectives downtown, sister."

"Geez, Chuck, there's no point in talking to it."

The officer grimaced. "Force of habit."

"I want to be free," Delta said, her voice soft, her anguish controlled.

"We all do."

Her anxiety reached a climax. She spread her arms, pulling against the constraint of the handcuffs. One of the links of the chain broke with a loud snapping noise. The two men stepped back, and Donny's gun came up to menace her.

Her arms were free. She was trapped no longer. She heard more sirens approaching, however, and knew that more men were moving in to surround her. She held up her wrists to look at the cuffs encircling them. She took one of the metal bands in the fingers of her other hand and twisted. The metal resisted, then gave way. In a moment, she had disposed of the other cuff.

The first policeman shouted at her. His words were indistinct from rage and fear, but she deciphered them quickly enough: "Stop, or we goddamnit shoot!"

She caused the upper part of her body, from the knees up, to become frictionless. Hobbling a bit, because of the pain in her ankle, she ran.

The loud report of a gunshot sounded behind her, echoing from the street and buildings. She hastened on, refusing to stop. Next she heard ringing footsteps as the two officers dashed after her. She ran into the street, directly into the path of an oncoming car. The driver was unable to stop. His car swerved, squealing noisily, emitting the stench of burning rubber as his brakes locked. The car fishtailed, and the fender slammed into Delta, knocking her sailing. Delta, with her hardened metal skin, slid across the road and up onto the sidewalk, slipping over the rough surface as if it were ice. Then she stood and pressed on, trying to escape the policemen.

Traffic came to an abrupt halt amid squealing brakes and sliding tires. Delta forced herself to ignore her pain and ran as fast as she could. Her ankle hurt her, however, and it seemed as if it could not possibly support her any longer. From all sides came shouts, the sounds of car horns, the rising and falling wail of sirens. Ahead, she saw flashing red and blue lights. To one side, more men leaped from a patrol car and pounded toward her.

She limped on, not daring to run, unwilling to be captured again. As the men stopped and braced themselves to shoot, she ducked into a storefront doorway, crashing noisily through the glass door she didn't know how to push open. An alarmed clerk stared at her in wide-mouthed dismay. Delta looked at the shoes, shirts, hats, and ties standing on display racks. Perplexed, she tilted her head to one side and thought for a moment.

People wore clothes. She didn't. The difference, although it had been evident to her from her first encounter with men, had never been made so clear. Clothes come off and go on again. She darted through the store, grabbing here and there at pants, vests, jackets, shoes and socks, scarves and hats.

The door to the back of the store was open, a dark rectangle that led to the storeroom, the rear entrance, the back alley, and freedom. Delta, having been indoors only once, envisioned the dead-end trap of a jail cell with iron bars and turned and hurried out the front again.

The street had been cordoned off by police emergency units, working efficiently. Officers with bullhorns shouted at her, demanding that she surrender. Men crouched behind their cars, aiming rifles at her.

She began to dress herself.

Slowly, cautiously, the police moved in on her. They watched, wondering, as she pulled pants over her shapely metal legs and wrestled with a silken shirt, trying to fit it over her arms, both at the same time.

Police units closed in, moving from cover to cover in an almost chesslike series of maneuvers. Although she tore the shirt along one of the seams, Delta fitted it on at last and worked on the jacket. The street was raucous with the sound of police radio traffic, men calling softly to one another, and the distant wail of approaching sirens.

A man with a bullhorn stood and addressed her directly. "Stop what you're doing and put your hands up!"

Delta raised her head, smiled hopefully, and raised her hands. "I'm dressed. I'm one of you now."

The officer waved, and a team of men jumped forward. They threw themselves atop Delta and tried to wrestle her to the ground. She resisted until her ankle betrayed her. She fell heavily, her metal banging noisily against the concrete of the sidewalk.

"No," she said, shaking her head. "I'm one of you now. I'm wearing clothes."

"What the hell difference does that make?" one of the team muttered. The handcuffs he fitted her with were of a heavier, sturdier metal.

When Delta heard the ratcheting sound and felt the cuffs about her wrists, she arched her back, throwing the men from atop her. She had released her frictionless defenses while trying to don the clothes, but now she let her surface go slippery again. The clothes rode up her torso, slithering over her breasts; her pants slid down, and she hastily kicked them free.

"What do you want from me?" she demanded in a loud, unhappy voice. "What will it take?" She stood and looked at the men who had captured her. "What must I do to live here?"

The officer lowered his bullhorn and heaved a deep sigh. "Get into the car," he said, his voice weary.

*   *   *   *   *

"Police activity," Sam said cheerfully to himself in his cramped electronics closet at the Quentin Corey Museum. He hummed a little tune under his breath and turned the volume up on the police scanner. There seemed to be a huge gathering of police units in response to an emergency in East Commerce Street. Radio discipline was slack; cross talk and useless comments fled back and forth. One word was repeated several times: "Robot."

Well, if a robot is on a rampage in downtown San Antonio, I, for one, want to be there to see it, Sam thought and hustled into his jacket.

"Where are you moving, such hurry?" Madeline asked, pulling her glasses closer to her eyes. Sam looked around the museum. The lights were off again, which meant that there were no visitors.

"There seems to be a disturbance downtown. I thought I'd go take a look."

Grant poked his head from behind a display case, where he was working on an electrical connection. "Disturbance, eh? What say I tag along? Two alert men are always safer than one."

"Neither of you go seeking 'disturbance,' " Madeline fleered. "You are forgetting personal safety, go voyeuring after riots and parades." She pushed her wheelchair closer to Sam, then leaped out of it and stamped forward. "Do you think how I got to become this old? I chase riots?"

"Madeline," Grant said softly, "the lad has a right to seek adventure. You and I—"

"Were fools!" Madeline's anger melted, as it always did, into a smile of resignation. She threw herself back into her wheelchair. "I am weak and broken up, and wheel myself fro and back. For this I hithered off to the war?" She shook her head at Sam. "Be wary-full. Don't stand caught in the cross fire. When howitzers speak, lie down on floor of street."

"I wish I could go with you, lad." Grant indicated Madeline with a quick tilt of his head. "But someone ought to stay here and keep the fortress against the foeman."

Madeline spun to face him. "I curate here! I keep fortress. Go with Samuel, see that I care! Go! Go, *Va-t-en!* Clear the field. Go, and to devils with those of you!"

Grant smiled a secret smile of triumph at Sam and put down his tools. "Only if you're sure you don't need me."

"Sure? You? I have needed you since nineteen thirty-one? Pooh! Go and have fun. Fix electricals another time."

Smiling a wry, ironic smile, Grant nodded to Sam and started to follow the younger man. Then he stopped, and his face grew serious. He turned about. "Thanks, Maddy," he whispered, then spun and chased after Sam.

CHAPTER TEN

Grant Alexander and Sam Taramasco arrived at the rear of the crowd watching the street spectacle. Sunlight painted the storefronts into bright pastel colors—pink and green, blue and yellow. A profusion of specialty shops clustered in a row.

Clean white vans with the logos of news stations painted neatly on their sides had pulled up and were parked on the sidewalks. Cameramen stood atop them, focusing in on the newsworthy scene. A large crowd of people had gathered to gaze in fascination at the unusual activity.

Grant, although diminished by his years, was still taller than most people ever get during their lives. Standing on his tiptoes, he peered over the heads of the crowd. What he saw rankled his sense of honor.

"Damn!" He rubbed his upper lip with a dry knuckle. To Sam, who was struggling to see and whose shorter stature denied him Grant's viewpoint, he explained the situation in short, crisp sentences. He sounded like a soldier bringing in a dispatch.

"Woman—silver skin, naked, hands cuffed behind her back—trapped against wall. Police officers, armed, giving her a bit of a roughhousing. Guns everywhere—revolvers, some assault rifles, shotguns at standby. Don't like it."

Sam looked up at him in astonishment. "Silver skin? Is she a robot?"

Grant frowned, and stood and shaded his eyes. "By thunder! Nothing else!"

Sam didn't waste another moment, but instead began pushing his way rudely through the crowd. It was incredible to him how many people had come out to watch. The stores must have been emptied. He gritted his teeth and shoved on through, pushing people aside left and right. In a moment, he found himself at the informal barricade the police had set up.

An officer stood, radio in hand, his back to the crowd. No line of sawhorses, no strip of tape stood between the crowd and the arena where the police were beating their captive into submission. News cameramen stood as far forward as the police would permit, their heavy shoulder-mounted cameras focused on the scene.

Sam saw Delta, and he took an involuntary step forward. She was startlingly lovely, exotic, even erotic, and he would have been taken with her under any circumstances. Now her nudity under the harsh handling of the policemen made her appear helpless, forlorn, vulnerable.

"Vulnerable" would have been the last word the police officers would have used to describe her. Eight men

now held her down, sprawled across her body, sliding
off, grasping for a purchase that could not be found. Her
ankles had been cuffed, and chains had been cinched
around her knees and her waist. Her wrists were still fastened behind her. But still she struggled, rolling from
side to side, throwing the officers from her with a lithe,
athletic agility. The men cursed and swore as they sought
to hold her. She remonstrated with them, seeking to understand. But she also struggled with all of her might.

A high, noble fury took hold of Sam. He dashed past
the officer and ran up to the detective in command.
"Stop this! Stop it at once!"

The detective snapped Sam a cold glance. "Get out of
here, boy."

"You're damaging my robot!"

At that, the detective backed off a step and looked
Sam up and down. "Your robot, son?"

"Yes, sir." Sam glared defiantly at the man.

Smiling, the detective repeated himself. "Your robot." He grimaced, an expression of distaste erasing his
smile. "You build her yourself?"

"Yes. Yes, sir." Perhaps Sam's dislike of the honorific
showed through in his expression, in his voice. Perhaps
his lifelong hatred of figures of authority could not be
hidden.

On the sidewalk, the men tried to fix a dark bag over
Delta's head. Sam saw, and started off in that direction
to try to stop the injustice. The detective caught up to
him in one bound and grabbed him by the arm.

"Hold it, kid." His voice was iron, and his grip was
unbreakable.

"I can talk to her, sir." Sam didn't have to feign desperation. "I built her. I know how she works."

"A junior-college science project?" The detective's sarcasm was broad and obvious. He dragged Sam back to shelter behind a patrol car.

The bag had been dragged over Delta's head; she gripped it with her teeth and began fighting against it. Two more men slid from atop her, landing roughly on the sidewalk.

Sam talked fast, giving the most desperate pitch he had ever made.

"I made her. I'm no schoolkid. I worked in the research division of Cook Chemical Industries for two years, and I've done a lot of independent work. That's a highly sophisticated robot. I've put a lot of innovations into her. You can see how slippery she is: I've used a new Teflon derivative to prolong surface life. The articulation is advanced. There's a lot of computing power in her, just to make her walk." He gazed into the face of the detective, who stood listening, his eyes half-closed. Taking a deep breath, Sam continued, lying as he had never lied before in the whole of his imaginative and creative life.

"She's not fighting your men to fight them. Not to hurt them. She's programmed to work her way free from entangling things. Barbed wire. Vines. Water weeds, too; she can work underwater. And she acts smart but really isn't: her artificial intelligence capacity is low-grade. A programmer would be able to tell the difference, but to an untrained observer—"

The detective held up his hand. "Can you stop her from struggling?"

"Yes, of course. She knows my voice."

Holding Sam by the hand as if he were a young child,

the detective dragged him forward.

"Okay, boy. Stop her."

What do I call her? Sam wondered, but only for a moment. To the officers dog-piled atop her, he snapped in irritation, "Back off. Get away from her!"

Some of the men looked up at the detective; others had their hands too full with Delta's struggling form.

"Okay, men. Get away from her. C'mon."

"Get the sack off her head," Sam added. He wondered who had really built this magnificent machine. "Innovations," had he said? This was the most technically advanced machine he had ever had the honor of examining.

The very best of the Detroit automobile plant robot working arms couldn't begin to compare with the smooth elegance of this robot's arms. He looked at the complex way the metal plates had been formed to slide under and over one another; he marveled at the articulation of the joints. And the hands—he could see one of her hands, pinned beneath her rump and caught by a heavy-duty handcuff. It was as lovely and graceful as a true human hand. The fingers were jointed in perfect duplication of the human model, thickened slightly at the knuckles, slightly flattened at the ends to simulate a nail. A master metal sculptor, working for a year in a private foundry, might have been able to craft the body. An engineer with computer-assisted design might have been able to produce the motors to make it move. But that would have left no space for the filing-cabinet-sized computers that would have been needed to coordinate those motors.

Proprioception—she knows where her arms are. Sur-

face tactile feedback, internal pressure feedback, changing resistance feedback . . . in real time!

He stepped closer and smiled into her face.

No face? But a mouth? Clearly this flat surface is a visual plate of some kind. . . .

"Hi. It's me, Sam. Everything is going to be okay. It was a mistake. Please stop fighting."

"Hello, Sam," Delta said, her voice soft and warm, indistinguishable from the voice of a real woman.

Sam had to fight to control his facial expression, but he had succeeded, so far. Delta had ceased to struggle.

"Don't worry. We'll get you free in just a moment."

To the detective and awestruck officers, he turned and delivered a withering stare. "So. That's all it takes. Which of these brave men hit her first?"

"Seems like we have quite a bit to talk about, boy," the detective muttered. "My name's Johnstone. I've got quite a few charges I could press, seems like."

Sam sneered. "Charges? Let's look them over. Creating a public nuisance? Disturbing the peace? Let's get something straight, Johnstone. Your men started this. My robot didn't."

Oh, god, let that part be true! Sam knew the official mind well enough, however, to know he was on somewhat secure ground.

"We've got public endangerment, resisting arrest, and shoplifting to add to those. You want to discuss it back at the station?" Detective Johnstone looked Sam in the eye. "Maybe it isn't your robot, but you, who ought to be in handcuffs."

Sam looked at the ground, feigning a contrition he didn't even begin to truly feel. "Well, maybe . . ."

All of my previous encounters with officialdom have gone sour. Always. Now I need to stay in control. I must! his mind raced.

"Did you just send her out, without any remote-control box?" Johnstone shook his head. "What were her instructions?"

"Not shoplifting, I can assure you that." Sam looked the man in the face. "What did she steal?"

"Clothing."

Sam crossed his arms on his chest. "Again, that's the fault of one of your officers. He came up to her and said, 'Why are you naked?' and she took that as an instruction to get clothed." He thought for a second. "Hmph. More likely, he looked at her and said, 'Get some clothes on!' "

Delta remained silent. Sam glanced at her and smiled encouragingly. She smiled back, or at least her lips widened and curved upward. It was an expression that was eerie on her otherwise blank face. Sam shivered.

"Perhaps I can help a little here," a thin voice sounded from the edge of the crowd.

Sam and Detective Johnstone turned. Grant Alexander came forward slowly, favoring his old joints.

"Are you responsible for this young man?"

"Sam's quite responsible for himself, I daresay." Grant fixed Johnstone with a clear eye. "But I heard you mention a shoplifting offense, and that's one matter I can help with."

"How?"

"I'll pay for the merchandise, eh what? I've never met a shopkeeper yet who would rather have the lawsuit than the profit."

Johnstone turned to one of his officers. "Sergeant, go

bring the store manager." To Grant, he smiled thinly. "What's your name?" He looked at Sam. "And yours."

"Grant H. Alexander, Captain, Twenty-eighth County of London Regiment, the Artists Rifles, pensioner, sir!" When he spoke, and when he snapped to attention, everyone present looked at him in amazement.

"World War Two?" Johnstone asked, slowly, grudgingly, as if he resented asking the question that Grant's introduction had begged.

"One, sir," Grant said and did not smile.

"Right . . ."

"And this is Sam Taramasco, my young protege. I've taught him everything he knows."

What the response to that would have been, from either Sam or Detective Johnstone, was never to be known. A police sergeant came up, with the clothing store manager in tow. "This is the manager, sir. He lost his front door and—" he checked his note pad—"one pair of pants, one pair of shoes—"

"Bother!" Grant snapped. He dove into his pocket, brought forth three small coins, and flipped them to the shopkeeper. "That'll even the reckoning, I daresay. One more matter that never needs to get into the books."

The shopkeeper bent his head, examined the coins closely. Reluctantly he looked back up at Grant. "These are gold!"

"Yes, they very well are." Grant snorted. "Can't imagine why your country is so set on banning imports of the things, either. They're good, solid coins to carry about."

"But—but it's gold!" the shopkeeper went on. "These are worth—"

"We don't need to discuss the shillings and pence, my good man. Is it sufficient to cover your damages?"

The shopkeeper's eyes grew wide. "Sufficient? Um . . ."

"Good." Coming from Grant's mouth, the word was a dismissal.

The crowd, which had gathered to watch one spectacle, stayed to gape at another.

"We still have several charges to file here," Johnstone said testily. "I'm going to have to place Sam under arrest."

Sam, who had been stunned to learn that Grant had been carrying gold coins, shook his head. Gold now stood at nearly four hundred dollars an ounce. What else had the old man, whom he had thought so garrulous, never told him? He collected his wits quickly.

"I'll go with you. My robot, which you have damaged sufficiently, can go back with Grant."

"No way, boy. That robot is a very dangerous piece of machinery."

"So's a threshing machine, sir, or an automobile. If someone drives a car through a lamppost, do you arrest the car?" He inhaled deeply and moderated his surly tone. "You're only thinking of it as intelligent, as independent, because it's human-shaped." He smiled and spread his hands. "It's just a puppet. A mannequin. Your pet dog is its superior in brainpower."

"It put up quite a fight there."

"Automatically. On its own, it can barely walk."

Johnstone hesitated. "Is this true, Mr. Alexander?"

"Indubitably." He favored the detective with a friendly, knowing grin. "Sam is a genius, to be sure, but hardly in the same class as Dr. Frankenstein, or as Daedalus or Hephaestos, either." He looked Delta over. "Not bad workmanship, though, and I speak as a man with a bit of experience in metalsmithing."

Leaning forward aggressively, Johnstone put his face very close to Grant's. "This nice piece of workmanship has just terrorized most of East Commerce Street."

"Naturally," Grant said softly. "Your cars, men, guns, and flashing lights, however, might be a complicating factor." He held up his hand. Johnstone swallowed the retort he was about to utter.

"The robot is a delicate and expensive piece of machinery. I can control it. If you take it into your custody, any damage to it would be assessed against the city. Furthermore . . ."

"We can't just let you—" Johnstone began.

"Furthermore," Grant went on, his voice only a fraction louder, "the machine requires maintenance on a very rigorous schedule. I must insist on retaining control."

Johnstone threw up his hands. "All right. I give up. Release her."

"It," Grant corrected him. "Release *it*. Ships are 'she,' and that's as far as we have the right to go in personifying our tools."

Two officers reluctantly unlocked the heavy cuffs and chains binding Delta.

Sam took hold of Grant's wrist. "Grant . . ."

"Eh?" He looked at Sam. "What is it, lad?"

"You'll be careful, won't you?"

"I'll be all right, lad," Grant said heavily. "Go with the officers and get the details all straightened out. Call me at the museum."

"Thank you, Grant." Sam let an officer help him into a patrol car and sagged in relief. He loved Grant and knew that he would do anything, anything at all, to repay the man.

Johnstone wasn't finished yet. "I'm going to let you keep control of your robot, but I'm assigning an officer to go back with you to your museum. I don't want that machine out of his sight at any time. I can't have the city endangered. Do you understand?"

"Quite. You've made your position abundantly clear." Grant's cool smile took any insult away from his words.

"Officer Pruitt!" Johnstone's bellow produced a clean-shaven officer, a small, tanned man with bright, cheerful blue eyes, clean brown hair, and a small button of a nose. He had laugh lines at the corners of his eyes, a sign that Grant found highly reassuring.

"Fletcher Pruitt, sir," he introduced himself to Grant.

"Most pleased to make your acquaintance," Grant responded.

Johnstone turned and left in disgust.

With a wail of sirens and a screeching of tires, the assembled emergency vehicles scattered. The crowd, fortified with a true nine-days' wonder of a tale, dispersed. Newsmen crowded around Grant, took an entire album of snapshots, and pestered him for details. He explained at great length, telling them everything they could possibly want to know and more. He promised them interviews with Sam, if they would but come to the museum—"The Quentin Corey Museum of Antiquities," he reminded them all very carefully—first thing in the morning. Eventually the newsmen went away as well.

Then, almost as unmindful as he would have been in an afternoon stroll alone, Grant H. Alexander and Delta walked side by side toward Pruitt's patrol car.

Pruitt held the door open for them. Delta hesitated but was encouraged by Grant's comforting touch. Pruitt slammed the door, then went off to make some last-minute reports to Johnstone before pulling out.

Grant looked at the strange robot by his side. "Bit of a limp you have," he said after a time.

"Yes. I hurt my foot."

"Um-hm." Grant fished in his jacket pocket for a cigarette, until he remembered that he'd broken himself of the habit nearly half a century ago.

The two waited in silence, the man and the machine.

Grant looked away, his face almost as devoid of expression as hers was.

"So. Who are you, really?"

"I am Delta."

Grant nodded, as if that had been the answer he wanted. Before long, Pruitt came back, started the car, and drove the two away to the museum.

CHAPTER ELEVEN

Omicron was gone, and the darkness closed in on Edward Busk. He made several groping circuits of the cavern, running his hand over the jagged crystals of the cave wall. The floor was rough, heaped with sharp, tilted plates of stone. How had he been brought in, anyway? How had Omicron gone out? Squinting into the darkness made his face hurt.

The cave was larger than he'd thought, big and circular, with rugged walls. It was probably very lovely to see, but he had no way of making a light. He felt at the walls and walked softly. Every noise he made echoed, and the echoes were horrible. They sounded like distant chuckling noises, like goblins laughing behind the walls. His sleep had been haunted by evil dreams, but his awakening was just as bad.

He understood how cave animals could become blind over the long years. His eyes merely seemed a hindrance to him. Eyes closed or eyes open, the view was the same. Any relief from the heavy blackness would comfort him, would prove that he had not been blinded.

There was nothing to lift the dark curtain that seemed to hang just in front of his face. He pulled his radio from his belt and listened. Only the rushing noise of background static came out of the small speaker grille.

I'm really in the soup. I'm as good as dead, he thought desperately. His skin was beginning to peel. He'd lost track of time, but he thought it was the fourth day since he'd been kidnapped.

At least my hair isn't falling out . . . yet. And I don't have diarrhea . . . yet. He reached up and pulled gingerly at his hair. It felt funny, as if any really hefty pull would drag it away from his scalp, which, like the rest of his skin, itched.

He was ravenously hungry.

A sudden terror gripped him. He was buried alive, in a cavern miles beneath the desert. Then, in a sudden burst of realization, he knew where he was. He almost laughed aloud. He was beneath the test range! Underground nuclear bomb tests sometimes left bubbles in the rock, which cooled to form deep, radioactive caverns. Intense heat from the nuclear fireball spalled massive flakes of rock off the walls. These fell to the floor, creating a mound of detritus, a rough, uneven surface. Most of the radioactivity was pent beneath, but that which remained in the cavern made the sites dangerous for years afterward.

Better hope this is an old one, say Nineteen-fifties. Busk tried to calculate the diameter of the cave and deduce the yield of the bomb that had formed it. He shook his head. He didn't know enough about explosive yield formulae.

He knew the procedure of the tests. Somewhere above him, partway up the cavern wall, would be the melted end of the access tunnel. He wouldn't find it here, down in the bottom of the chamber. He'd have to do a bit of climbing.

He'd covered about half of the cavern, climbing the walls as high as he could and working his way back and forth around the perimeter, when Omicron returned.

"Little Busk?" Omicron demanded. The faint radio-active glow that had rendered Omicron visible to Busk had by now completely faded. Omicron was only a voice in the darkness. As before, his voice echoed eerily from Busk's radio.

"I'm here." Busk smiled helplessly in the darkness. Where else would he be? But if he could find the entrance to the tunnel—the tunnel that Omicron must be using to enter and exit—then he'd be able to get far, far away from this monster.

"I have brought three men to you. You have power over them. Find out how I will get power."

In the darkness, Omicron came closer. Three human bodies fell with heavy thumps onto the rocks. Omicron backed away. Busk, in amazement and terror, crept near them.

One man was dead. Busk bit down hard on his lips and cheeks to keep from shrieking. His outstretched hand had brushed against the gaping crack in the man's forehead. Nausea etched his throat with acid. He wiped his hand on his trousers, panicking for a moment.

The second man was dead also, but Busk gave thanks

after examining him for a moment: no gross external injuries were evident. He wasn't sure he could stand the feel of torn-open skulls or dragging guts or . . . He reined in his imaginings and did what he had to do.

The third man still breathed. Omicron had dumped him crudely onto the rocks. The fellow would be a wretched mass of bruises in the morning. He was alive, however, and none of his limbs seemed broken. His breathing was shallow. Busk didn't like that.

He stood and bravely faced the darkness. "Two of these men are dead."

"Dead?"

"They have no power. They cannot move. They won't ever be able to help us. They can't hurt us, either. They're dead."

Omicron thought. Busk listened to the thoughts on his radio.

Dead. No power. Power makes dead. Power destroys power.

Hey, Busk thought, *that'll be enough of that!* He spoke aloud, hoping to distract Omicron from this train of thought. "The third guy is okay, just unconscious. He won't be able to talk to us for a while."

"His power is not gone?" Omicron asked, his voice horribly neutral.

"No. It will return and grow, and he'll be okay."

"His power will *not* grow." Omicron's words gave Busk the warning he needed. He leaped back away from the third man just as a hot beam of glowing amber light leaped from Omicron down to the unconscious soldier. The man melted, draining away into the rocks. The light faded.

Just like that! Busk thought, horror-struck. He stood in shock. *Without a care. No compunctions. He fried that guy, and he did it because of what I said. Oh, god . . .*

The brief flash of light had given Busk what he most needed—a brief respite from the unending darkness. He had seen the outlines of the chamber, a hemispherical dome in the rock, partly filled with rubble. He saw the molten stone above, frozen again into dull, blunt curves. And he had seen the black gap of the access tunnel, about twelve feet up one wall, behind Omicron.

It was dark now. The light was gone. But Busk had marked in his mind the place where the tunnel came out, and he knew he would not be able to forget it.

"How does power grow?" Omicron demanded.

"Only within fixed limits. That man would never have been nearly as powerful as you. He wouldn't even have been as powerful as me. You shouldn't have destroyed him. You've seen me asleep; that's how you carried me here."

Little Busk powerful. Threat?

Busk shivered.

"No human being will ever be as powerful as you. You're safe. You don't have to worry." He inhaled deeply. "Look, Omicron. You've got to tell me what it is you want. I'll help you. I have some kinds of power you don't. Little things." He added that last in haste. "Like . . . I can tell you which men have more power, and which have less. And devices . . . devices have power, too. And—"

"Power can increase?"

"Yes."

"It can be destroyed?"

"Yes."

"I have a very large amount of power."

"I'll say!"

"Can I be destroyed?"

Darn! Think fast. "Some of your power could, possibly, be destroyed. But you have so much that every human on earth, working together, could only destroy a small fraction of your power." *Buy it, Omicron,* Busk prayed. *Buy it!*

In the darkness, Omicron thought. *Power all Earth. People all Earth. Destroy.*

Busk didn't like the sound of that at all.

"Tell me where I go to get nukes."

"Nuclear weapons?" Busk gasped.

"Yes."

Busk shook his head, a gesture that Omicron did not see in the darkness. "Well, you're in the right place for those, I'll tell you that much."

He faced his first dilemma in dealing with the power-mad monster that had captured him. If he guided him to the weapons bunker, Omicron would become the most deadly force on Earth. But if he lied, Omicron would only kill him and capture someone else. Eventually someone would tell him what he needed to know. It was also possible that Omicron could conquer and kill all humanity without any weapons at all.

How powerful is this heat beam of his, anyway? Busk shook his head and gave in.

"The weapons bunker is in the inner compound of the east group of buildings. You'll be able to recognize it by the big white building. . . ."

I don't want to be a traitor to the human race, but I don't have any choice! At least if I play along with this guy, maybe I can trick him.

Omicron turned and left.

Once he was gone, Busk quietly climbed up the sloping wall and ducked into the mouth of the access tunnel. It stretched on, rough going at first, then smoothed out. Fifty yards later, the tunnel ended at an elevator.

Omicron, not knowing how to use an elevator, had simply torn it away. The ruined metal cage had been trampled and shredded. The cables dangled loose in the shaft.

Busk knew that he could never climb those cables. He was at least a quarter-mile beneath the surface, and he was fatigued from mental anguish and weakened by hunger.

He pulled out his radio and called for help, but the rock shielded the weak signal.

Resigned to his fate, he made his way back along the tunnel and climbed back down into the cavern.

Shortly thereafter Omicron returned. The last time he'd come back, he'd dropped three men roughly down onto the rocks. This time he tossed down two large, heavy metal weights. In the blind darkness, Busk heard them strike the cavern floor and clatter to a stop. He didn't need to see them. He knew what they were.

* * * * *

Two other prisoners shared Sam Taramasco's holding cell in the police station. One was old before his time, worn down from liquor and exposure. Once given a meal and released, he would waste no time in finding or stealing enough money to get drunk again. The cycle had only one exit. The other prisoner was a sullen, fringe-bearded youth, wearing a short-sleeved T-shirt and ragged cutoff jeans. Sam had the impression that the young man was in for something commonplace, perhaps burglary or assault.

The charges pending against Sam were legion: disturbing the peace, assault, creating a public danger, and a long list of others. Sam's personal favorite was the charge of willful disregard for public safety. He felt that it had an almost poetic ring to it. The phrase ran through his mind over and over: *willful disregard for public safety, willful disregard for public safety* . . .

At least I calmed the robot down. No one else thought of speaking gently to it. He closed his eyes and thought about the robot. It had been lovely, sensual, delicately formed. And, he recalled, it had been damaged. There were scars along its leg, and its ankle was twisted.

It was a lovely machine. Sam didn't regret having rescued it, despite his present circumstances. He peered around his cell, seeing the stainless-steel toilet shining in the center of one wall. The bearded young burglar looked up, noticed Sam looking at him, and made a face.

An hour slid slowly by, and another.

An attendant in uniform stepped up outside the bars. "Sam Taramasco?"

"Yes?" Sam stood.

"Come with me."

The man unlocked the door and slid it wide. Sam stepped through. The man slapped the door shut and bolted it securely again. He caught Sam tightly by the upper arm and escorted him brusquely past rows of holding cells, each filled with two or three men awaiting booking.

They passed through another barred gate, then past a guard station. On this side of the barrier, police officers strode about, hurrying to and fro on their missions. Overhead, shielded lights shone on bulletin boards filled with notices and photographs of wanted men. The corridors were narrower here than they had been in the jail, and the floor was covered with woven rattan matting. There was an orderly chaos about the place that appealed to Sam's sensibilities. Papers were strewn about everywhere; coats hung over the backs of chairs; coffeepots gurgled near stacks of plastic cups.

The warder shoved Sam down onto a chair by a desk. After a short wait, an officer in plainclothes came to sit in the desk chair. He was large, florid, clean-shaven. Fortyish, he was fighting a losing battle with fat. His cheeks were pink and slightly puffy. His eyes were a clear, attentive blue.

"Sam Taramasco?"

"Yes, sir."

"I'm Detective McStay." He held out his hand, and Sam reluctantly shook it.

"Okay, kid," McStay said, running his hand over a stack of papers as he read them, "this looks like an unusual case. I've never seen anything quite like this." He looked up at Sam, and his smile faded. "In fact, it's a damned unusual case. You built the robot?"

"Yes." Sam gritted his teeth. Was there any way he could push his lies far enough to escape detection? This man was trained to catch even the smallest contradiction in a suspect's story.

"You made it out of spare parts?"

"Motors and other stuff. I wound the armatures myself." Sam looked up at the man, a sincere look of unhappiness in his eyes. "It's good workmanship. Good stuff. Metal plates, hammered over wood frames. Automobile batteries in the torso. Independent microprocessors to keep the limbs in synch. Getting a machine to walk is a lot trickier than you'd think."

McStay looked at Sam. After a long time, he said softly, "Your robot would make a pretty powerful soldier, wouldn't it?"

Frowning, Sam shook his head. "No. Of course not."

"Does it have any weapons in it?"

"Hell, no. Not inside. I suppose it could use a gun if you put one in its hand, but it wouldn't be able to aim it properly."

"Why not?"

"Getting a robot to see things is even more tricky than getting them to walk. Computers don't process visual information the same way we do."

"Have you lived in San Antonio all your life?"

Sam smiled. "I've never been farther from here than Carlsbad Caverns."

McStay snorted. "I've heard they're overrated."

A twinge of anger passed over Sam's face. "No, sir. They're lovely . . . very lovely."

"Hm. You used to work for Cook Chemical Industries. It seems you had a bit of trouble with Mr. Cook. The court record shows you owe him several hundred thousand dollars."

"Yes, sir," Sam said softly.

"Speak up." McStay leaned forward. "It says here you slandered him. Why?"

Sam swallowed before he could trust himself to speak. "I didn't like him, sir."

"Hm. You were a chemist?"

"Research chemist. Yes, sir."

"Is that where you learned to build robots?"

"The only thing I learned from Cook Chemical Industries was abuse, sir." This time he was unable to hide his anger.

McStay looked at him. Sam returned his look bitterly.

"The court records say you're currently under no obligation to be making payments to Mr. Cook."

"That's because I have no money."

"Right." McStay flipped through the papers for a few more minutes.

"Did you program your robot to go into town and do some shoplifting?"

"Of course not." Sam spread his hands, trying to be reasonable. "Look how far it got before you caught it. I'm not stupid."

"Hm . . . That's not what your court record says."

Sam bit off the words that he wanted to say, a task as difficult as any he had ever undertaken.

I have a big mouth, Sam reminded himself. *My temper gets me in trouble. Shut up. Shut up. Shut up!* Aloud, he said, through clenched teeth, "I've apologized to Mr. Cook. I don't have to apologize to his company. Are you going to press charges against me, or are you going to release me?"

"You're mighty angry, kid. Mighty angry." Without

another word, McStay stood and walked away. Sam sat alone and seemingly forgotten. Eventually, someone came along, took him in charge, and walked with him to another room.

"Taramasco? Sam?" called out a man behind a glass window. Sam walked up and stuck his face near one of the small circular holes in the glass.

"Yes?"

"Sign here." The clerk shoved a batch of papers through a gap beneath the window. Sam read them over. They committed him to appear at a preliminary hearing to be held late next month. Looking closer, Sam saw that he was being released on his own recognizance—the phrase "release o.r." recurred throughout the papers—and no bail was being required of him. He signed.

"Through there," the clerk said, gesturing with his head toward a door.

This building is nothing but doors and tiny rooms, Sam thought bitterly. *They've completely honeycombed the place into microscopic cubicles. We're all being held in cells, policemen and prisoners alike.* In the next room, which was nearly as small as his workroom back at the museum, a uniformed officer behind a counter gave him back his belt, wallet, keys, and some coins. He took the hefty fifty-key keyring and examined it closely.

"Everything still there?" the officer asked.

Sam shook his head, not in denial but in helplessness. "Everything's here, but . . ."

The officer leaned forward. He was suntanned, with a warm, seamed face and oversized Texas mustachios. "You're thinking that we might have made copies of your keys?"

Sam shrugged. "Yeah."

"Well, that'd be against the law, now, wouldn't it?"
The man winked at Sam.

Despite himself, Sam smiled back. "Yeah."

"Go on, son. Git goin'." The officer pointed at a
door. Through it was a corridor, at the end of which was
yet another door. Above it, a green "Exit" sign glowed
invitingly.

Sam wasted no more time. Back at the museum,
Grant was waiting. So was his robot.

* * * * *

In the police station commissary, detectives McStay
and Johnstone talked the matter out over sandwiches.

"You're a fool to let him go." Johnstone sat hunched
forward over the small table, a torpedo sandwich
gripped tightly in both hands. "That robot could do any
number of dangerous things, cause all kinds of damage."

McStay leaned back in his chair, fiddling with an unlit
cigarette. Grimacing, he broke it in two and threw it to
the floor. "Maybe. Maybe not. Did you read the kid's
file or just skim the high points?"

Johnstone sneered at him but kept listening.

"Okay. The kid's a loudmouth jerk." McStay listed the
points while making marks on the table with his pen.
"Crabby, cranky, but this is the big one: He's a genius.
Cook would have given anything for the boy's loyalty.
So?"

"So you shouldn't have let the robot go."

McStay pounded his fist on the table. "I don't have
enough cause to impound the damned thing!"

"The kid's a criminal."

"His slander was a civil matter."

"Same thing."

"Look, it just isn't in him to go and build a murder weapon. That robot's got to be a five-, six-year project. Do you think maybe he wants to murder Mr. Cook 'cause he owes him so much money? Nope."

"I had twelve officers playing bouncy-bouncy with that goofy machine. Tossed 'em around real good. Too dangerous."

"Nobody got hurt, though." McStay smiled nastily. "Suppose you tried having twelve officers tackle a bulldozer or an elevator car."

Around a mouthful of sandwich, Johnstone muttered, "Yeah, yeah. So what do we do now?"

"Leave things just the way they are. Pruitt will watch things at the museum. We'll go fishing for more evidence. Way things are now, we don't prosecute."

"Except for the nuisance charges?"

"Those?" McStay stabbed his pen back into his pocket. "Who gives a damn about those?"

CHAPTER TWELVE

Officer Pruitt's patrol car pulled up smoothly into one of the parking spaces behind the museum. Sunlight shone down on the tall, whitewashed building. The architecture was a hybrid-milieu mixture of Mexican-Spanish missions and Old-Spanish alcazars. Florid sculpted friezes of a bellicose motif ran around the building, high under the overhanging red-tile roofs. At the very top of the building, a ridiculously tiny belvedere stood.

"Everybody out," Pruitt announced.

Grant helped Delta exit the car. As he did, he brushed his fingers softly over her lips, in time to silence what she might next have said.

It wouldn't do for her to ask, "Where are we?" he thought. *No, that simply wouldn't do.*

"Come along, then, Mr. Pruitt." Grant took hold of Delta's arm and looped it over his shoulders, so that he could serve as a crutch for her injured foot. "Come along, Delta."

"Delta?" Pruitt watched the two walk. "What the heck kind of a name is 'Delta'?"

Grant smiled. "What kind of name is Fletcher Pruitt? Or Grant Alexander? I knew a man named Larrabee Lazenby McGonigle MacAuliffe." He glared at Pruitt as if daring him to doubt it. "We called him by his nickname, of course."

"Yeah?" Pruitt said.

"We called him 'Steinmetz.' But you had to earn the right."

Pruitt looked at Grant and began to shake his head. He saw the way he helped Delta walk. It was a small thing, an everyday act of gentility. How out of place it seemed in a world where civility and thoughtfulness were artificial, abstract concepts.

"Go ahead and fling wide the door—be a brave lad." Grant and Delta walked along the gravel path from the parking lot to the side door. Tall trees lined the street on both sides. The few drivers who passed by paid little or no attention to the sight of an elderly man helping a silver robot to walk.

" 'The Quentin Corey Museum of Antiquities,' " Pruitt read from the black lettering fastened to the museum's east facade. A long, wide ornamental bank of stairs, twice interrupted by landings, led up to wide double doors. "I haven't been here since I was in school."

"Yes," Grant said, his voice dry. "It took us hours to scrape the chewing gum from beneath the railing."

Pruitt had the grace to blush.

"Go ahead, Mister Pruitt. Tell Maddy that I'm back

with Delta." He smiled secretly to himself. Maddy was a hell of a lot smarter than she let on. She'd know enough to keep her peace.

Pruitt, pausing partway up the stairs, turned and looked at Grant. "Maddy? Old Miss Schenk? You mean she's still the curator?" He smiled. "Man, she had us terrified. We'd come here on research trips, and she scared the living daylights out of us. She's still here?"

Grant smiled lopsidedly. "Just go ahead and tell her, will you do that, lad? There's a soldier. Leave the door propped open for us."

Pruitt threw a mock salute, as stiff and formal as he could make it, and spun and sprinted up the stairs.

"Calls that a salute, does he? The dog of the day would be clapped in irons for a salute half as sloppy as that, back in the Twenty-eighth," Grant muttered, shaking his head. Turning to Delta, he began to whisper quickly. "I'm Grant. Maddy's inside. We're trying to deceive this Pruitt bloke. Try to say nothing to give away our game. The story is that Sam Taramasco built you. Did you see him back there?"

Delta's voice was soft, a gentle, kindly voice. "Yes."

"You understand what I'm saying? You can play along with this necessary deception? It keeps you free."

"I will say nothing."

"Good soldier!" Grant helped her up the last of the stairs and through the glass-paned doors.

*   *   *   *   *

Delta found herself wondering and amazed at the complexity of the human mind. The television shows she had watched, in the cold winter snowdrifts outside Mrs. Gessenby's home, depicted human motivations as serialized conflicts that were always resolved in a short half-hour span. Now it seemed as if television and reality were two different things, linked only metaphorically to each other.

When Grant offered his help, lifting some of her weight off her ankle, she was astonished. No one had ever aided her before.

And what of the younger man, Sam Taramasco? That was the name that this old man had mentioned. Delta had only seen Sam briefly. He'd calmed her, speaking kindly and rationally to her. Then he had gone off, seated in the back of a police car. He had been taken away to the containment that was meant for her.

She grieved a little then. Something in Sam had called to her.

At the top of the stairs, she hesitated a bit. The museum was dark. Then, trusting Grant, she went inside with him.

The complexity of the interior layout stunned her. Everywhere stood high display cases, filled with astonishing things. She quite forgot her distress and her pain, and pulled slightly away from Grant in order to look more closely. The purpose of the clear-glass displays was instantly obvious to her. Here was a place where instruction was taken through observation.

A section of anthropological exhibits stood before her. She strolled slowly through them, looking to left and right. A cutaway grass hut lay exposed behind glass: within it, mannequins huddled together, facing a small simulated fire.

They wear clothing, Delta saw. *And their home has windows. They watch the moving light.* Either of them could be Mrs. Gessenby, in her home in the snow. Impulsively, she stood on tiptoe to see if anyone could be seen peeking through the window behind the two mannequins, the way Delta had peeked through Mrs. Gessenby's window.

On the other side was a scale model of a medieval siege. A crenelated castle wall supported several archers, who discouraged the charge of a band of mounted men-at-arms. Already familiar with television, Delta wasn't disturbed by the concept of model on a reduced scale, but she was fascinated with the men in their flexible metal armor.

When she moved only a step to her right, she found herself facing a full-sized figure, a suit of plate armor. It was a full suit of ornate Italian plate, high-helmed, broad-breasted, and burnished to a gleaming silver shine. The helmet had only the narrowest of slits for viewing through; to Delta, it seemed as if it had no face at all.

"Hello," she said, speaking politely to the first person she'd yet seen here who was at all like herself. The display of armor made no response.

Hesitantly Delta reached out and touched it, running her hand up to the face. She felt at the visor, saw that it was hinged, and lifted it.

The head was empty.

A sharp thrill of horror passed through her. She felt as a man might feel when, invited into the home of his host, he finds a skeleton dangling from a gibbet. Was this what they intended for her? Would her life and her strength be drawn out of her as it had been from this thing?

Or . . . Delta calmed her panicky thoughts. *Am I already hollow? I never thought to wonder. Are things made up of no more than their surfaces?*

She turned and walked back to where Grant, Madeline, and Pruitt stood.

*   *   *   *   *

Madeline Lenoir Schenk sat in the wheelchair that had become for her almost a part of her body. So much of modern museum operation was a constant appeal for funds. Her correspondences were far more likely to be financial than scientific or historical; requests outnumbered inquiries. This museum had become a home to her, and she would do what was needed to keep it afloat. The high overhead lights were off, and the only illumination for most of the hall came through the windows. Long slanting beams of sunlight shot straight through one window, spotlighting the rearing skeleton of a cave bear in the main lobby. A small brass lamp with a low green shade lit up her cluttered desk.

What I would not give to hire a secretary, she thought wearily. Her letters were all handwritten, and she insisted on using a crow's-quill pen and India ink meticulously scraped from a small block. She was not unaware of the fact that in this museum of antiquities, her own techniques of office-keeping were antique also. She chose not to devote the time to retraining herself to newer methods, however. She believed that typewriters were soulless.

Behind her, in the east entrance, one of the doors banged open.

Is not Grant. Grant pushes doors open with more gentleness. She smiled. *That is because he is the one who must rehinge them when they break.*

She backed her wheelchair around and looked down an aisle. She saw Officer Pruitt. He hurried toward her, having left the door wide open. Madeline frowned in disgust at his poor manners. The museum furnaces hadn't been fired up in decades, but there was no reason to let it become colder in here than it was already. Pruitt half-walked, half-ran toward her, then stopped and approached her with a bit more dignity. In the dim light, all that Madeline could see for certain was that the man was a policeman.

That sort of man who has little class, but in this sorry age, no one could be expected to show good manners. Little by little, gentility died in the world. It, too, was an obsolete and antiquated mode of behavior.

"Miss Schenk?"

"*Oui.* You are to be who?" She didn't wait for his answer but went on, her voice rising. "And why is the door leaving open? Were you born in the stables?"

Pruitt's eyes went wide. "Uh . . . Grant Alexander is coming right in behind me, ma'am. . . ."

"And he does not know how to open this doors?" Madeline wheeled herself toward Pruitt, who backed off a step.

"He—he asked me to leave the door open." Pruitt pulled off his cap and held it in front of him. "Please, ma'am. He asked me to."

Madeline looked up at the young man. "Then I am

the one who has faulted and will owe you my apology." The contrition she felt was deep, sincere, honest, and it showed on her face. "I made assumption defaulting from wrongness. I misaccused you. Can you please take tea, perhaps, or coffee?"

"Oh, nothing, please. I'm here on business."

Just then Grant appeared at the doorway, aiding a svelte young woman. Madeline could only see their silhouettes against the brightness of the afternoon. What she saw made the short hairs at the back of her neck bristle. The woman with Grant was nude. She was silver. And she had an injured right ankle.

Grant left the woman and hurried down the aisle toward Madeline. Madeline could not tear her gaze away from the silver woman. There was a strangeness about the way her knees and elbows were articulated; no extreme of arthritic disease could explain the elegant slimness of those joints. This was not a human woman.

Grant came up to her, slightly out of breath. Madeline looked up at him. He was wearing his stern, worried expression, looking at her with his face slightly lowered, his eyes wide and serious.

He wants me to keep silent, lest I give away the lies he has already told this policeman, Maddy sensed.

When two people have worked together for over fifty years, they grow to understand this kind of teamwork. Madeline knew that Grant could never lie to her, no matter how he might try, and she knew that he understood her far too well ever to be deceived by her. That sort of companionship was a far warmer thing than mere love.

"Good afternoon, Grant. Persuade with me this policeman to take coffee."

"Coffee!" Grant boomed. "Just the thing! I'll fetch the cups."

"You must state your business, M'sieur . . . ?"

Pruitt swallowed. This was the deadly Miss Schenk, who had frightened him so badly when he was young. It was both reassuring and disturbing to see her still alive, for she had been very old when he had come here as a schoolchild. But she had changed little, and the museum had changed even less. It was still as dark and as quiet as a tomb.

"I'm Officer Pruitt, ma'am."

Madeline smiled and held out her hand. Pruitt took it and shook it gently. He saw that she was still waiting for him to explain his duty here.

"Well, ma'am, there was a disturbance downtown involving Sam's robot." He wiped his hand nervously on his trousers. "You do know Sam Taramasco, don't you?"

Grant returned at that moment with three cups of coffee, the saucers balanced precariously along his arm. In his free hand, he held a fistful of wrapped sugar cubes and a small pitcher of cream. Madeline took one cup, and Pruitt gratefully caught up another. Grant dribbled a precise measure of cream into Madeline's cup, then set the pitcher within Pruitt's reach. He left his own coffee black.

"Sam's a good boy," Grant snapped. "His robot never hurt anyone and never will. Sam doesn't build things to hurt people."

"*Vraiment*, too true!" Madeline frowned and cast a quick glance at Grant. "Sam builds things to learn, to listen. Is scientist."

"Well, I'm assigned to keep an eye on this robot,"

Pruitt said. "Grant's going to have to show me how to work her."

"Simplicity itself!" Grant's voice was loud and boisterous. "The robot is voice-actuated. It can obey several simple commands."

"Oh, and here she comes now," Madeline observed, unable to keep a note of fascination out of her voice. *A robot? In a museum of antiquities?*

The design was marvelous. Madeline looked with great interest at the intricacy of the robot's form. The machine had no face, and yet had a humanlike mouth. It had breasts—high, well-formed breasts—above a flat belly and wide hips. Madeline wondered whether she should think of this vision as an "it" or as a "she."

"Please," Delta said then, in a soft, inquisitive voice.

Madeline made up her mind. This machine might be a robot, a computer, a machine and nothing more, but she was definitely a she.

"Are things made only of their surfaces," Delta asked, "or do things have internal structure?"

Madeline was the first to speak. "Only when you look behind a surface does structure become revealed. Things over their outsides are appearance, but things in their insides are reality."

"Surfaces reflect, then? Interiors reveal?" Delta tilted her head to one side in concentration.

Pruitt gaped. "That's—that's *philosophy!*"

Madeline, Grant, and Delta all looked at him. His eyes went horribly wide.

"Of course is philosophy," Madeline said. "Not everyone is born already knowing these things. If we don't ask questions, afraid of seeming foolish, foolishness is certain winner." She smiled and sipped at her coffee. "Scholar's duty is always clear. Slay ignorance. Vanquish illiteracy." Her eyes gleamed with dedication and fervor.

"But she's . . . smart!" Pruitt pointed a finger at Delta. "You're smart! That's . . ." He stopped. He didn't know what it was: An intelligent machine was as alien to him as a talking dog would be.

Grant spread his hands, a gesture meant only for Madeline. She quickly understood that Delta's intelligence was a revelation that would have best been kept from the policeman.

"Pointing fingers is impolite," she said fussily. "You are smart and serve the city as a *gendarme*, policeman. I am smart and hold antiquities in old museum. Grant is not smart—"

"I say?" Grant interrupted.

Madeline winked at him. "I tease. Grant is okay smart, never genius. I read that they taught a gorilla to talk, so perhaps anything should happen."

"Teaching gorillas to talk," Grant intoned solemnly, "is a far, far easier task than teaching the same to a Frenchman."

Madeline sputtered in outrage. "*Non!* A insult! I outrage!"

"Please stop," Delta said, her voice low and unhappy. Grant and Madeline put aside their mock feud instantly. "We only argue on surface, do you see?" Madeline explained to her. "Not for real. Look beneath surfaces."

Pruitt closed his eyes and shook his head. "It's all too much for me." He picked up his coffee and wandered off into the maze of museum display cases.

Madeline leaned forward and spoke in a low voice so that only Grant and Delta could hear.

"What is this about, then, for really?"

Grant explained it all to her swiftly and succinctly. Madeline, slightly bewildered but willing to accept it, nodded in general comprehension.

"We will keep M'sieur Pruitt overbalanced, then, until Sam comes again." She smiled thinly. "This task is not a hard one."

CHAPTER THIRTEEN

Sam Taramasco arrived back at the Quentin Corey Museum of Antiquities shortly after six-thirty in the evening. The twilight air was warm, but the warmth was brittle. A chill hung high in the air, waiting to descend. This part of the city was sparsely lit; a scattered handful of stars fought back against the glow of streetlamps and headlights. Purple and crimson streamers of pale light still showed in the west. Sam walked, whistling saucy Irish folk songs and keeping his eyes open.

There was the museum, a dark shadow of a building, only a faint glow coming from its high windows. Sam smiled. Home, for him, was a museum, and his family was made up of its two elderly curators.

The front doors were unlocked, as always. Sam dragged the lefthand door open a little way and edged within. The vast interior of the building was dimly lit, with huge shadows standing high against the walls.

"Is Sam," Madeline's voice sounded from her small office behind the display of bronze spear points. "Come welcome, Sam."

Into the aisle between display cases, Grant stepped slowly. He was only a silhouette, but Sam detected a hint of direness in his stance. "Come on in, lad, and meet Officer Pruitt."

Sam smiled to himself. It was so like Grant to issue the first warning. There would be no freedom of speech tonight.

The museum was an odd home, a cavernous, spacious place, given over to the hallowed past. When Sam walked, his footsteps echoed; when he spoke, his voice rebounded from the cold marble walls. Grant disappeared again, going back into Madeline's office.

Sam hurried down the aisle and swung into the office himself. The only light in the entire vast building came from Madeline's shaded desktop lamp, and the only warmth from a small kerosene stove. Grant sat on a low wooden crate, holding the cold white skull of a zebra in his hands. He was polishing it, running an oil-slicked rag over and around it. Madeline looked up and smiled when Sam came in, then returned to her letters. She was thickly bundled with blankets over her wheelchair, and she wore a thick wool sweater. Her silver-gray hair was tied behind her head in a simple ponytail.

"Hello, Sam." Officer Pruitt stood but did not offer Sam his hand. There was obvious emotional strain on his face, and it was clear that he would welcome a friendly word. Almost despite himself, Sam smiled at the forlorn man.

"Officer Pruitt?"

"Yep." The man beamed. He sat again, heavily, clumsily. "Fletcher Pruitt. Call me Fletcher. Geez, I . . ." He might have said more, but he stopped when he saw Sam look at Delta.

She, like Grant and Pruitt, was seated upon a bare wooden crate. She was still naked, and Sam found himself stunned by her beauty.

She was sexy; Sam could never have ignored her obvious physical presence. She was female, in form and in posture, and she was lovely. But she had no face. A tiny *frisson* sped up and down Sam's spine.

"Delta's okay, Sam." Grant spoke casually, his voice controlled. "Her ankle is twisted pretty bad, but Pruitt swears it was that way when the police first spotted her."

Swallowing, Sam fell into the act with natural ease. "Then it must have happened earlier. I'd like to know how."

Delta stood slowly, favoring her right foot. "I fell into a swift-moving stream." Her voice was soft and warm and very human. Sam felt the hair at the back of his neck begin to stand stiff and bristly, a sign more of reverence than of fear.

"Did you get your foot caught in the rocks?" Sam asked, his own voice suddenly scratchy and nervous.

"Yes."

"I told you it wasn't us who damaged her," Pruitt asserted.

Sam shook his head. "That's okay, then, Fletcher." He tried to smile but could not. "It isn't your fault." He stared at Delta in rapt fascination.

The small area between the display vaults was warm, dimly lit, and friendly. It was like a small nest, feathered with memories, with Grant's hair-raising tales, with Madeline's ghastly malapropisms and her penetrating wit. Fletcher Pruitt was only a minor distraction, but Delta was completely out of place in this warm spot in Sam's universe.

Sam needed to go out; he needed to get away. But he needed to talk to Delta far more.

Delta. Is that her name? It says nothing about her, and yet it fits her so well. . . .

"Delta, come with me, please." He spoke peremptorily, almost brusquely. Madeline, listening carefully, nodded without turning her head. She could tell what strain the boy was under.

Delta stood and followed Sam as he backed slowly away from the small office. Pruitt started to rise but was stopped when Grant looked up and grinned at him. "Amazing, isn't it? Scrap plate and stepping motors, and you'd think she was alive." He forestalled Pruitt's objections with a theatrical stab in the air with a thick, gnarled finger.

"But that's no paradox. Not at all. In the Great War, when the first tanks came over the battlefield toward us, we knew they were more than just machines. Dinosaurs, we thought, or dragons. It took a man of iron nerve to stand and face those monstrosities. . . ."

Delta followed Sam out into the dark aisles of the museum. Grant's sonorous voice echoed from the high vaults of the ceiling.

In and out of the many paths between library stacks of books, Sam led and Delta followed. In the darkness, her hand slipped into his. His flesh was warm and strong; her metal was chill and impossibly solid. Sam felt completely bewildered. Was this a woman or a robot? Physically she was lovely, but what kind of mind did she have?

He stopped and turned to face her. They looked at one another, surrounded by darkness and the dusty weight of the ages.

"Who are you?" Sam whispered.

"I am Delta." She knew how little this was by way of an answer, but it was all she knew to say. "I am not an enemy."

"Where do you come from?"

"Forever ago; forever away." Her voice was troubled. "There was a sky-filling antagonism. Something of me was there, but only a part. . . . The world was so different!"

Sam heard the pain in her voice. It sounded very human. He wished he had some way to comfort her. He squeezed her hand more tightly, just as he would have with a real person. Woman or robot or whatever she might be, he couldn't just sit and watch her suffer.

"How did you come here?"

Delta thought. "I don't know. The rules changed. I knew of a light that was so unlike the light of this world, and a time that isn't anything like time here. But the light and the time were at war. I was a part of the war." She continued in a hushed, awed voice. "I was only the smallest part of it. I was one moving handful of water in a very big river. Or—or perhaps I never really was alive as me, as myself, until I stood on your snowy Earth."

"Delta . . ." Sam began. She turned her faceless face to him, and he saw the ghostly flat silver surface in the darkness.

"The war continues," she said. "It is an always-and-forever war, catching up all light, all time. I am a soldier, on your world to fight."

"You're not a soldier, Delta."

She removed her hand from his. The touch, the contact with his warm flesh, had been a comfort, although she could not understand it. Even so, she was leery of being contained. "I am. I am seeking another."

"Another like yourself?"

"No! Not like me in any way. Nor is he like you. He is . . ."

Sam waited.

Delta drew back a little way from him. "He is my opposite, who thinks only of breaking things open to disrupt their wholeness." Her mouth was small and frightened. "He is also your enemy, not only mine. But you are not a soldier."

"I can be," Sam said softly, "if you need me to be."

"He is Omicron, and he is an enemy. He would break the curve of your Earth. He would twist the geometry of your rivers. He hates the laws that make life possible and that make the world knowable."

"What does he look like?" Sam wanted to know.

In her mind, Delta groped for the source of her knowledge. She had never seen Omicron, but she knew what he looked like. She had never been near him, but it now seemed that she could hear his voice. She had never touched him, and yet his cold hands groped at her, ruining her metal where he touched it.

"I—I—" She stood, a bit too quickly, wrenching her ankle. Pain showed in her awkward stance, and she gripped the corner of a museum display case for support.

Sensing her distress, Sam stepped back. "Delta, I'll

do anything to help you."

She smiled, seeking a way to explain to him why he should stay out of this war, when her universe split into two lateral halves.

Omicron was far away, to the north and west. The cold voice that was like his but so very different was close, close nearby.

She whirled and tried to go to it, but bookshelves were in her way. She felt along them, trying to get past.

Sam was by her side in an instant. "What's wrong, Delta?"

She could not answer. It was as if she stood on two floors, saw both light and darkness at once, or walked both backward and forward. All referents had ambivalent meanings. She fought her way past the bookstacks and ran in the darkness across the floor of the museum. Quickly she slammed up against a wall.

Sam was beside her. "What's wrong, Delta?" he repeated. He kept his voice low, hoping that none of the others would hear.

"It is behind here," she whispered. "It is a small voice, and I must see it."

A shiver of apprehension thrilled through Sam. "My radio equipment is in there."

"Take me past this wall."

"All right." He took her hand and drew her a little to one side. Opening the door, he reached inside and flipped on the tiny overhead bulb.

Delta pushed past him, ignoring the sight of his computer, his radio receivers, his tuners and amplifiers. She knelt before his transmitter, a small device with two meters and several switches on its dark metal cabinet.

"Here . . ." she said, her face pressed close against it. "It is here."

My radio, Sam realized in pained amazement. *She was brought here by my radio signals!* He watched Delta. She lifted one hand to the panel facing on his transmitter and touched it softly. Her metal gleamed in the overhead light. Kneeling on the floor in a submissive, attentive pose, she seemed to be no more than a statue in cast silver. Sam was afraid that she would freeze thus and never move again; he was afraid he'd called her forth only to lose her.

The timing circuit switched itself off. The voice ceased. Slowly Delta stood.

"What is this thing?" she asked, her voice small and uncertain.

Sam looked at her, seeing himself reflected in her smooth face.

"Only a radio . . ." He turned the receiver on and demonstrated the equipment, bringing in a talk show from Kansas City. A caller was asking for advice on how to break up with her boyfriend, and a calm-voiced psychologist answered with useless platitudes.

"I can't hear any of this," Delta muttered. Sam smiled to himself, for it seemed that she was almost petulant.

"You can only hear the one frequency, most likely."

"Why did you speak with this voice?"

Sam explained. "I heard it myself, with this receiver, some twenty or so days ago. It was right here. . . ." He tinkered with the dial until eventually he found the chirruping radio whir. "Something out there is making radio noise on that frequency."

Delta froze, her mind whirling. The noise was a strange aural analogue of the knowledge she had of Omicron's position. It was wrong, horribly wrong, but it was also very strangely right. Omicron had spoken to this young man, and he, in innocence, had answered. She smiled to herself. She remembered answering when men had first spoken to her. "Who the hell are you?" they had asked, and "Who the hell are you?" she had parroted back. Sam was like her; he was made of the same mind, if not the same metal. She waited for him to straighten up from his instruments. Her bearing was stiff. "Do you know where it comes from?"

"No." Sam looked at her. He tried to smile but found he couldn't.

"It comes from that direction—" she pointed—"and from a distance of one million, four hundred and fifty two thousand, eight hundred of my paces. He is one hundred and sixty-nine thousand of my paces below us."

"He?" Sam thought he already knew the answer. "Who? Omicron?"

"Yes."

"Please wait." Sam left the room. Delta listened to the radio interpretation of Omicron's ever-present voice. The enemy had betrayed himself. Soon she would find him.

Sam returned in a moment with an atlas of the United States and a small compass. "What direction is he?" Delta obliged by pointing. Sam lined up the direction with his compass.

He looked at her legs and feet, estimated the length of her pace, and performed some quick calculations in his head. Delta, seeing him juggle the book and the compass, held out her hands to him and accepted the atlas as he gratefully laid it onto her palms.

"Here. He's here. . . ." Sam pointed to a spot on one page of the atlas.

"No, he's not." Delta held the book in one hand and pointed with the other. "He's that way—"

"No," Sam said and shook his head. "He's out there, but this is a picture of where he is." He looked at her, looked down at the map, and quickly switched the book around so that it was right side up for her. She looked at it without comprehension.

"Nevada," he muttered. "Right about here, at least within a hundred-mile circle. The estimate is a bit rough, but that's what I figure. Except that this whole region is higher in elevation than here." He looked at her quizzically. "But what I can't figure out is that you say he's below us. Almost a hundred miles down? Is that right?"

"Yes."

"But how . . ." Realization dawned on Sam. The earth is round. He moved his finger slightly farther out into Nevada. "He's here."

"No . . ." Delta began, then paused. "Oh." The realization was stunning to her. She pulled the book closer to her faceless face and gazed at it in amazement. "This is a depiction in miniature of . . . of . . ." She waved her hand. "Of the world?"

"Yes." Sam gripped her arm in excitement. "We're here." He jabbed his finger down on top of San Antonio. "And Omicron is here." He indicated the middle of Nevada.

Delta ran her own finger over the map, while holding

the book in her other hand. "I don't feel the mountains."

Sam swallowed and tried to explain.

The hours passed as Sam gave Delta more and more knowledge of the earth. Several times during the evening he dashed out and came back with more books—dictionaries, picture books, bestiaries, and travelogues. He showed her the path she'd taken, and together they deduced the point where she had first come to Earth. He showed her how rivers ran, how trees grew, and what cities and roads were for. She caught on more quickly than any human student could ever have done. Sam soon realized that she was smarter than anyone he'd ever met. She was even smarter than he was.

He admired her openly. He was attracted to the womanly shape of her body, the more so because of the perfection of her mechanical engineering. But he also very much admired her brilliant, inquisitive, seeking mind. Suddenly, sweeping aside the many books and pictures that he'd brought to show her, he reached impulsively for her and kissed her. Then, surprised and embarrassed, he pulled back.

"I'm . . . sorry, Delta." He held her hands. "That was wrong of me. It's crazy. It's just that you . . ."

Delta tilted her head to one side in a gesture very appealingly human. "Yes?"

"You're absolutely beautiful," Sam breathed.

"I'm afraid I don't completely understand." Then, her voice low and her head bent forward, she murmured, "But perhaps I do. . . ."

* * * * *

In the museum office, Grant talked of old hunts, old wars, and old feuds along the untamed rivers of the Far East, until Officer Pruitt, his reason almost blasted by the onslaught of thunderous new ideas, fell asleep in his chair.

Grant smiled and took a deep, heavy breath. "By Jove!" he sighed. He turned to see Madeline gazing at him intently, an expression of wonder on her face.

"Grant H. Alexander, you are my very favorite liar."

"Now, Maddy," Grant protested. "Most of that was true."

"Some things of it were, but other ones were not. Parts were a lie."

"A little," he admitted.

"One little. One big, big little. I love you anyway, for tales telling and putting little Pruitt to bed. He comes to museum when child, *non?*"

"I knew you'd remember."

"Out the lights. Museum pays for electricity." Madeline snapped off her desk light and wheeled herself off to her bedroom.

"Good night, Maddy," Grant said softly. He looked down in the darkness at Pruitt. "Good night, Fletcher, my lad."

CHAPTER FOURTEEN

Well before eight in the morning, the newsmen began to arrive. Newspapermen came first, driving up in rugged old automobiles. Later, closer to their eight-o'clock appointment, the camera crews pulled in, in vans tightly packed with electronic equipment.

Grant greeted them all, waving and making such grand theatrical gestures that one would think him the master of ceremonies at a state luncheon. The photographers took a few snapshots of him to be polite.

Inside the museum, while Madeline kept Officer Pruitt distracted, Sam coached Delta in the most current robot etiquette. In a quiet niche behind a towering map cabinet, they stood where none could see them. Sunlight filled the upper half of the building and filtered down softly to the floor.

"You have to talk stiffly," he explained. "Talk . . . like . . . this. . . ."

Delta turned her peculiarly blank face to him. "Why?"

Sam flushed. "It's what they expect. It really is best if we try to attract the least possible attention."

"By . . . talking . . . like . . . this?" Delta thought for a moment. "But it sounds so foolish."

"That was good. But you have to keep it up. And more nasal."

"More what?"

Sam looked at her. She didn't have a nose. "More atonal."

"Like . . . this?"

"Yep."

"Very well."

"More. You have to walk stiffly, too." Sam demonstrated a locked-knees robot gait.

Delta laughed, sounding utterly human. She covered her mouth with her hand. "Sam!"

"If you walk like a zombie and talk like an addlepated fool, then people might believe that I built you. There's no way they'll ever be able to accept your actual sophistication."

"Oh, Sam." She bowed elegantly, then took up a stiff, jerky pace, her arms swinging stiffly as she walked. She looked so utterly like a toy robot that Sam was hard pressed to stifle laughter.

"You think this is funny, don't you?"

"No." Sam bit his lips.

"Yes. You do."

"Well . . ." He came to her and hugged her. "Yes. I'm afraid I do."

"Perhaps it is." She smiled. "Very well. But Officer

Pruitt has seen me behaving naturally. Won't he make unwanted deductions?"

"Grant tells me that the man has never made a deduction in his life." Sam stepped back and paced up and down for a few moments. "I'm less certain. He's a policeman, and that means he's observant. But he's young. . . ."

"So are you," Delta noted, "and you're very definitely observant."

Sam grinned at her saucily. "You're younger than I am."

She drew herself up in haughty pride. "I wasn't born yesterday."

Together they went out into the museum. Madeline wheeled out in her antique three-wheeled chair and looked them over. After a moment, Sam began to become uncomfortable under her scrutiny.

"You fit together," she said at last. "I perplex, only at first. You two have sense of fitness." She smiled and adjusted her glasses. "Shall we go and tell big lies to newspaper cameras?"

"Yes," Delta said softly, "I think that's best."

Sam looked around. "Where's Pruitt?"

"Hiding in back, combing his hair, knowing newsmen will have photography. He thinks of himself on front page of the newspapers." Her voice was bitter. "Grant has more dignity."

"What will we tell him?" Delta wondered.

"Something like the truth," Sam said.

*   *   *   *   *

On the front steps of the museum, the press stood in packed array. Grant held them at bay, standing his ground like a British officer before an advance of Chinese Boxers. There was something magnificent in the way he doled out information about Sam, giving a useful word or two of news interspersed with paragraphs of colorful, unhelpful language.

One reporter had spent some time getting the exact spelling of "Taramasco." "What's his national ancestry?" he pursued.

"American, sir," Grant affirmed. "Spanish, Italian, Greek, Native American, and God knows what all else." He spread his hands. "All the Mediterranean in one boy. Hybrid vigor. Make some young woman a fine husband someday. It makes one proud, I must say."

"Are his parents alive?"

"Probably. He hasn't spent his whole life in San Antonio, as you well ought to know. He's traveled—"

A stir ran through the newsmen as Sam and Delta came out onto the landing at the top of the shallow stairs. Sam held the door open for Madeline, who in turn held it for Pruitt. Pruitt frowned at the sight of the many cameras and looked as if he would much rather go back indoors.

"Traveled, Grant? I've been as far east as Shreveport." There was a brief ripple of laughter at that. Grant allowed Sam to upstage him and drew back to where Madeline sat watching.

"You're the young man with the robot?" a reporter asked. Sam shrugged and tilted his head toward Delta.

"I . . . am . . . pleased . . . to . . . meet . . . you," Delta said in a voice totally devoid of inflection. She took two tottering steps forward, rotated half a turn to her left, and made a small, stiff bow. Sam knew that if he started laughing now he would never be able to stop.

The questioning began in earnest. How had he come to build her? Was it a "she," or was she an "it?" How had she come to be out of control on East Commerce Street yesterday afternoon? Were the police going to get a court order to have her dismantled? Did he have any response to the charges they had filed?

The sun shone in Sam's face, warming him, encouraging him. In the treetops, birds made small twittering noises, as important to them as the newsmen's chatter was to them. Occasional automobiles swept slowly by on the uncrowded street, drivers rolling down their windows to get a better look.

Sam played it down, without seeming unduly reticent. "It's a robot," he said, smiling. "What does that really mean? Gears? Pulleys? A microprocessor chip and an automobile battery? Well, yes, but more: It's a way of looking at ourselves."

"Can she compose music?"

"That's not in her programming."

"Can she hurt people?"

Sam held up his hand. "That's a very important issue. Yes, she can hurt people. But I think your cameras are just as dangerous."

He paused, knowing that they would all perceive the subtlety of his comment. Ideas, he knew, were dangerous. Publicity could be a weapon; communication of words meant communication of values, perhaps threatening ones. No one who worked for broadcast news could be unaware of this. But Sam just smiled vapidly and went on. "After all, you could drop them on some-one's foot."

Before long, the interview was over. Film had been ex-posed, videotape recorded, Sam's words jotted down. Delta had performed admirably, playing stupid as only a truly intelligent person can. A photographer had gotten a close-up of her metal hand holding an egg, displaying the fineness of her motor control. Sam shrugged. If it had been he playing at being a robot, he probably would have crushed the egg. Delta's show was less threatening, he realized.

She really is smarter than I am.

He stood on the step for a long time, watching the newsmen pack their equipment back into their cars and vans. Pruitt and Madeline went back into the museum, followed, after a time, by Grant. Sam was oblivious to the alert glance that Grant cast at him.

Soon he and Delta stood alone in the sunshine.

*   *   *   *   *

"Sam?" Delta's voice was blessedly normal.

He shook his head. "Woolgathering." And because he knew she couldn't know what that meant, he looked at her and forced a smile. "I was just trying to think. I'm not very good at it, you know."

"Nonsense." Delta's mouth twitched up cheerfully, almost comically, but the rest of her face was as blank as ever.

"You're going to have to go off to fight Omicron. I've promised to go with you." He looked away, then looked back. Struggling for words, he stepped closer to her. "I don't know what's involved. I don't like not knowing."

"Omicron is not your enemy. You can't understand him. He is a threat to your world."

"Then that makes him my enemy."

Delta held Sam, enclosing him in her arms, gently, lovingly. No one had taught her how to hug, how to hold another creature for emotional comfort. It merely felt right. Sam permitted it, and she didn't think to wonder what he must think. "No. You are not made—created with a sole purpose—as I was. I am hunting him. I have to—to contain him."

"Destroy him," Sam said.

Delta only held him tighter. "I don't know what destruction is. I have seen it on television, but I think the images aren't real. I feel that I only know the word."

"You're lucky." Sam leaned forward and, somewhat experimentally, kissed her. "You are blessed. Destruction is mankind's lifelong curse."

"I will leave tomorrow." Delta pulled back from Sam. "No. I have waited too long. I will leave now."

"Don't!" Sam cried. Delta paused. Sam bit his lip. "Not yet. I know so little of you. I—I like you, you know."

"I will wait, then, for a while longer with you."

Together they went back into the museum.

*   *   *   *   *

At midday, they crowded around a small television, which Sam had brought out from his electronics closet, to watch themselves on the noon news.

"Faster and faster," Grant noted. "The world has a

newer, faster pace every day. It tires a man merely to observe it. When I was young, we thought news was quite current if it was only a week or two old."

"This world is impertinent," Madeline agreed. "The week hasn't any end, and the seasons are hasty. Congress sets the clocks back, and, *voila!* is summer. Never anyone dawdles again, wasting time as is human privilege to do. Leisure is perhaps become dirty word."

Pruitt leaned forward, intent on the television. Delta and Sam sat by him, also watching. Sam pretended an indifference he didn't feel; he was still young enough that appearing on television was special for him.

Two news anchors on the screen introduced the next segment with a flippant joke about automation of the workplace making people obsolete, at which point the scene cut to a close-up of Delta's face. The camera pulled back, showing her full figure. An announcer came into the frame and began to explain.

"Oh, not cricket!" Grant complained loudly. "They cut me out entirely!"

Pruitt and Madeline hushed him.

". . . the same robot that terrorized East Commerce Street only yesterday," the reporter continued. "Built by Sam Taramasco, a twenty-six-year-old, self-employed inventor, the robot was intended for general-purpose work, including undersea salvage."

His voiceover continued while the camera showed, variously, shots of the crowd, of the museum, and of Grant and Madeline. One close-up lingered on Officer Pruitt, which both delighted and embarrassed him now as he watched.

"Gosh!" he murmured. "I'm a star."

The coverage finished with another close shot of Delta, speaking in her contrived mechanical voice. "I . . . am . . . pleased . . . to . . . meet . . . you. . . ."

Following this, the two studio news anchors took over, joked a bit more, and turned to a story on a stampede of goats in Del Rio. Sam reached out and shut the receiver off.

"Well done, lad—" Grant began, speaking heartily.

"But wait!" Pruitt interrupted. His face was perplexed. "She doesn't talk like that, not really."

"Talk like what?" Sam asked, looking at Pruitt as if it were the officer and not the robot who had been inconsistent in behavior.

"You know . . ." Pruitt flushed. "She . . . doesn't . . . talk . . . like . . . this. . . ."

Grant chuckled, and even Madeline cracked a smile at Pruitt's nasal, atonal impersonation.

"Of course I don't," Delta said and put a hand comfortingly onto Pruitt's shoulder. She turned back to Sam. "I still don't understand it, you know."

Pruitt blinked in stupid amazement. Nothing would ever make sense again, or so he desperately feared.

"It's really quite simple," Sam said, looking down at the floor for a moment before he meet Pruitt's gaze. "Suppose she spoke with a normal voice. Everyone would assume that the voice was that of a human woman, spoken through a remote microphone. The truth is too complex for the average television audience."

"Oh." Pruitt brightened. "Oh! And that's why you programmed her to walk stiffly?"

"Exactly!" Sam flashed a secret grin of triumph to

Madeline. "If her walk was as loose and as free as it really is, people would simply take it for granted that there was someone inside, wearing a suit of segmented metal. The effect would be lost." He held up his hand. "Perhaps the disbelief wouldn't be conscious, either, but unconscious disbelief is more deadly. The newspeople would approve of what I did if they knew.

"Also," he continued, with a quick nervous laugh, "I can promote Delta later as an 'improved model' without having to change a thing."

"Yeah . . ." Pruitt said slowly. He liked it.

* * * * *

Later in the afternoon, while Sam and Delta were wandering about the museum and while Grant took Pruitt off somewhere and filled him with further false-hoods, Madeline sat in her small office and went through her paperwork.

The museum was on shaky financial ground, although it was, for the present, secure enough. Most of its backing came from the Quentin Corey Foundation. However, the contributions from other sources were vital as well.

While Madeline sat worrying about the state of the museum's fiscal health, her telephone rang. She lifted her head and looked at it with an expression of puzzlement and disgust. No one ever called her; she made her distaste for the instrument abundantly clear.

She caught up the receiver and spoke directly into it. "Yes?"

Then she said nothing but only listened. The caller

had opinions, and did not solicit hers. The message completed, the caller disconnected, denying Madeline even the pleasure of hanging up on him.

She settled the receiver back onto the telephone, blinked a few times in anger and dismay, then reached up and turned off her lamp.

I save a few cents of electricity, she thought and crossed her hands upon her lap.

Then hurriedly, furiously, she backed her wheelchair up and guided it out of her office. Her hands slapped forward on the wheels; she shot down the aisles. "Sam? Sam Taramasco? Come here hither hence!"

Sam, startled, darted out into the aisle to meet her. They nearly collided, but Sam was able to duck one way while Madeline steered sharply in the other. Delta followed Sam and caught him by the arm to keep him from stumbling into a display case.

"Madeline!" Sam gasped. "What's wrong?"

"Cook! Ascendio Carlos Cook! He is a horse's mouth! He is a many-flusher! He has his will with young boys and old dogs! His immorality and conniving shame even the Bosch, and his blatancy has never equal!"

Sam, although dumfounded, still had the presence to answer. "That's what I said, and a jury awarded him two hundred thousand dollars."

Madeline looked at him. "Your crime was underestimating his noisome corruption, never slandering him. Such as he," she pronounced solemnly, "can never be slandered by word or work of man!"

Folding his hands across his chest, Sam asked casually, "I heard your phone ring. Was that him?"

"His lawyer. Phoo! No man should be too self-important to deliver his blackmail in his person." She looked up at Sam. "He wants your robot."

Sam straightened as if slapped. "He—"

"He wants Delta."

"He can't have her!"

"I know that. You know that. Delta knows most of all that." She twisted her mouth. "But Cook has hold you and is twisting his knife."

"Did he threaten you, Maddy?" Sam demanded, his voice low and angry-sounding.

"Me? No, but also yes. He said—" she looked away in fury—"he said he would cut off his support of the museum."

Inhaling sharply, Sam narrowed his eyes in cold rage. Using the power of the law against a man was cowardly enough. Legally obtained court orders were regular and inescapable. But to resort to an act this base, this callous . . .

He let out his breath. His shoulders slumped. "Hell," he said, his voice weak. "He's got me."

Madeline looked up at him in dismay. "But no! You will fight, yes?"

"How? He's got more lawyers than I have shirts. He's already got the law on his side. You know why he did it this way, don't you?"

"No, I do not know." Madeline's anger was gone, completely submerged in her concern for Sam.

"He could have gotten a court order, but then I could respond by taking out a patent on Delta. I'd sell the rights to someone else and pay Cook off in cash. He doesn't want the cash."

"This would be if you had actually made Delta."

"Yes." Sam turned to Delta and buried his face in her breasts. "If."

Madeline nodded. "It must be worth two hundred thousand dollars to slander such a man."

"No," Sam said, trying not to cry. "No, it isn't. Nothing is worth this much pain."

Delta said nothing, but held Sam gently in her arms. She thought she was beginning to understand the word "destroy."

CHAPTER FIFTEEN

.Busk discovered that he was able to lie to Omicron. He told him to dig down, into the earth, to gain power.

Thus Omicron took the earth in his hands and tore at it, ripping boulders away from their sturdy matrix, clawing holes in solid rock. The tunnels he hewed twisted through the rock, heading always downward. A maze developed, tortuous and strangely subtle for having been dug by his ungentle hand. He also dug new exits and adits that let out onto the desert floor so high above. Busk's rising hopes for freedom suffered a setback, however, for Omicron never left him alone long enough to attempt an escape up any of these new tunnels. The cruel, strong giant wasn't about to lose his best source of information about this world.

Busk had showed him how to use the nuclear weapons he had stripped from the desert testing ground above. Busk had also warned him to keep the weapons far away from his small, weak body. Omicron, vast and strong, humored his companion, knowing that the man had curious powers and wisdom that Omicron himself lacked.

"If you use this weapon anywhere near me," Busk said, fear in his voice, "you'll lose me. And I can still help you."

Omicron paused, deep in thought, never realizing why Busk listened to his radio so carefully.

If Busk can help me, then I am weaker without him.

"I have power, too," Busk went on, as if unaware of the trend of Omicron's thoughts. "But I have no power over you."

Omicron, not sensing that Busk's words were a cool lie, was reassured.

"How are nuclear warheads utilized?"

Busk gave that some thought. "The heavy metal inside needs to be compressed, and that's what the explosive pads are for." Nuclear physics in baby talk. Busk shivered.

Omicron had supplied him with light. A huge flame burned against one wall of the cavern. By the opposite wall stood a small pyramid of oil drums. Fresh air entered, and smoke escaped, through some of Omicron's newly driven tunnels. Busk hoped that the army would spot this smoke and come to investigate. In the meantime, he had to breathe the hot, fume-stinking air of the cavern.

Busk wished the place didn't look so much like hell.

"Is there enough rock between you and the nuclear warhead?" Omicron asked, his voice ill-equipped to express polite solicitation.

"I'll have to look," Busk responded. He stood with

difficulty and plodded weakly down the tunnels, counting his paces. He quickly lost count. The tunnels twisted back upon themselves so often that the only direction he was certain of was up.

He didn't dare appear indecisive. "From here, tunnel another hundred yards straight down. That's where to plant the warhead. Remember to seal the tunnel behind you, or else the flame will crawl right back up the tunnel and fry me." He gritted his teeth and cast his dice. "You have nothing to worry about, of course."

"What do you mean?" Omicron's voice was dire.

Busk spread his hands, acting as if the conclusion was obvious. "The closer you are to the center of the blast, the stronger you will become. You want to be right on top of the warhead. That will maximize your power."

Oh, god, let him destroy himself! Busk looked at Omicron and listened to his thoughts.

Power from center of warhead. Maximize power.

Somehow Busk found the strength to climb back up the maze of tunnels to the cavern high above. It was strange, but he had come to think of it as "home."

This isn't my job, he thought, weak and almost delirious with the contradictory pangs of hunger and nausea. His hair had thinned, but it had not fallen out in clumps as he had feared. The radiation dosage wouldn't kill him just yet.

I could probably climb out of here, up one of his exit tunnels, and get away. But he wasn't sure and couldn't find the courage to try. Omicron came back to check on him every so often and always seemed suspicious.

Once the monster had found Busk asleep and had been sorely startled when he saw the soldier awaken.

Since then, Omicron had been careful to mangle the bodies of the men he killed, pulping their corpses with unwholesome thoroughness. Following that, he melted them with the strange beams of powerful light and energy that were his to command.

Busk thought about it and closed his eyes, trying not to be sick. Omicron brought human bodies down to him regularly now. He was reminded of the way a cat will bring offerings of dead birds or mice to the doorsteps of their owners.

I don't own him. Busk gritted his teeth. *I'd give him away to the pound if I did!*

The irony was too much for him. Omicron, a beast, kept Busk, a man, as a pet. He stretched out on the hard, cold rocks and tried to sleep. The flickering oil fire warmed him. Only in sleep could he find comfort.

*   *   *   *   *

Below, Omicron puzzled over the warhead. He'd peeled away its outer casing, exposing the inner works. The tight-woven bundles of wires and the triggering tubes meant nothing to him. In fury, he directed a harsh blast of heat at the weapon. The chemical explosives that were intended to drive the plutonium into a critical state burst blindingly harsh white flares in Omicron's darkness. The plutonium was only pushed around, and most of it was scattered. Several milled chunks coalesced into subcritical masses, releasing floods of radiation and heat. Had Omicron been a man, he would have died more thoroughly and more quickly than anyone had ever died before, dead to his last cell. Being what he was, Omicron

fed upon the heat and simply shed the particles, slough-
ing off the neutron rain without concern.

He scooped up the plutonium fragments, some
melted, some nearly intact, and tried to mold them in
his hands. Killing radiation sleeted forth, and the metal
glowed blue-hot. The light nourished him, but there
was no fission explosion.

Raging, driven to extremes of anger, he turned his
wrath upon the rock and drove several miles of new tunnels, heading always downward.

He glowed now, as he nearly always did, from internal
fires of his own. The first blast, deep underground, had
fed him. He wanted more. His skin had absorbed the radiation and most of the heat by the time he climbed
back to the highest cavern, the attic of his underground
mansion. If he had not been able to absorb it, if he had
been made of normal everyday matter, Busk would have
died within moments.

"The warhead failed." Omicron's announcement,
booming and echoing in the cave, startled Busk awake.
The fire burned brightly, puddles and pools of oil burning warmly, filling the top of the high dome with pungent black smoke. The wall where it burned was stained
with streamers and columns of black soot.

"The warhead . . ." Busk shook his head, trying to
clear it. "The warhead failed? How?"

"Do you have power over the weapon?" Omicron demanded.

Busk frowned. "Only this. I know, in general terms,
how it works. But I don't know the particulars."

*How could I? I'm only a patrol private, with a military
occupational specialty in telegraph operations.*

"I am going to find out," Omicron stated flatly, and he turned to leave. Busk started to rise, knowing what Omicron must have in mind. The monster was going to go up into the military base and kidnap people until he got a nuclear weapons specialist.

"Wait!" He controlled himself, straightening his grimy clothes and trying to appear confident. "Tell me just what you did."

Omicron described his misadventure with the weapon. Busk gaped, dumfounded. "The weapons are delicate. You can't just go hammering on them like that, or they'll fail. Even I know that much."

Learn what little Busk knows before killing him, Omicron thought, and Busk heard it through his radio.

Swallowing, Busk stepped closer to his tormentor and tried to explain the workings of a fission bomb. He described, as well as he could, the way the triggers had to be detonated in precise simultaneity. He did what he could to describe electronic primers and fusing circuits. Inwardly, he didn't know whether to laugh or despair. The knowledge was so common that even he had a good working understanding of the triggering mechanisms of the world's most deadly instruments.

"You can tear through rock with your bare hands," he finished, "but there is a great power in complexity. A computer has the power to think very quickly. And it's a kind of computer circuit in the warhead that triggers the detonators."

"Power in complexity?" Omicron sounded suspicious. "How many kinds of power are there?"

You single-minded bastard! Busk cursed silently. *There are powers you never dared to dream of. There's love. There's faith. And there's courage.*

Oh, how I wish I had the courage!

"There are only a few kinds of power. Only one or two, really. You just haven't learned how to use them. You have to think like a human."

Omicron looked at him with a cool, evaluating expression. Busk suddenly feared that the monster was more human than he appeared. Once he became suspicious of his small human ally, the game was over.

Omicron retraced his steps down through the tunnels and was lost to Busk's sight. The private sought solace in sleep, but he was unable to find it. He waited, a cold dread tightening in his chest. He huddled near the fire, watching the pools of oil burn down slowly.

From far below came a sharp, upward-moving shock. It felt like an earthquake, slowly growing. The cavern shuddered as the stone protested noisily. Shards of rock fell from the roof and clattered heavily onto the rubble below. Busk wondered if Omicron had sealed the tunnel, or if hot, flaming gases were even now rushing up the tunnels, seeking to broil the skin away from his bones.

Finally the earth stopped trembling, and the rocks ceased to groan. Busk uncovered his face and looked around. The oil had splashed a bit, but it continued to burn, warming the cavern.

Busk waited. How had Omicron fared? Could even he have lived through direct exposure to a multi-kiloton fission warhead?

The silence stretched out, but Busk knew a sinking despair in his heart. He could not force himself to hope that Omicron was dead.

Deep below, he heard further rumblings as rock subsided, as vast slabs of stone settled.

Then he heard, on his radio, Omicron's voice, thinking. *Power. Power. Power.*

I hope you choke on it! Busk snarled silently. He wondered idly why the many yards of stone failed to block
the radio transmission, then he concluded that it wasn't
any ordinary radio wave. Omicron violated too many
known laws of nature. Either the laws needed revision,
or Omicron was supernatural. Busk didn't know which,
and he didn't care.

Power. Power. Power.

Would it be too much for him? There was a monoma-
niacal perseveration in the way Omicron repeated himself. Perhaps the power had hurt him without killing
him.

On the other hand, perhaps he basked in it, immers-
ing himself in molten stone, bathing in the radioactive
glow.

Busk shivered and moved closer to the fire.

Several hours later, Omicron came back up to his cave.

He glowed a white-hot glow, like semiliquid iron
brought out of a forge. His body shone. Busk could feel
the blast of the heat all the way across the cavern, a merciless, searing heat. He caught a whiff of the hot iron
smell before the air scorched his nose and he had to
breathe through his mouth. His eyes hurt when he
looked at it.

*If that stuff is radiation, I'll be dead in about fifteen
minutes,* he realized. His throat grew parched, and for
some inane reason all he could think about was ginger
ale.

"Power," Omicron said, and took a step closer.

"Get back!" Busk shrieked. He gasped and scalded his throat on the hot air. "I—I can't live with your power." Controlling his voice, he went on. "Go away from me until you've cooled down, or I'm a dead man."

Omicron nodded, slowly and solemnly.

The tunnel he took led up to the desert floor.

*   *   *   *   *

In the Quentin Corey Museum in San Antonio, Grant prodded Sam awake.

"Hm?" Sam squinted at his watch. It was nearly midnight. "What is it?" he asked sleepily.

Grant saw how Sam and Delta shared Sam's small workroom, and how she lay near him, nestled by his side, but outside of his sleeping bag while Sam was tucked within it. It wasn't hard for him to see how the boy felt about the robot. Grant smiled thinly. He felt a little of the same himself.

"The network radio news just reported a nuclear accident in Nevada."

"What kind?" Sam was suddenly wide awake.

"Omicron," Delta said softly. "He has been getting steadily stronger for the past four hours."

Sam looked at her in distress. Grant watched them both, his eyes narrowed.

"You'd better explain that to me, Delta," Grant said and sat on the floor, Indian fashion, at the foot of Sam's bedroll.

"No," Sam put in. "Let's get the television news on first."

He leaped up, wearing only the underwear he slept in.
From a high shelf, he fished down his small-tube television set. Only that morning they had sat together and
watched themselves on the same set; now they saw the
works of their enemy.

The film was black and white, taken by army cameramen under trying circumstances. At the bottom of the
picture, a message was superimposed: "Department of
Defense Film."

There wasn't a lot to be seen. Flashes and flares where
munitions burst, a column of smoke lit from beneath, a
tracked vehicle hurrying past from right to left.

An army spokesman explained the circumstances in a
voiceover. "We don't fully understand what caused the
explosion. And I must emphasize that the explosion was
underground. There is no leakage of radiation into the
environment. The test was unscheduled. The Department of Energy was planning more tests during the
spring and summer, but none were scheduled until late
April, at the earliest."

He went on, trying to minimize the shock of the report, but being candid nevertheless and not denying the
public the information. Sam sat on his bedroll and
watched in horrified amazement. Delta faced the set,
the cold blue light of the tube reflecting off her flat,
blank face. Grant looked on impassively. He'd seen such
things at first hand and had grown resigned to them.

"Fifty people are known dead at this time," the
spokesman went on. "At least three hundred other people are casualties. We can definitely rule out any possibil-
ity that this was a terrorist attack, either from agents of a
foreign nation or from domestic nuclear-protest organi-

zations. We have not been attacked, but beyond that, the cause of the explosion is completely unknown."

As he spoke, flames shot high into the air, followed by a skyrocket flare of glowing sparks.

The scene switched to a news anchorman at his station in the New York network headquarters.

"For more information, we take you to the Pentagon, where correspondent Robert Vincente has this report."

Sam leaned forward and switched the set off. He smiled weakly. "When they start interviewing rear admirals, you can tell they're out of fresh information."

Grant laughed, a hearty, booming sound. "You know the military as well as the most seasoned regular, lad. I have to say, I'm glad you never joined."

"Oh, god, me, too!" Sam breathed.

"Who is Omicron, then?"

They both looked at Delta.

CHAPTER SIXTEEN

The sounds of water pervaded Sheriff DeSoto's office in Pyramid, Wyoming. Snow had fallen last night, and the sounds of dripping snowmelt were loud, falling into puddles on the macadam parking spaces outside, thudding onto the wooden porch in front. When he was very still, his eyes unfocused in a thoughtful trance, he was sometimes brought back to awareness by the distant sound of the creek. Already swollen by rains and melting mountain snow, the creek roared, a low, rolling noise unlike any other. The sound was a part of his childhood. It anchored him in reality.

The town of Ramshorn had been a part of his childhood, too. And the thing that had murdered that town was now free, running the ranges, skulking.

I had it in the palm of my hand! he fretted. *I had it cold.* He dragged his hands roughly back through his red hair and gnawed for an instant on the middle of his mustache, a habit that went a long way back. Then he collected himself and sat, still and stiff, only his mind racing. Coffee percolated in the antique coffeepot atop his old iron stove. The acrid aroma of the coffee did more for him than the hot liquid would later.

DeSoto had learned how to wait. When hunting as a lad up in the stony hills, he'd learned to sit stock-still, with timeless patience. But he'd learned how valuable time was and how deadly it was to sit and let time slide by. He knew how to wait, but he still itched to act.

There's a silver-skinned killer out there somewhere, he thought, and his eyes narrowed. *A lovely, deceitful, woman-shaped killer.*

His phone rang; he grabbed it with one hand while the rest of him remained completely motionless. There was something almost robotic about the way his arm and his body worked independently.

"Sheriff DeSoto speaking." He waited.

What he heard brought him fully to life. He slewed about in his chair and ground the receiver tightly against the side of his head. "Yes, I reported a silver robot. Two weeks ago, come Tuesday."

He listened intently. The call was from the state sheriff's office in Cheyenne. A robot fitting the description he'd given had turned up.

"San Antonio? No fooling?" He took a deep breath. "No, I don't have a fax. Describe it."

He waited, his large hand poised on the edge of his desk.

"That's her, all right. Six-foot-four, silver skin, no face, bad right ankle. Kill it, goddamn it! That's the monster that killed eleven people in Ramshorn!"

After that, there was a long pause in his office while he listened. He was used to giving orders, not to receiving them, and taking reprimands was worse. He bore it. The murdering machine was within reach again.

"Right." The one word was a grudging admission. The state sheriff's office didn't want him to get involved. His word of identification was all they wanted.

It sure as hell wasn't all he wanted.

"Okay," he said and pulled the phone around closer to him on the desk, poising his finger over the cradle to shut off the voice on the other end. He had more he could tell them, but it didn't seem as if they wanted to hear.

"'Bye." He shoved down on the cradle, breaking the connection.

Leaning back in his chair, he thought about what he had just heard.

I could call San Antonio, but what could I say that the state office won't? Nobody's going to listen to a hillside sheriff. Nobody ever listens to us out here.

"Ben?" he snapped suddenly. Where the hell was his deputy? . . .

DeSoto stood, clapped his hat onto his head, paused only long enough to set the coffeepot off to one side of the stove, and pounded out the door.

The street was wet, and the shoulders were piled with slush. He tramped across the highway to the general store. The door opened silently; the storekeeper had wired the little bell up out of the way of the door's swing. DeSoto could understand that. The little jingle, coming with a blast of cold air, could get annoying mighty fast.

Ben, a skinny, thin-haired man with bony fists, stood

leaning over the counter, peering into a hand-held slide viewer. He looked up and, seeing DeSoto, set the viewer down.

"What's the trouble." He grabbed his hat, but didn't don it just yet.

"They've found our silver robot woman. San Antonio." He smiled without humor. "Texas."

"Long way to walk on a busted foot."

"She's a robot." DeSoto shrugged. "She's tough."

"Okay." Ben puffed out his cheeks. "What'd she do in San Antonio? Kill somebody?"

The disgust in DeSoto's face put Ben on alert. "She got on the goddamned evening news. A novelty. A new toy, just in for Valentine's Day." He looked up at his deputy, his face torn. "Ben, that thing killed eleven of the finest people I've ever met. And they're treating it like a movie star!"

Ben put on his hat and straightened. "They haven't even locked her up?"

"It isn't a 'her,' Ben." DeSoto's eyes were cold. "That killer's an 'it.' "

"Right." Ben looked away, then looked back at the sheriff.

"They say we haven't got enough evidence. The footprint casts don't make sense. And she didn't give us any trouble."

"Broke jail like slipping out of school for an afternoon, that's all." Ben rubbed his jaw with a knuckle. "The footprint casts . . . now, that's something else."

The killer in Ramshorn had had large, flat, humanlike bare feet, with five fat, splayed toes. Delta's feet were delicate and high-arched, and the toes were articulated in a segmented fashion. Robot's toes.

"I agree. But . . ." DeSoto shrugged. "Well, we've got to do something about this, and do it now."

"What do you want me to do, Boss?"

"Nothing just now. Stay here. See to things. I'm going for a drive."

"Texas way?"

"I'll phone you." DeSoto cracked a weak smile. "Don't let anybody start any fires."

Ben nodded. The forests were soaking wet. It was DeSoto's way of telling him to do nothing. Sit. Mind the store.

"See you in a week or so, then." Ben set his hat back down.

* * * * *

DeSoto climbed into his car. It had taken him a few minutes to make up his mind, but he felt right about his decision. It was his own private car, a '74 Chevy, light blue, with some mileage on it but still going strong. He knew it and trusted it, and was aware it would attract less attention than a county sheriff's vehicle.

He eased onto the road, driving slowly because of the water. In shady places, it could turn to ice.

The boys in Cheyenne don't know how it is here, he thought. *Different kind of people. Evidence is important, but a man's got to check things out with his own eyes.*

He'd been up to Ramshorn on the day of the killing. He'd collected the evidence. He'd made those footprint casts. And they didn't match.

Fine. Maybe the silver-skinned bitch has got a boyfriend.

He'd collected other evidence. Smelly gelatinous splatters of red goo that had once been people. Pink human bones blackened by flame, but already picked clean of flesh. Skulls with frightened eyes, still lying on the pillows of their beds, scoured and stripped by some impossible weapon.

They didn't pay any attention to the cattle mutilations, he thought. *They tried to palm this off, too. If it happens in the hills, then it's just folks getting panicked over no big deal.*

Friends of mine died at Ramshorn. They were people I was supposed to protect. I can't sit back and wait. No man could.

He kept his anger behind his eyes, never letting it run down his shoulders and into his hands. Driving angrily was stupid, and Sheriff DeSoto was never a stupid man.

* * * * *

Ben waited for a good long while, biding his time in the store. The slides were shots of New England, taken by the store owner while on vacation. It seemed to be a pretty enough land, but Ben wondered how anyone could enjoy living next to a cold and wintry sea. For him, the mountains were enough.

The store owner came back out of the cold-storage locker.

"Good slides."

"Thanks, Ben."

"You hear what Sheriff DeSoto said?"

The storekeeper's eyes glinted. "The robot that killed the Tullys, up at Ramshorn."

"You knew Mr. and Mrs. Tully?" Ben wouldn't meet the storekeeper's gaze.

"Everyone round here did. You know that."

"San Antonio's not too awful far." Ben's voice was soft.

"Four days. Maybe three, if you push it." The storekeeper nodded. "I'll give Andy Welty a call."

Ben picked up his hat. "Old Andy? Last I heard he was trying to start a new hauling business in Grand Junction."

"We keep in touch." The storekeeper smiled, an expression cold and humorless in its ferocity. "Maybe he's got business in San Antonio."

"That's what I was thinking." Ben shrugged. "None of my affair, of course. But tell 'em to keep out of Sheriff DeSoto's way, okay?"

"I'll pass it along."

*   *   *   *   *

Duncan Cantrell got the message only a few hours later. He phoned his cousin Hank. Texas seemed like a mighty interesting place to visit all of a sudden. The word passed up and down the middle way, running the high Rockies on phone lines, along the interstate highways, and up and down the narrow back roads.

The word was select. Not all who heard cared. Ramshorn wasn't even a name to most, and most heard and forgot. Those who needed to hear heard.

The word was inexact. One farmer by the fork in the

road up in Whalebone heard it that a sheriff, DeSoto by name, had already arrested the murderer and was bringing her back to Cheyenne for trial. "Good thing, I suppose," he muttered, and told his wife. Her church group learned it that way. The misinformation spread.

The word was singleminded. Talk of the silver-skinned whore would give way to the troubles over in Nevada. Men in truck stops swore and laughed and traded gossip, and never connected the stories. There didn't seem to be any point in it, and the world was full of too many odd things. No one could link the ones that fit together without seeing conspiracies behind every coincidence.

"Meet you at the post office in an hour, Hank," Duncan said. "We got a second chance at that robot woman."

"For all the good it'll do us," Hank complained. "What do we do, when bullets just slide off her?"

"I don't honestly know. I'm bringing my rifle, but I've also got a good coil of rope."

"Which she'll saw through with her eye beams, I guess."

Duncan chuckled. "I guess."

"Okay, I'll be there." Pausing, Hank came up with another thought. "You know, those New York newspapers will be calling us 'vigilantes.' "

"Well, that's fair enough. Isn't that what we'll be? And who ever said that was a bad word?"

"Right. See you an hour from now."

* * * * *

In San Antonio, Detective Johnstone looked up Detective McStay in the downtown police station.

"Word on the robot."

McStay, who had been about to rise up out of his chair from behind his desk, settled back down instead. "Word, huh?"

"Ever hear of a little town up in Wyoming called Ramshorn?"

"Nope." He held up his hand. "Wait. I got one for you. You ever hear of a basketball player, six-foot-four, a center, named Wallace Pointer?"

Johnstone frowned. "Nope. How's it tie in?"

"It doesn't. Now we're even. Come by again sometime, and we'll play some more." He crossed his legs and leaned back in his swivel chair. "Stop playing mysterious with me and tell it straight, okay?"

Johnstone made a face. "Funny guy. Ramshorn, Wyoming. Eleven people dead . . . horribly. Skin melted off their bones. And—get this—a naked silver woman robot was seen in the area the next day. The local sheriff even caught her, but she got away."

"Well, we know firsthand about that. She's slippery."

"Joke if you want to. Joke all the way to the museum. But grab your coat, because that's where we're going."

"Are we going to haul her in, big buddy? Just you and me? When ten of our best tripped all over themselves trying to grab her?"

Johnstone leaned forward and placed his hands on McStay's desk. "Just you and me and Officer Pruitt. And his job is to hold the door."

"Fine." McStay spread his hands. "Let me make two phone calls first."

"Phone calls? Who do you want to be calling?"

"Pruitt first, to let him know we're coming. Officer

Kellen second." He looked up from the phone. "She co-ordinates the hospitalization plan for the city."

"Call Pruitt," Johnstone muttered.

*   *   *   *   *

The phone in the Quentin Corey Museum of Antiquities rang more often these days than it normally did. Madeline answered it, as always, with one word, more a demand than a greeting. "Yes?"

It was another of her peculiarities. When composing a letter, she would begin it with the most formal of salutations: "My Dear Colleague, Mister Kemper," and close with a charmingly out-of-date series of complimentary closes: "In anticipation of any further means by which I may be of assistance, I remain your humble and obedient servant, Madeline Lenoir Schenk." But she answered the phone like a surly cook taking deliveries at a back gate.

Perhaps her abruptness was not an ill-chosen manner. After listening for a moment, she pushed the receiver away to arm's length and stared at it as if the instrument itself had been the source of the offense. Frowning tightly, she set the receiver down gently upon her desk and wheeled her chair out into the museum.

"Officer Pruitt?"

"Yes, ma'am?" Pruitt had been relaxing, almost dozing, stretched out upon a wooden bench.

"The telephone, he is for you."

"Oh," Pruitt said and began to smile. He quickly saw that Madeline was not in a smiling mood and swallowed. "Thank you, ma'am."

"Only answer it, this costs nothing. If you needfully make calls, I require a deposit. The museum, he has fall on bad times."

"Yes, ma'am." Pruitt followed her and lifted the receiver. He listened for a few moments. "Yes, sir," he said at last and hung up quickly.

Madeline looked at him. *He never says anything else? "Yes, ma'am. Yes, sir." Woeful times for the eloquence of a nation who spawned John Joseph Pershing.*

"That was Detective McStay," Pruitt said unhappily. "They're going to have to take Delta downtown."

Madeline, who had not asked, only nodded. "Very well. Let us go and see her prepared."

"Spit and polish?" Pruitt joked.

Madeline twitched the tiniest smile. "Something like that." She looked around and saw Grant on a high ladder, polishing the western windows. "Grant! Come along here, if you would, please."

Grant waved and descended the ladder.

She and Pruitt found Sam and Delta in the east wing, poring over maps of the world.

"Sam?" Madeline began softly.

Sam looked up. Delta did also, in a motion almost the parallel of his.

"Officer Pruitt has something to tell you."

"Well," Pruitt began, after a brief stammer, "Detectives McStay and Johnstone are on their way over here. They're going to take Delta downtown." He spread his hands. "I dunno . . . maybe you want to get her ready. A new battery charge or something?"

Sam took a step forward, his fists knotting at his sides. "You—"

"*Non!*" Madeline spoke sharply. "That will not be doing. None of assaulting officers in my museum unless it is on my say-so!"

Grant came up then, wiping his hands on his cleaning rag. "What-ho? Is the game afoot?"

"Grant," Madeline said, spinning her wheelchair about to face him. "Cosh this man, noggin-pop, one-two, straight-the-way."

Grant blinked, then shrugged. Pruitt had only a moment to gape in alarm before Grant's gnarled fist crashed down on his crown. Eyes crossed, teeth gritted tightly, Pruitt sagged to the floor.

"What the hell?" Sam demanded. He looked back and forth between Grant and Madeline. "Have you both gone mad?"

"Mad, son?" Grant smiled at him and flexed his hand a couple of times. "One can't fight when one is angry. Strong emotions dull the senses. A controlled man is a man to be respected." He looked down at Madeline and smiled. "How much time have we got?"

"No more than minutes, I am think. Five. Maybe the ten."

"On the run, I take it." Grant smiled. "Just like old times."

Delta looked at Sam. Sam looked at her and saw his own blank expression reflected in her smooth faceplate.

CHAPTER SEVENTEEN

Grant H. Alexander and Madeline Lenoir Schenk sprang into the most astonishing activity that Sam had ever seen. Although Sam, being human, knew more about humanity than Delta did, he was as perplexed as she was.

While Madeline wheeled off on a hurried round of the museum, Grant rolled Officer Pruitt over and began to hog-tie him with intricate and expertly made knots. Pruitt, unconscious and now trussed inextricably in four yards of stout cord, could be considered safely out of the picture.

"Grant, what does this mean?" Sam asked plaintively.

Grant just smiled. "No time." He stood and looked about. "Not yet noon. Traffic will be light." He nodded in satisfaction. "It will have to do."

Ignoring Sam's feeble noises of protest, he leaped up

and dashed back into the display stacks. To Sam's horror, the sound of broken glass echoed malevolently throughout the high-ceilinged museum.

Grant returned in a few moments, bearing a large handful of diamonds.

"Grant! Those were on display!" Sam's world was overturning. The shock of finding an intelligent robot of alien design was nothing compared to the sense of wrongness he felt watching his friend upset the work of decades.

Winking at Sam, Grant tucked the diamonds into his pocket. "Don't worry, laddy. Everything's under control. But . . ." He paused. "You might want to get packing, eh, now?" Tugging at his mustache, Grant hurried off.

Sam staggered after him. None of this made sense.

Grant turned down an aisle of large mounted animal specimens. Sam followed.

Pausing before an enormous stuffed yak, Grant whipped his utility knife out of his belt pocket. He closed one eye, aimed the knife toward the yak, and plunged the knife deep into its throat. Sam choked and came to an abrupt halt. Behind him, unseen, Delta watched in fright.

"Where are you?" Grant muttered, looking away while he reached into the yak's neck. He groped for a bit, then his face lit with exultation. "Right where I left it!" He pulled his hand back out, and in it was a leather sack the size of a softball. Pulling the thongs loose with his teeth, he peered inside.

"See, lad? Gold. Bane of the wise, downfall of civilizations, the price of men's souls. Gold." His face was serious, but merriment played behind his eyes. "Be wary of the stuff, lad, for 'tis almighty treacherous!"

Sam blinked in dismay.

"A pretty specimen, eh?" Grant indicated the yak with a sweep of his hand. "I potted this one in April of 'twenty-two, in High Assam, when the snows were just beginning to melt. He'd gone rogue, you know, and there are few things as dangerous."

"Grant!" Sam wailed.

"Eh? Yes, lad?"

"You've gone rogue yourself!" Sam stepped forward, unmindful of Grant's knife, and took his friend by both shoulders.

"Well, yes." Grant looked a bit embarrassed. "When a man goes rogue, it's a bit more dangerous than when a yak does." The fire in his eyes returned. "But the time for regrets is never at the beginning of a journey, my lad." He tossed the bag from one hand to another, guessing at its weight. "Gold," he muttered, his eyes shadowed and wild.

Sam ran in a panic through the museum, seeking Madeline. She was like a mother to him; she wouldn't go rogue. Delta waited a last moment, looking at Grant. Then she hobbled after Sam.

Madeline was making a thorough sack of her desk. Paper money and travelers' checks were in one box, and a collection of small bound notebooks was in another. From the lower shelves of a high closet, she pulled forth odd items one by one and dropped them into an open satchel.

"Grant is never practical man," she muttered. Looking up, she smiled. "Hello, Sam. Have you all packed?

Non? Electricals, chemicals, I don't know whatever else. Too little time."

"This is insane!"

Madeline snapped her head around to stare at him. "Insane? Yes, perhaps you would think it is." She spread her hands. "So little you know of us. Old people caged in museum, friendly people, warm people, but you think we were born here? You think this is our only place?"

Delta, standing behind Sam, spoke softly. "This place had you contained. You now burst free."

"Contained?" Madeline nodded. "Trapped. Total life support in hospital is less inhibiting. . . ." She spread her hands. "Or maybe not." She returned to the closet, fishing out clothing, soaps, shampoo, a bulky first-aid kit, sunscreen lotion, a fire-starting flint and steel, a small tin of water-purification tablets, and more survival gear than Sam had dreamed of. She tossed four empty canteens over her shoulder. "Fill these."

Delta bent low and brought them up. "Fill them?"

Madeline spoke without turning about. "They contain water."

Delta nodded. "Yes." She walked away, out toward the mop closet where an iron-stained sink stood.

"Maddy . . ." Sam wanted to ask her why but couldn't find the nerve.

"Grant is not practical ever. No thought to efficiency of body. He is not young man who once he was, tallying over Himalayas of ignorance. He gets cold now, pneumatic fever, breaks ribs coughing. No Serbians come warm him in yurt."

"The Serbians don't have yurts," Sam said, his voice

soft. He thought he was beginning to understand.

Slowly he walked back to his electronics closet. This was all going away. It was a part of his past, lost, the way his family was now lost, and every other home he had ever known. He pulled open the door, flipped on the high, bare light bulb, and gazed over his setup.

Tears stung him, welling up behind his eyes. He rubbed his sleeve across his face roughly, angrily. *I won't cry!* he swore, and bit his lip. What equipment would be most useful? He began to pull his apparatus apart, component by component.

The collection of recorded music would have to be abandoned. He ran his hand over the tapes, feeling the music slip from his fingers. Orff. Telemann. Kurt Weill. David Munrow. He reached out and touched the shielded antenna wire running up to the ceiling. There was no way to bring the omnidirectional antennae along. He gripped the wire and tore it loose. It felt as if he had cut an umbilicus.

He smiled sadly, wryly. It was like being born. The museum no longer contained him. Delta would understand.

Behind him, Grant spoke, his voice uncharacteristically low. "It hurts, I know. And I don't know which is worse—losing everything, or being given five minutes to decide what part of your past to bring with you."

Sam whirled. "Grant, I—I can choose." He looked up at the taller, older man. "I can do this."

"Yes." Grant looked back, pride on his face. "You can, because you must. Nothing makes a boy into a man as fast as need."

Then, slipping back again into a smiling and boisterous mood, Grant reached down beside the door and held up the biggest gun Sam had ever seen in his life.

"Sam, meet 'Hohenfriedberger.' Seven-fifty Nitro Express. Elephant gun. Nothing as big has ever been made since. This blighter could put a thumb-sized slug all the way through one of these marble walls and still kill two tigers on the other side."

"Nitro?" Sam murmured.

"Just an expression." Grant whipped the rifle up to his cheek and aimed it into the air. "It uses gunpowder, like any other rifle."

"That's a relief."

"Bring your chemistry lab anyway," Grant said cheerfully. "We might need it still." He went off to zip the gun up in its leather case.

Delta came by, with the canteens filled. She set them down carefully on the floor and took Sam by the hand. "I don't understand any of this."

"It's strange," Sam admitted. "They're being unpredictable." He shrugged. "Well, I suppose you'll get what you want. It sure looks like we're going to Nevada, and I guess we'll find Omicron there."

"You will help me fight him?" Delta sounded hesitant yet hopeful.

"I will. I can't speak for Grant or Maddy."

"Thank you," Delta said breathlessly. "Thank you so much!"

"Well, sure." Sam shook his head. "Let's hurry, then, and get some of my stuff packed."

* * * * *

It took them three trips out behind the museum, where Grant's car was parked. It was a 1952 Ford Roadster, a trim convertible that had once been quite a flashy and stylish car. The bright red paint had faded over the years to an almost gray tone with a subdued red tinge. The chrome parts had faded as well, now dull and drab. Delta looked at it with suspicion. Cars were meant to contain people, and she could not feel comfortable with that.

Buildings, too, contained people, and had exits. And she had twice exited cars that she'd entered. She set her reservations aside. She liked the way the trunk was made to contain cargo.

Madeline was the last to come out, after locking the doors to the museum. Grant helped her gently out of her wheelchair and walked slowly with her around the car. She slid into the driver's seat. Grant quickly knocked the retaining pegs out of the wheelchair and folded it away, the last item into the trunk. The two large wheels fit exactly.

Grant had not yet slammed the front passenger side door before Madeline gunned the engine and started the car rolling. She shot out of the parking lot, careened left onto the street, and blasted away north on Pleasanton Road.

Sam held on tightly to the back of Grant's seat in front of him and gritted his teeth. Delta, at his side, found herself tossed violently about by Madeline's brutal swerving.

"Not calling any attention to yourself, are you, Maddy?" Grant asked, his arms stiff and his hands on the dashboard.

"Oh, *oui*, I forget." She slowed to a pace only moderately faster than safety would suggest. "I have not drive car since Great War." She turned and spoke over her shoulder to Sam. "No, that is not terribly true. I drive now and sometimes."

Watch the road, Maddy! Sam thought, his teeth and throat aching.

"Only this last gauntlet," Grant announced, "and we're free."

Somehow Madeline's driving escaped official notice, and they obtained a space on the freeway without incident. Now her skills as a driver were more evident, and on the long central Texas freeway the car was safe, just one more anonymous car, although older than most.

Their first hour of driving was mostly silent. Each thought about what had been lost. The Quentin Corey Museum of Antiquities, a point of stability in a world shocked by its own progress, was gone. The past was past.

The pain of the loss hurt Sam in a way he couldn't completely understand. He had always been rootless, a young man lacking any sense of family or cultural history. But the museum had been home.

Finally, as the dry miles sped by, he leaned forward and spoke to Grant and Madeline.

"I'm sorry for getting you into this trouble."

Grant turned about. "No, lad. We got ourselves in trouble long ago. What are you thinking? That Maddy and I have lost our jobs? That we've ruined the comfort we had in the museum? No." He reached out and roughed up Sam's hair, a friendly gesture that, from anyone else, would have had Sam in an instant fury.

"No, it didn't take any great gift of prophecy to see what was happening there. The museum didn't have five years left. The money was just drying up." His voice sank. "And Maddy and I were drying up. We'd talked about getting out, you know. We'd talked about making off into the night. . . . You noticed how little time it took us to pack."

"Grant . . ." Sam began.

"Lad, you've never lived. Maddy and I, well, we've done things together that you couldn't credit. Someday I'll tell you about fighting the K'Krakti in central Africa. Someday I'll tell you about Quentin Corey and the tunnels under St. Louis."

"Grant," Madeline said, her voice sharp. It was a word of warning.

"Well," Grant hurried on. "Someday." He shifted in his seat. "The point is that we tried to retire, as the elderly are expected to. A museum was a good place for it. Twenty-two years we spent there.

"Twenty-two years in prison, shackled hand and foot, waiting to die." His eyes were bright, and his voice was bitter. "For the love of god, lad, don't be apologizing. We should thank you."

"Maddy?" Sam asked, looking at her face in the rearview mirror.

"Yes. Grant can speak of me, as also. Curating museum paid poorly in money, but the just living also grew worse and worse every year. M'sieur Cook and his blackmail . . . well, perhaps we could have taken it. Perhaps not." She grinned, a sharp, feral grin. "But when he threatens our new-come friend and yours, *la* Delta, it is not to be borne!"

Several more miles and minutes slipped by.

"Thank you," Delta said. "I have learned that I was right. Containment is a trap."

"Exactly right!" Grant agreed. "And I, for one, loathe traps with an unutterable abhorrence."

* * * * *

As the afternoon grew warmer, Grant first, then the others, rolled down their windows. Finally, as Madeline slowed the car, Grant cranked back the collapsible top. Sam and Delta caught it and stowed it in the well behind their seats. Madeline took the car up to full speed again. The air whipped Sam's hair into his face, ruffled Grant's mustache, and pulled tufts of hair loose from Madeline's tight coiffure. Delta raised her face up into the slipstream and sat that way, entranced, for almost an hour.

"It flows like water!" she said at last.

Grant snorted and fished into his pack for a deck of cards. "Ever play 'Trench,' Sam?" He had to raise his voice over the rushing of the air.

"No."

"It's like 'War,' but you get to choose your card. Twenty-six each." He dealt the cards, holding carefully to each in the wind. "Discard the aces and— Hell, I've got three. Give me a card; there's the lad. And we have to each have two kings. Okay? We each turn over a card, and high card wins. Kings are best."

"Hm?" Sam thought for a while. "I think I get it. I can beat a two with a king, but it's a waste of power."

"Right. All in the psychology." He and Sam each showed a card: Grant's five lost to Sam's Jack. At the end of the first round, Sam held twenty-two cards and Grant held twenty-six.

"You're in the trench now," Grant said, giving Sam what he considered fair warning.

They played for several more rounds, until Sam was down to his two kings and two other cards, a losing configuration.

"Care to try it, Delta?" Grant invited.

Delta, who had been watching, opened her mouth as if to answer, then stopped, suddenly struck by a thought. She examined the logic of it and leaned forward in excitement.

"The point is that I don't know what you will show?" Her voice was bright and eager.

"Exactly. You have to try to guess."

"At the same time, you are trying to guess what I will show?"

"Right." Grant smiled and began to deal the cards.

Delta accepted her twenty-four cards, shuffled them as she had seen Grant do, and held them facedown on her lap. Grant frowned, pulled a card, and waited for Delta to pull one. She did so without ever looking at it.

Grant's eight took her three.

"You're supposed to choose your card with a deliberate strategy in mind. It's a game of intellect."

"I have applied my intellect. You can't predict what you can't know. I will choose my cards unpredictably."

Grant's frown deepened.

"The word you want is 'random,' " Sam said, his face full of wonder. "And if the cards were circularly ranked—a two beats a king, for example—and if they were replaced after each showing, you'd be right." He taught her the game of "Rock, Paper, an Scissors" and explained a little of the mathematics of randomness to her.

When he had finished, Delta smiled at him, raised her head up into the rushing air, and again stayed that way for nearly an hour. Meanwhile, Sam gently plucked the cards from her hand and proceeded to lose game after game to Grant.

"You ought to stop giving her ideas, lad," Grant muttered. "She may find some use for the idea of randomness."

"Yes . . . she probably will." Sam shook his head. "But she needs every weapon she can get her hands on to fight Omicron."

Not long after that, Delta pulled her head down out of the wind.

"How is the game supposed to be played?" she asked.

"Intelligently," Grant snorted. "It's essentially a measure of intellect. Can you predict, based on my past actions, what my future actions will be?"

"Is that why you can consistently defeat Sam?"

Sam made a wry face. "Age and experience count for something as well."

"Very right." Grant chuckled. "Age and treachery will always beat youth and skill."

Delta took the cards from Sam, careful to control them in the roaring wind. She lost the first few games, then began to win. By nightfall, as they neared the state line, she was winning two games out of every three.

"She's smarter than you are, Grant," Sam said, his awe taking any pleasure out of the observation.

"Yes," Grant admitted simply. "Yes, she is."

Madeline put in her first remark for nearly five hundred miles. "A robot woman comes from future and stars and makes it alive into city in mid-Texas, and you think she maybe is unintelligent? Of course she is smarter than we."

"I have to be," Delta said quietly.

CHAPTER EIGHTEEN

In desperation, the army launched an invasion of Omicron's subterranean lair. Soldiers dressed in fully self-contained chemical warfare suits lumbered forward and climbed painfully down the rough-floored tunnels.

Stringing ropes behind them, the advance units moved slowly. Their thick rubberized gloves made all movements clumsy; their thick-lensed goggles made vision tight and difficult. The suits grew almost unbearably hot inside. The men trudged on.

Omicron had last burst from the ground only half an hour ago, to spread wanton destruction everywhere he touched down. Among his more curious thefts were two horses. Military planners, overseeing the touchy defense of the nuclear test site, had noted that Omicron usually raided at widely spaced intervals. Thus, while fires still burned and emergency crews were still sweeping bodies into sacks, a counterattack took to the desert tunnels.

Stumbling down the steep slopes, the men worked to keep a tight timetable. Another group, even now, was being lowered down the straight elevator shaft to the bomb-test chamber.

* * * *

"Buster" Busk sat, head bowed in misery, in one of the lower chambers, where Omicron had carried him. He sat facing a slow-burning flame, tending a slowly-cooking piece of horsemeat on a bone spit. The meat was coarse and red. It dripped into the fire, and gobbets of fat sizzled as they burned. Busk was horrified . . . but his stomach overrode his preferences. His mouth watered at the scent of the cooking flesh.

Across the chamber, Omicron stood, unmoving, still glowing with a cool bluish light. More oil barrels lay stacked near him, and a larger fire burned, sending a sooty cloud of smoke roiling up the twisted walls. Smaller fires burned, little pools of oil with orange flames dancing slowly on their surface. Several flames had been set up on the walls. Others drooled and snaked across the churned-up rocks of the chamber floor. The dismembered carcass of the horse lay discarded against the wall as far from Busk as he was able to drag it.

Omicron had hollowed out this chamber by hand, scooping out the stone with huge sweeps of his gray, cabled arms. The floor slanted down in a steep incline, until a small tunnel dropped off at the bottom. To Busk, being in the room felt like being inside the entrails of some uncaring stone beast. He looked at the parallel grooves in the stone: Omicron's talonlike fingers had swept through solid rock like chisels.

Well, he got me what I asked for, Busk thought with a shrug. He pulled the meat from the fire and, unable to wait for it to cool, tore into it with his teeth. A sense of great shame filled him. *I asked him for food. I had to have food. But how do you explain "food" to a thing that eats heat, light, and neutrons?*

Hunger had guided him. He had asked for Omicron to bring him something four-legged. It was easier than trying to make his captor understand grocery stores or canned rations.

The horse was dead when he brought it in, Busk reminded himself over and over. He wished he could forget the sight of it when Omicron had thrown it down. It had been no burden for the humanoid robot. He had carried it over his back in a ludicrous parody of a fireman's carry. The horse had lolled, limp, floppy-legged. Its eyes had been wide open, the whites showing, and its lips had been drawn back from its teeth. The horse had looked at Busk with a dead look of madness.

Busk had butchered it with nothing more than sharp rocks and roasted its flesh on a spit made of its own long bones.

God help me, it tastes good! Busk hated Omicron with the cold, bitter hatred that a slave feels for an uncaring master.

"Will you live now?" Omicron asked.

"Yes. I'll live." Busk was sullen and morose. He had to help defeat this monstrosity. It shocked him when he realized that he would gladly give his own life if, before he died, he could see Omicron taken down as well.

Time to begin, Busk guessed.

He turned about, wiped his chin, and looked at Omicron. "You know, you're going about this all wrong."

"Wrong?"

"You've got too many tunnels."

"You told me to dig."

And thank god I did, Busk thought. *Suppose he were free above, with perfect mobility.*

"Yes. But you've dug twisted tunnels. They branch and meet again. It's too complex."

"You told me that complexity was a kind of power."

The army is going to come in here after him. I've got to help them defeat him.

"Yes," he explained patiently, "but in simplicity there is a greater power. For example . . ." He groped for an analogy that Omicron could easily grasp. "Well, is it better to kill an enemy with a hundred small injuries or with one large blast?"

He almost didn't need his radio anymore to hear how Omicron thought. Behind his enemy's face, the thoughts were obvious.

"With one large blast."

Of course. A being that worshiped energy would answer that way . . . if it were simpleminded enough.

"That's why your tunnels are wasteful. You want one tunnel that goes down, at a gentle slope, and comes to a blank end."

"Why?"

Busk crammed more horsemeat into his mouth and chewed hastily. He could feel his stomach beginning to cramp from the unexpected meal, but he felt stronger already.

"The tunnel must be a single tunnel, with no

branches, in order to gain the power of simplicity. It can't be too steep, or else I can't move along it. And it has to end . . ." He smiled. "Well, it has to end, because it can't go on forever."

He waited. Omicron was thinking. Busk thought also. *I want people to get around behind him . . . but I want him to get his retreat cut off.*

"What should I do?"

"Don't do anything about the tunnels you've already dug. Changing things you've done is the greatest waste of power there is. We will have to simplify your tunnel system, however. All routes must lead here. This is where we'll centralize the network. Starting right about here. . . ." He stood and paced slowly to a place against the lower wall. "Right about here, start digging downward at an easy slope and go about a hundred and fifty yards. Connect the paths."

"Why?"

Busk spread his hands. "It focuses your power."

Omicron was silent for a long minute.

"This is where I come if I am attacked?"

"Yes."

For the next thirty minutes, Busk trembled against the opposite wall while Omicron pounded at the rock with his hands. Shards flew out of the tunnel, breaking into splinters as they hit the rubble-choked floor. Omicron drove the hundred-and-fifty-yard tunnel in half an hour, then emerged.

"Is this as it should be?"

"Yes. That's—"

Omicron denied him the opportunity to finish. He turned his back on Busk and trod heavily up the slope, out of the chamber. Busk froze, then whipped up his radio and listened closely.

Omicron's voice came coldly from the speaker. *Men. Sounds. Nearing. Many. Destroy.*

Men? Busk thought. *The army*, he realized with a pang. He'd almost tricked Omicron into trapping himself, and now . . .

He was still weak, but desperation lent him strength. He followed after Omicron, forcing his legs to carry him up the rock-tumble that floored the tunnel. Once past the light of the flames, he groped his way in darkness. Before long, he saw wan flickers ahead of him, high above. He toiled toward them.

Exhaustion slowed his legs. His chest ached. On he pushed, through one bomb-blasted pocket and up into another.

Far ahead, far above, he heard the sounds of combat. Rifle fire popped, the reports faint and distant. Grenades banged, a sound he'd never heard before in enclosed areas, but unmistakable nevertheless. Automatic-weapons fire joined the chorus of martial sounds.

For a moment, Busk's courage failed him, and he paused. He rallied quickly. Men were fighting up there, trying to beat Omicron. Could they win? Could he be beaten? He struggled up the slope, deciding between left and right branches as best he could, judging by the sounds of the gunfire.

He arrived at a high chamber, only two or three levels beneath the surface. Strangely, the weight of the rock overhead seemed greater. The cavern was a large one, which had been boiled out of solid stone by one of Omicron's stolen warheads. It was brightly lit; a rocket had struck a pile of oil barrels stacked by one inward-sloping wall, and giant gouts of flame licked at the very ceiling of the chamber.

Busk stood in a low point in the cave. Omicron was on a pile of slag in the very center. In two groups in high tunnel mouths, soldiers stood, directing their fire at the robot.

Bullets flew, singing noisily as they ricocheted off Omicron's impervious surface. It almost seemed to Busk that he could see the thick streaks in the air where lead coursed. The deep thump of a grenade launcher gave a background heartbeat to the cacophony, and a series of concussions reverberated at Omicron's feet.

Squinting, Busk tried to make out more details of the men. Their bulky chemical and biological warfare gear made them look even less human than their enemy. Their gas masks had tiny protruding eyes and insectlike snouts, and they were tightly wrapped in rubberized clothing. But they were unquestionably men, and Busk loved them for it.

He stood and waved, then ducked back down again, out of the way of stray fragments of metal.

Some of the men pointed and jostled one another. They had seen him.

Almost as if taking that as a sign to counterattack, Omicron lifted his hands and played narrow streams of energy over the cave mouths where the soldiers fired their weapons.

The firefight ceased. Then slowly, one or two guns at a time, it picked up again. The soldiers kept farther back, deeper out of sight. Omicron unleashed more of his strange, flickering beams of death, and again the fire slackened.

Busk had to cover his eyes, and tears slid down his face when he looked again. The light from Omicron's hands was strong, a brilliant violet light that seared afterimages upon Busk's vision. It was a silent attack, and yet the light itself seemed noisy, as if the silent flash clapped against the eyes. Omicron stood motionlessly throughout, guiding the beams with his outstretched arms.

He switched attacks, aiming a low, bone-shaking sonic pulse up at his enemy. Busk quickly understood that the weapon was not ordinary sound; he saw rock quiver and flow wherever Omicron pointed.

He watched with horror as Omicron stepped forward, pacing casually into the teeth of the fire. There was no way he could follow his captor. There was also no way the soldiers could withstand the onslaught.

Again and again the cold, buzzing beams leaped out. Omicron reached a point directly below the tunnel entrances and began to climb. Something in his posture made Busk pause in wonder. Again he listened to his radio, trying to hear Omicron's thoughts over the shrieking of gunfire.

Power. Destroy. Weakness. Destroy.

A trio of soldiers dashed forward, almost to the lip of the tunnel, and poured a sustained burst of fire directly into Omicron's face. Busk's heart leaped. *They've got him!*

His hope was short-lived. Omicron faltered a moment, then climbed more quickly, almost catching the men in his deadly hands. They fell back, firing as they went. Omicron ducked into the tunnel in pursuit.

The sounds of battle receded.

Busk settled down to wait.

Perhaps an hour later, Omicron returned to the cavern bearing loose, floppy bags in each hand. Busk saw that they were rubberized environment suits, partly filled with some odd liquid that pooled in the dangling gloves and boots.

Liquified men.

Busk wanted to vomit, but his stomach would not relinquish the first food he'd had in five days.

He walked slowly back down the tunnels, with Omicron pacing measuredly at his heels.

In the low cavern, Omicron stood much too close to Busk, waiting for his power to focus, as Busk had promised him it would.

* * * * *

"Who hit you?" Detective McStay asked, helping Officer Pruitt to his feet.

"Grant."

"Grant?"

"You know. Grant Alexander, the caretaker."

McStay looked at Pruitt with disgust. "He's at least ninety years old, Pruitt. How could he have knocked you out?"

Pruitt, rubbing his head, could only stare at the floor in embarrassment.

"Detective?" another officer called from deeper within the museum. McStay cast one last glance at Pruitt, then went to look at the shattered glass of the museum cases.

"Diamonds?" McStay wandered back to where Johnstone led another team over the tiny office space. "What happened here?"

Johnstone looked up at him bleakly. "They packed in a hurry and left."

"Do you think Pruitt tipped them off?"

Johnstone grimaced. "Who else?"

"Grant owns a car. Pink or red, I remember . . . old Ford convertible." McStay jerked a thumb at an officer. "Go check out in the lot."

"Yes, sir."

"All-points bulletin?" Johnstone asked.

"Sure. On a red Ford with a robot, a cripple, a great-grandfather, and a loudmouth."

He grabbed up the phone on Madeline's desk, then snarled a curse when he discovered the receiver was dead. He yanked at the phone cord. It had been neatly cut, right at the wall.

* * * *

Traffic on I-10 was light, and the speed was quite high. The official limit was a standing joke. Not many people got a good view of the old roadster and its unusual crew.

One truck driver, passing on a long, level stretch, looked once, then turned his head and looked again. He smiled. Not long after, playing around with his CB radio, he described what he'd seen to another trucker. A third man, listening in, broke the channel and asked for details.

The word shot up the middle way. In Pyramid, Wyoming, Sheriff DeSoto's deputy took a phone call. The news interested him greatly. Later that evening, when DeSoto checked in by phone, he was given an update.

"Howdy, Boss. I've got news."

DeSoto wasn't the only man he told. Others were interested, too.

Interest shifted west. Guns were readied.

No one connected Delta's flight with the news from Nevada. DeSoto would be the first to make that leap, early the next day.

CHAPTER NINETEEN

Grant fretted more and more as the open-topped roadster bounced along the rutted dirt road. Madeline was back at the wheel, after having traded back and forth with Grant on the two-day trip out. Sharing driving duty had hastened their trip. Sam, however, had noticed that they never offered to let him drive.

Delta watched. She scanned the horizon as it moved past them. She looked down at the road beneath, seeing how it changed from interstate highway to concrete to asphalt to oil to gravel to dirt. She watched the sun slide along its course; she watched the stars.

The road pitched and swerved, running in and out of scrub brush and clumps of spiny cactus. The horizon was closed in now, and had been since they last topped a rise, several miles back. Delta spoke now and again, giving Grant the exact bearings and distance to their foe. Grant craned his neck, gazing all about him, watching the terrain. Delta's navigation was valuable, but his own knowledge of campaigning was just as important. His eyes were narrowed, his lips compressed.

Finally he leaned over to Madeline and spoke. "Here."

"Very well," Madeline agreed. She slewed the car off the road and brought it to a crunching halt in the midst of a large patch of low, stiff weeds.

Sam was startled by her acquiescence. When had she ever accepted direction from Grant? Always she had made a great play of stubbornness, and her back talk was lively and saucy.

They aren't playing anymore, Sam realized. The thought chilled him.

"Five minutes to unpack," Grant snapped. "Latrine facilities east for men, west for women. Once unpacked, two minutes to get the car covered."

"Covered?" Sam asked, standing slowly in the backseat and stretching his stiffened limbs.

Grant rounded on him with a harsh and terrible expression, a burning rage in his eyes for the common soldier who showed the temerity and lack of wisdom to question his orders. Then he softened, and his mustache drooped a bit. The wars, the never-ending wars, had not yet touched this lad. Obedience of any kind was alien to him, let alone the blind, unthinking obedience of an army private. "Yes. Well." He rubbed at his lower lip. "We'll cover up the car with these long weeds so it won't be quite as visible from the air." He forced a smile. "Up, lad, and let's get to work!"

They pulled Madeline's wheelchair from the trunk, then dragged out their boxes and bales of equipment.

Grant sorted it all out on the sand and rocks of the desert, then assigned packs with a rough equality. One look at the terrain dashed any thought of the wheelchair, however, and he folded it back inside the trunk.

"Up to the walk, Maddy?" His voice was calm, but even Sam sensed the seriousness of his manner. Maddy would walk, or she would be left behind.

"Of course I am!" Madeline sneered. She leaned against the car, tying her share of equipment into an easily carried bundle. "I slow you down, some bit, you know this. I tire quickly. I am weak. So, *hop-la*, I am least, last member of party, endanger us all, require the rescue, all fail, you blame me." She made a face at Grant. "You knew this all in Texas. Is now your perceptivity to only begin to realize what is obvious to your face? Some military leader!"

Grant faced her, his fists on his hips. "Let us venture to add, rounding out the inventory of accusations, that you are as familiar with Nevada's topography as I am."

Sam blinked in distress. This was the closest he'd ever seen Grant and Madeline come to having a fight. Delta walked hesitantly toward the two.

"Why are you fighting?" she asked, her voice low and gentle.

Grant and Madeline looked at her, their faces blank with incomprehension. "Fighting?" Grant snorted. "Thunder! That wasn't a fight." He grinned at the robot. "Sometime we'll show you a real fight." He stalked off, moving around the car and ripping up large handfuls of dusty gray weeds. Tossing them roughly on top of the car, he set about the job of camouflage. Sam began to help him.

"Blasted women! Robots and cripples," Grant muttered to no one in particular.

"How can you say that?" Sam asked.

"As easy as truth." Grant had nothing else to say for some time. He checked the action on his heavy rifle several times, opening and closing the breech.

Delta watched, her sympathy obvious, as Madeline walked about, her impaired legs stiff and clumsy. As she exercised, she gradually regained a bit of control over her movements. Delta's own painful limp, although still a constant nuisance, seemed minor and unimportant in comparison. "Why were you so hard on him?"

"On Grant?" Madeline looked up, her expression clouded. "Hard on him? I gave him only what he deserved." She looked away. "When we have set out, I will explain, I think." A hint of a smile played about her lips when she looked back. "Grant is numbskull, and times I curse him. Leave it at this."

Delta backed away and began attending to her own pack.

Before long the car was buried beneath a thin covering of weeds, and the four adventurers were equipped and ready. Grant had taken the diamonds and his gold and buried them in a spot he knew he could find again, fifty yards from the car. Now, still fretting, he stepped off into the desert, leading the others at a pace he knew they could all maintain. Slowly they filed out into the desert hills, moving into the restricted area of the Nevada nuclear test range.

*   *   *   *   *

"I might as well explain," Grant said during a short rest stop nearly an hour later.

"Yes," Maddy agreed. "Sam deserves to know, and Delta is curious, too."

"Well," Grant began sheepishly, "Maddy and I worked all this out some years back."

"Some decades, yes?"

"In nineteen-nineteen, to be precise—the year after we first met." He swallowed and went on. "We found that there's a fight in any trip. It's just the way people are, I should reckon, and Madeline agrees."

Sam goggled. "So you—"

"We get it out of the way early."

"Contrition comes later." Madeline couldn't meet Grant's gaze, nor he hers.

"What a stupid way of going about your preparations!" Sam snapped.

Grant and Madeline each whipped about to face him. "I daresay it's great wisdom like yours that can surpass our poor adaptations," Grant growled.

"A young fool condemns old folly," Madeline cut at Sam, "with the same ease he cuts at old wisdom. Maybe you are just a horse's eye and we should leave you here."

Sam bit back his cold rage and stalked on ahead in sullen rancor. Grant and Madeline followed at a more moderate pace. After a time, Sam slowed, resting while the others caught up to him. He had nothing to say, however, nor did anyone else break the bitter silence. They took up the march again, heading west into restricted government land.

* * * * *

Nearly four hours later, as the sun began to set before them, Sam gently raised his voice. "By golly, you guys were sure right!"

"Eh?" Grant turned. "What do you mean, lad?"

"A fight at the beginning of the trip puts things into perspective. It lets us see where we stand."

"You fell into habit of thing like one long experienced," Maddy agreed. "You are born fighter, perhaps."

"It isn't that." Sam groped for words. "We're going off to meet an enemy that might kill us. He might rip us to shreds and leave us torn but alive." He put his arm around Madeline. "But nothing anyone could do to me would hurt as badly as that fight."

Grant lumbered up and embraced them both. "That's how I feel. It's good to let off a bit of the day-to-day steam, but it's far better, for me, to be reminded of how valuable you two are to me."

Delta stood back and watched.

Sam brought a final smile to the robot's lips when he stepped away and muttered, "But I still say you two are utterly crazy."

"Sanity is what you make of it," Grant pronounced, unlimbering his rifle from his back. It was a sign to make camp, and he insisted that Madeline take the first watch.

* * * * *

The dawn broke early and cold over the desert. Even after having spent the predawn hours awake on his watch, Grant was quicker and more alert than the others, save only Delta. She strained forward, almost like a hound pulling against her leash, once having caught the scent of the quarry. Grant smiled. The contretemps and feuding of the past day were gone, lending an almost nostalgic warmth to the team's awakening.

And yet Grant still fretted. His gaze was everywhere, and his eyes were troubled.

"Are you afraid the army is going to find us?" Sam asked as they set out on their second day's march.

Grant paused, then tightened the strap of his massive gun and stepped more heavily for a time. "I don't know how to answer that question," he said at last. "They know we're here, I should think. Today, or perhaps tomorrow, they'll find the car. But they're onto us, as it stands now."

Feelings of panic pricked at the back of Sam's neck. "Spotter planes?"

"Yes, lad. Nasty things, spotter planes. I haven't had any peace with them since nineteen-fifteen, and I find my detestation is not lessening with the passage of the years."

"Can they see us?" Sam waved his hands in useless gesticulations. "Can we do anything?"

"We can maneuver to elude pursuit." Grant made the maxim seem a small, easily accomplished thing.

With the first afternoon's recriminations out of the way, Grant never once brought up Madeline's condition. But he and Sam were aware that she would require four days to cover ground they could cover in one.

Delta, too, slowed them. Her steps were always tentative, especially when she placed weight on her right foot. The pain of every step, and the agony of each misstep, was visible in the way she stood; it showed in the stiffened set of her shoulders and in the way she lifted her elbows to counterbalance her strides.

Grant, watching carefully, shook his head in resignation. Delta might be only a mechanical maid, a toy windup robot, but she obviously felt pain, and that made her just a step removed from human. While she plodded and Maddy toiled, Grant took advantage of his relative strength to make extensive side trips, scouting far ahead and ranging behind. Sam took to accompanying him on some of these outings and was amazed to discover that Grant, at more than three times his age, had the superior stamina.

Delta stood fast by Madeline, sensing in her the superior intellect of the three humans and the greatest insight. She also felt linked to her by their shared disabilities.

"Omicron is a terrifying thing," she confided in the late afternoon.

"He is not like you," Madeline said shortly.

"But he is like me. He does not belong to Earth."

Madeline looked at her. "You belong here, with me, in middle of desert. I am as far from the France of my youth. New Mexico? Where is purpose of New Mexico? But you and I, together, belong here. Nothing is out of place in its place."

"I don't understand," Delta said apologetically.

Madeline drew in her breath sharply. "Where does Grant belong? Where there is hardship, trouble, things to be killed. Where do I belong? Near where Grant is, but not too close. Where does Sam belong?" She frowned. "I never know answer to that one. Sam is every kind of immature. But you will see. Things, people, places, all have logic to way they are made." She looked around her as she trudged painfully along. "Even this dry damned desert and sand in my shoes."

* * * * *

On the third day, Grant spied a low-flying spotter plane and drove the team into cover behind a sharp ridge of low, bladelike stones that shelved up from the clay. Not long after, they came upon the first fence they'd seen. Until now, it was, in theory, possible for them to pretend, if caught, that they didn't know what rules they were breaking. The desert was vast, and the warning signs at the perimeter of the base, although prominently posted, had no fences to go with them. This one, however, was a high, thick chain-link fence, topped with two coils of barbed wire and sensitive with detection alarms.

Grant brought Sam up to it and showed him where he wanted to cross. Sam nodded. On hands and knees, he crept forward, then lay flat. He had his electronics kit in hand. Working quickly, he disabled as many of the sensors as he could and bypassed the others. Then he snipped out a small low hole in the fence and bent the wire back.

He ducked through quickly. Grant followed. Maddy squeezed beneath the sharp ends of the cut wires, although with some difficulty. Delta slid through with agile grace.

"We become felons in the eyes of the law," Grant announced portentously.

"Not for first time," Madeline muttered.

"Nor yet the last." Sam grinned.

The four of them, three determined humans and one duty-fated robot, pushed on through the desert. Once out of sight of the fence, they found no difference in the terrain. Scrub and weed and bramble knew no distinction between enclosure and freedom.

Delta saw this and was heartened. Containment could not prevent life from thriving.

CHAPTER TWENTY

Late that day, at Grant's insistence, they put into effect their alternative traveling arrangements. As the sun westered, they clambered into crevices in a vast, low outcrop of brittle stone.

With Grant and Madeline supervising, they found positions that were secure from visibility. Sam took extra care with his own hollow, knowing he would be spending quite a few hours there. First he scouted it carefully, looking for scorpions or rattlesnakes. Grant had assigned him to a crack between two flat plates of rock. It looked suspiciously like a grave, and Sam informed Grant of this resemblance.

"Hm?" Grant scowled. Then his face lit up with a jolly thought. "We'll be traveling at night, won't we? We'll be nocturnal creatures of evil, now, won't we? Be a good vampire and retire to your crypt."

"I'm not evil," Sam protested.

"Neither are all vampires," Madeline spoke from behind him, so close by that cold shivers ran up and down his spine. When he turned about, she was nowhere to be seen.

Grant smiled at his amazement. "When Grant H. Alexander hides you, you are well hidden."

Sam tossed up his hands and crawled down into his resting place with no further protest.

"It's okay to talk," Madeline assured him. "No one is going to uncrevice us for noisy."

"A nice round of twenty questions, anyone?" Grant's offer met with no enthusiasm.

"Delta?" Sam asked.

"I am here."

"Where is Omicron?"

Delta had learned to gauge distances the way humans did. "Twelve miles away, almost due west, and five hundred yards beneath us."

Sam blinked. "Five hundred yards?" Curvature of the earth wouldn't explain that. Perhaps the terrain was a factor. . . .

"That can't be," Madeline objected. "I look at map. Elevation that direction is higher, not low." She paused. "Subterranean delvings?"

Grant and Sam had the same thought at the same time. The bomb tests.

"He's found himself one devil of a hiding place," Grant remarked coolly.

"I don't have any radiation meters," Sam said. "No geiger counters or exposure film. I looked for something I could use, but we didn't have time to adapt it. The last test was only a few days ago. Add to that the havoc that

Omicron's causing right now, and we might get ourselves a bit cooked."

"No one's here who doesn't want to be," Grant said.
That fairly well settled that. They played a few half-
hearted rounds of twenty questions, then composed
themselves for sleep.

*   *   *   *   *

The news coverage coming out of the Nevada nuclear
testing range was confusing, conflicting, and grim. Large
portions of four states had been evacuated, but only fit-
fully, the evacuation procedures beginning, only to be
canceled, then implemented again. No one seemed to
know where the evacuees ought to be settled or what
kind of emergency service workers ought to be left on
site. The harried Las Vegas Police Department, merely
trying to follow orders, found itself making three round
trips to Barstow in escort of the gambling town's citi-
zenry and two more on their own behalf. Gambling men
themselves, they finally opted to stay in town to guard
the wealth that had been left behind. A handful of
looters tried to call their bluff and paid for it.

Sheriff DeSoto spent a long day in touch with the police detectives in San Antonio, explaining how he believed the events in Nevada tied in with a renegade
robot. Further phone calls to federal authorities proved
futile. No one wanted to listen to a crackpot with another UFO story.

In his motel room in Winslow, Arizona, DeSoto
spread himself out on an overstuffed bed and tried to
keep his temper. His bare feet fidgeted, and his hand

twisted the phone cord into tight, kinked knots.

"All I want is information, sir," he said, kneading his scalp with his other hand. He held the phone clamped tightly between his shoulder and his ear. His beard ground against the mouthpiece where he held the receiver tight against his chin. He resented badly having to say "sir" to damned near anyone; the Energy Department military aide he'd finally gotten connected to demanded respect from the beginning. "Yes, I've got information that will probably be useful to you."

He waited a moment. Then his face twisted in disgust. "Yes, I can hold."

After four minutes waiting with a dead telephone against his ear, he yawned a huge, frustrated yawn of helpless fury and banged the instrument down.

"Getting nowhere," he said aloud. "Absolutely nowhere."

Fishing out his wallet, he thumbed through his well-worn list of phone numbers, looking for the number of his sheriff's station back in Pyramid. His deputy took the call.

"Teton County Sheriff's office in Pyramid, Ben speaking."

"Morning, Ben." DeSoto rested, lying on his back in the cold room. It was good to talk to someone with common sense. Ben didn't have a long supply of it, but he had a little, and that pack of useless men in Washington didn't seem to have an ounce to share among them.

"Hey, Sheriff, good to hear from you."

"Any problems?"

"Heck, you know. Nothin' *but* problems, sunup to sundown. McManus's bull got out onto the road and got hit by a pickup. Nobody hurt, other than the bull."

DeSoto looked up at the ceiling. "Killed him?"

"Hauled him to the meatcutter this morning."

"Nothing you couldn't handle?"

"Old McManus is pretty mad. He figures the guy had room to stop. Hard to say, up on those hairpins. The road was dry when I got there, but the fellow says it was iced up. I wrote everything down, made a note of the exact spot. They want to go to court, that's their business."

DeSoto relaxed. It was good just to hear Ben's voice.

"Fine, Ben. I'll see you in a while." He leaned over to drop a hand on the cradle, to shut off the short conversation.

Ben, hesitantly, put in a quick word. "Boss?"

"What do you have?" DeSoto wondered if he really heard a bit of worry in Ben's voice.

"How you doing? Where are you?"

"Winslow, Arizona. Heading into Nevada, if I can ever get some clearance."

"Well, yeah, that's a trick, ain't it."

DeSoto sat up slowly and lowered his legs over the side of the bed. Ben was worried, was hiding something. He waited. It would come out.

DeSoto kept on talking normally. "Officials are running things in Nevada. They're running around in circles, it seems like to me. They aren't interested in anything I happen to know about our silver-skinned murderer."

"Well," Ben repeated, "I guess not."

DeSoto waited. Finally Ben caved in.

"I knew people were interested. You know—people who lost friends up in Ramshorn, people who . . . Well,

I told 'em what you'd guessed, about how the Nevada thing and Ramshorn might be related."

"Yeah? And?"

"A bunch of 'em set out two, three days ago. They figured on getting in close, over the desert. They're going to try for Warm Springs tomorrow. Then . . ."

"Ben, are you helping these guys?"

"Well, kind of." Ben sounded forlorn and helpless. "I've been keeping in touch with 'em."

"Who have we got? Who are these jokers?"

"You remember Duncan Cantrell? And Andy Welty?"

"And Duncan wouldn't go out without Hank." DeSoto leaned forward and gripped the phone. "You call them back, you hear?"

Ben was by now openly miserable. "Boss, you know they wouldn't listen to that."

DeSoto closed his eyes. *Nope. They wouldn't.* He bit down on his temper.

"Tell them I'm meeting them in Warm Springs. It's small enough; we'll find each other."

"Boss, that won't do any good either. They aren't gonna let you bring 'em back." Ben's voice darkened. "They lost family in Ramshorn, and they're going in."

"Yeah. And I'm going in with them." DeSoto went right on, overriding Ben's protests. "That's right. Straight. No tricks. I'm as responsible for losing Ramshorn as anyone, and I've got a right to be with them." He grinned humorlessly. "Besides, maybe I can keep them from getting killed."

"Goddamn," Ben muttered. "Should I join you?"

"You do and I'll thump you. Stay there, keep order,

and get Andy on the phone. Call back here when you get him."

"No tricks?"

"No tricks."

DeSoto hung up and lay back on the bed again. Even in repose, his muscles were tense. He didn't feel much like relaxing.

*   *   *   *   *

Clouds overhead threatened to develop into a cold rainstorm over the desert. Grant was on the point of suggesting the team look for higher ground. By evening, however, the clouds had passed over, and now the ground was as dry as ever.

Setting caution aside, Sam leaned up out of his crypt of rough stone to watch the sunset. He glanced at Delta, who, likewise entranced by the colors in the west, sat up. They were two Lazaruses, reborn from tombs of desert rock.

The sunset shimmered; layer upon high layer of clouds burnt red and orange from below, curdled purple and dark gray above. Sam watched the colors reflected in Delta's featureless face and waited, enraptured with the beauty of her form. He knew himself a fool, and named himself a dolt. But he was in love, and he saw the glory of sunset in the face of his love.

"Time to move on," Grant said at last, when the sunset had faded away into the gray silence of night.

"I must think you will be leaving me here," Madeline said, her voice sad yet realistic in the darkness. "I do not believe I will be able to travel farther."

Sam and Delta both leaped to aid her from her hiding place.

"We can't leave you behind, Maddy," Sam said, fear tingeing his voice.

"I'm muscle-twisted, all sore." Madeline's hand on his was warm. "The days of travel, the sleep all jammed over bump-field of rocks, have conspired thus to weaken me."

Grant likewise was attentive. "Can you stand? You can lean on Sam and me."

"I can stand . . ." Madeline staggered to her feet. "Just barely."

Delta stepped forward, bent, and caught Madeline up in her arms. She held her like a mother holds a child, her arms supporting Madeline's back, holding her tight against her breast. Sam saw the silhouette of the two against the deepening sky. He saw the stars of the east reflected in the smooth dome of Delta's head. He loved them both so much that he almost wished to weep. .

"Can you carry her far like that?" Grant muttered. He stroked Madeline's hand.

"I can."

"Is nicer than wheelchair," Madeline muttered. Sam detected a trace of embarrassed shyness in her voice. No one had lifted her for quite a long span of years.

Grant heaved a sigh. "Onward, then, into the eye of the west. What awaits us, we cannot foretell." Sam thought he might have been quoting from something, but he was unable to guess what the source might be.

The trip through the darkness was dreamlike for Sam. He knew that army patrols must be seeking them, that a monster tore up the desert in front of them, and that his life and works back home were already devoured by the man who had ruined his young life. Here, however, there were only stars and the uncertain footing of the desert hills.

Grant crunched through the gravel ahead of him, feeling his way with a hillman's skills, learned in Pakistan and high Kashmir. The stars gave the old man light by which to steer. Behind, Delta trod less noisily, more solidly, bearing the extra weight of Madeline as if it were no burden. Her steps were still slow, still agonizing. Her right ankle was still bent awry. It made little creaking noises, metal squealing against metal every time Delta lifted her foot. Still she kept on, heading toward her duty, abiding the pain because she must.

Madeline, exhausted from having pushed herself well beyond her limits, slept soundlessly. As they walked, Sam began to hear other noises—little sounds, tiny hints of the nighttime life of the desert. He heard scrabblings and snaps and scrapes in the dark. He looked about him. Sharp-edged hills showed in silhouette on the horizon, their jagged rims lining the nearly black sky. Sam thought he saw faces in them, reposing faces gazing upward into the darkness. Above, the stars shone down like spiders' eyes, watching him, watching Grant, watching Delta—watching with a cold, immortal malice.

*   *   *   *   *

A murmur from Grant broke Sam out of his hypnosis. He had been stumbling along, paying less and less attention to his surroundings. Now he was wide awake, fully alert.

"Look there, lad."

Sam turned and saw, across the plain, a tiny flame burning brightly, limning the underside of its own smoke with pale orange.

"Omicron's work," Sam said.

"Yes."

"Then that's where we have to go?"

"No." Delta spoke, her own voice soft. "We have come to the right place." Gently she jostled Madeline awake.

"Where and in what night are we?" Madeline turned her head from side to side in perplexity before she remembered where she was. "What miles? We have come to where? And what burns, so smokes? Put me down."

Delta deposited her gently onto the sandy desert floor. Madeline caught her balance and stood, slowly regaining her poise.

"Omicron is very near us," Delta said.

Sam felt the hairs at the back of his neck stirring. "How near?" His voice was but a whisper.

"That way—" Delta pointed, but Sam could not see her arm "—fifty yards."

"Yards!" Sam yelped, then clamped a hand over his mouth. *Oh, god, no . . .*

"She knows better than we," Grant said grimly. In the darkness, working by feel and by the memory of the mechanism, he twisted the lever that broke the gigantic hunting rifle at the breech. Surely, swiftly he inserted two massive rounds, then snapped the rifle together again.

"Does he know we're here?" Sam whispered.

"He knows," Delta answered.

"Sam?" Madeline came forward and took Sam's arm. "Back here. We are noncombatant people."

The soft rustling noises of the desert continued, then ceased. The darkness was unrelieved; the silence was absolute.

"He is here," Delta said, her voice sad and regretful. This was her purpose, when she would much rather have lived to discover a purpose of her own choice.

"What direction?" Grant asked.

Delta stepped forward and guided his arm.

"Grant!" Sam hissed. "Wait a minute! That gun! It'll tear your shoulder off if you shoot it!"

"Perhaps," Grant admitted. Then, in a louder voice, he bawled, "Stand to, Omicron, or taste three ounces of spinning lead!"

Delta added her command. "You have been found, Omicron. I am your end."

Sam saw what he had overlooked before—a faint glowing shape in the dark. It looked vaguely manlike, and it walked upright. It gained in definition as he stared at it.

"Delta?" In the darkness, Omicron's voice was deep, hollow, and malevolent.

"I warned him," Grant murmured, and pulled his trigger.

The snap of the hammer clapping against the firing pin was nearly as loud as the report of most normal caliber guns. There was, however, no detonation. Grant pulled the other trigger, and again the hammer fell with a loud, useless snap.

"Damn!"

"Grant!" Sam shouted. A wave of fury warred with

the helplessness he felt. "When did you load those cartridges?"

Grant's voice was level and even. "June . . . or perhaps July. Yes, July. July of the year of our Lord nineteen hundred and thirty-five."

"Nineteen thirty-five!" Sam fell to his knees. Gunpowder can be depended upon to lose its potency with time.

"A man can't think of everything," Grant muttered.

Omicron moved closer in the darkness.

Delta bounded forth to meet him.

CHAPTER TWENTY-ONE

"Down!" Grant snapped, his voice astonishingly crisp. It was a whipcrack of an order. Sam and Madeline obeyed instantly, diving for cover. The pair of older adventurers burrowed, splaying their legs and nestling their facedown heads behind their elbows. Sam had never eaten dirt before, had never hugged the earth to survive a bombardment, had never been strafed. War was an alien fancy to him, as foreign as fear or hunger or true despair.

He watched and was nearly blinded when Omicron erupted with flames. A vast circle of desert sand was thrown into harsh, flickering relief. Sam saw the small, twisted shadows of low-lying scrub. He saw the sand take on a subtle blue color, the shadow of Omicron's blazing red fire.

With the light came heat. Tears sprang into Sam's eyes, tears of pain. His face felt blasted by the scorching breath of oven heat. And still, not knowing to drop his face to the cool sand, he watched.

Delta shone like molten silver, burnished red in Omicron's red-orange fire. Barefoot, naked, unarmed, she sprinted forward to close with her foe.

Omicron lifted his hands, his gesture one of warding. To Sam, it looked almost pathetic, as if the monster were afraid.

Bright, narrow beams of terrible brilliance leaped from Omicron's hands. Twin swords, or two searchlight beams, they shone an arctic white. They glanced away from Delta's midsection, sparkling and scattering. Where they struck the desert floor, sand melted in little glowing pits of heat.

As quickly as the beams had sprung forth, they ceased. Darkness reclaimed the desert night. Sam blinked and groped in personal darkness, his night vision destroyed. He lifted himself up on hands and knees, starting to rise.

Omicron unleashed another field of deadly power. Sam saw the glow and fell heavily to the ground. This time the light was a soft, pink luminescence, but it grew more and more painful. Sam saw Delta silhouetted against it; he saw the light playing about her, reflecting from her, surrounding her. He narrowed his streaming eyes. The light hurt, in a way that ordinary brightness should not. He started up, then dropped down again when Grant and Madeline scrabbled, low on knees and elbows, across the scrub to join him cowering behind Delta, depending on her shadow for protection.

"I wonder if we're seeing the future of warfare," Grant said softly.

Sam's mouth opened in astonishment. It seemed so strange to him that the lights, blazing and fiery, were silent. So blinding, they should have been deafening. But Grant's voice came to him gently in the cool dark.

Madeline, beside Sam, reached out and took his hand. Her message, one of touch, was more reassuring, more personal. Sam squeezed back, taking strength from Madeline's gnarled, warm fingers. On his other side, he took a grip on Grant's jacket and held on for his life.

Delta, in the midst of a bitter, flaming glow, strode slowly forward. Omicron, his hands outstretched in a desperate attempt to hold her back, gave ground step by grudging step.

His onslaught increased. Now even Sam, who might have wished to watch, had to bury his face against his shoulder lest he become blinded by the scything lights.

Alone, coldly resolute, Delta moved toward her enemy. Her superhardened skin reflected away the lancing shafts with which Omicron tried hopelessly to smite her. The cold sand and empty sky drank his energies.

Delta reached out a silver hand and, for a moment, touched Omicron's palm with her fingers.

Omicron spun and, riding a pillar of smoking flame, blasted into the sky. His departure, unlike the combat before it, was stunningly loud. His flight started with a thunder, a roar that grew and peaked before it trailed away into the sky. Twigs and sticks and blowing sand whipped over the desert, then fell still.

Sam leaped up, watching Omicron arc off into the night. Then all illumination failed, and he groped in chill darkness.

Delta met him and took him by the hand. He pulled her to him and hugged her with a desperate, lonely grip.

Madeline hooked a flashlight out of her carryall and shone it around the small battlefield. All of the plant life was dead, the stiff, spiny desert plants soft and flat and melted into sticky gray-green spatters splashed over the sand.

"As if digested," she said, so softly that only Grant, by her side, heard. Kneeling gingerly, she plucked at a strand of dead weed. It came up covered with sand. It was dry, desiccated, like seaweed left too long on a beach.

Grant touched her arm, indicating Sam and Delta locked in a frightened embrace.

"She's a shield."

Madeline turned about to face Grant, shining her light downward so that she could see his face without him being dazzled by the beam. His deep-seamed face was more grim than usual in the indirect light; illuminated from below, he looked ultimately dire.

"*Non.* She is a friend."

"Yes. That's so."

"Still, it is that you are right; she is as a shield. So then what is needing is a sword," Madeline observed.

"I daresay." Grant preened his mustache with his free hand. "The three of us shall have to serve her in that capacity, wouldn't you say?"

"Save batteries," Madeline muttered and switched off the handflash. To Grant, it seemed ambiguously like an editorial comment.

*   *   *   *   *

The fight could not have failed to draw the army's attention. The lights had certainly been noticed. Grant led the team onward across the desert in a desperate night-time forced march. Delta carried Madeline in her arms, and her weight seemed to be no burden at all. Delta's footsteps were still irregular and awkward, but she bore up under the pain with a soldier's sturdy courage.

Sam wondered, while trying not to. He fought to drive the thoughts from his mind, but always they returned. What manner of being was Delta? He had thought her vulnerable, and yet that was the one quality she exhibited least. In his mind, he reviewed the attack upon her. She had advanced into the flames, resolutely driving Omicron back. He, as powerful as he was, had been afraid of her. Sam wondered if he, too, ought to be.

In the night, he heard her footfalls, brushing through the sand and crunching down on brittle plants. He thought of her metal skin and her hard metal arms; he thought of Madeline held in that bruising embrace.

*   *   *   *   *

Sheriff DeSoto found his three friends standing in the blue morning light, bunched up in a parking lot behind a liquor store. They were leaning back against a paint-faded pickup truck. DeSoto saw the rifles in the rear-window rack.

The town of Warm Springs didn't consist of much beyond the store and three or four other buildings. It wasn't much more than a wide spot in the road, but to DeSoto, it was an important place, and it stirred protective thoughts. Ramshorn had been as small, as exposed, and was now dead.

"Duncan." He smiled. "I haven't seen you in a while."

Duncan Cantrell smiled back, but DeSoto could see it was a tight, unhappy smile. He leaned forward, shifting his weight off the truck. "I've been around."

DeSoto accepted this. He nodded to the others. "Hank. Andy."

The others looked back at him, silently accepting his greeting.

"I'm glad you waited for me."

"Yeah." Duncan wasn't glad at all.

A space of uneasy silence followed. The three men arrayed against DeSoto stood in sullen repose, their boots on the gravel, their elbows back. Andy pulled a beer from a paper bag and flipped the cap off the bottle. There was insolence in the gesture, and yet he relented first. Deeply ingrained notions of hospitality came to the fore; he pulled out another brown-glass bottle and tossed it to DeSoto with a forced smile.

DeSoto caught it, twisted off the cap, and drank deeply.

"So. What's the story? You fellas really want to go trespassing on government land?"

"There's something in there, Sheriff." Duncan's voice was level. "We don't want to let it get away."

"Have you been listening to the news? That place is pretty active right now."

Andy leaned forward and gestured with a broad hand. "Best time for us, I'd say."

"I'm not going to stop you."

The three looked at him, already knowing full well that he wouldn't have.

DeSoto looked down. "I'd like to go with you."

The tension shifted. Duncan saw it instantly and the other two a moment later. Which of the two would be the leader? Duncan thought for a second. Did he want to refuse this man, this friend of his past? The idea passed.

"Sure. Get your stuff."

The others relaxed. It was clear now tht Duncan was in command. That was all that really mattered. DeSoto couldn't cause any trouble, and he knew quite a bit about tracking.

"I have something to say first." DeSoto looked at the men. "Is this really worth it?" He was speaking the unspeakable, and he knew it. He wanted revenge as much as the others did, maybe more. It was his duty, however, to uphold the law. "Is it worth the cost? Ramshorn . . . it was a tiny place. The folks there are dead."

Only DeSoto's strength of personality let him say that and keep any respect at all from the others. They knew how much the death of Ramshorn had hurt him, and they knew how hard he'd tried to recapture the silver-skinned killer.

"We're going in," Duncan said, his eyes cold. "Get your stuff."

"Sheriff?" It was Hank who spoke. "Duncan and me, we faced it on a mountaintop. I shot it—it or her. She's beautiful as a silver razor, Sheriff. I shot her. She got away." He looked down. "I want a second shot."

DeSoto cast a sharp glance at Duncan. He saw that the older man, like the younger, needed a second chance at the silver woman who'd shamed them.

"Okay. In we go."

* * * * *

The progress of the small party of men was much swifter than Grant's and Sam's had been. They were four strong men who knew the terrain and how to cross it. They made good time for six hours, paused for half an hour, then pressed on. No one complained; there wasn't much talk at all.

DeSoto got a good feel for their moods. Duncan was here for the best reason—because he felt he ought to be. It was a matter of pride and honor. Someone had hurt a lot of people he liked. Revenge was as natural to him as breathing. He'd always been a lonely, secluded man, and this kind of job called out to him. It wasn't personal; it was just mechanical.

Duncan, in his way, was a little like a robot himself. Hank was the force behind the mission. He wanted that robot in his sights. Shame drove him. DeSoto kept clear of him during the march.

And Andy—surly, sharp, and wise—he was here to cause trouble. He'd bring the robot's head home on a pole. He'd talk to reporters and end up incriminating all four of them. He'd also likely try to make some money on the deal.

And me. DeSoto looked at himself in his mirror of solitude. *What the hell do I want?*

He stamped his boots on the rocks as he went. He was here for nearly the same reason Hank was: He wanted a second chance. He wanted to know that it hadn't been his fault that the robot woman had gotten away. Hank wanted to rape her with his rifle. DeSoto merely wanted her dead.

Shortly before nightfall, they came up against a fence. It was the northern section of the same fence that Sam had cut through yesterday.

The four men stopped.

Duncan reached into his pack and pulled out a pair of fenceman's tools, a hammer-headed wire-cutter. The fence opened up before him. He ducked through. The others followed, DeSoto just behind Hank, just ahead of Andy.

They paused. Trespass was a serious crime where they came from. It gave them all an uncomfortable feeling to stand on the wrong side of anyone's fence.

DeSoto recovered first. "Well, let's get a move on. The fence was probably rigged with some kind of alarm."

He didn't say any more, but he didn't need to. They all knew they'd broken the law. He was a sheriff. He was with them, and he'd made himself responsible for them.

Duncan looked at him sidelong and shook his head. He moved his jaw back and forth, then spat. He should have expected it. Another day, another fence, and DeSoto would be leading this ride.

*   *   *   *   *

Omicron fled down the tunnels, looking about him, looking behind him. The caverns were strung out, one above the other, sloping down into the earth like over-sized pearls on a short string. Near the bottom, he found Busk.

Busk looked up to see Omicron rushing down toward him. He had only a moment to wonder if his time was up, when Omicron plunged to a halt.

"I am weakened. Delta comes."

Busk's facial expression was that of human annoyance. *So what?* he thought, tired and hungry and sick and unhappy. He forced himself to stir.

"We can stop it." He paused and looked puzzled. "What's Delta?"

"My enemy. My end."

Busk frowned. Omicron was whimpering like a baby. He set his teeth. That was fine with him. It made betraying and destroying the fiend that much easier.

"Your energy is depleted?"

"Yes."

"We'll have to restore it." Busk was tired, exhausted as he hadn't been since basic training. He was tired of serving this monster. He was tired of living in fear. It was time to start telling Omicron a new set of time-wasting lies. A sly, malicious grin stole over Busk's face. He'd been thinking of a joke for the past few hours and decided to implement it now. Why not? He was probably going to die anyway; why not do it with style? "We'll charge you up with *magical* energy." He looked at Omicron, his face serious. Any human would have been able to tell he was playacting. Omicron had never yet learned to see through his lies.

"What is magical energy?"

"The strongest of all powers." Busk stood. "It involves symbolic manipulation. And it's subtle. You might not feel anything, but be assured, your power will be incomparably great."

For the next six hours, he led Omicron through a series of inventive rituals. Omicron carved pentagrams into smoothed-over stone floors, ignited flames at the corners of the pentagram, repeated syllables of mock-Latin after Busk, and sought to find the spiritual center of himself through repetition of a mantra. Busk had impishly given Omicron the mantra, "Kiss my ass." It did him good to hear Omicron repeating this over and over again, in a deep, solemn voice.

Again and again, Omicron objected. "I feel no power."

"The power is metaphorical," Busk insisted. "It relates to similarities between perceived elements."

Fatigue and desperation had given him the daring to speak this way. For most of his life, he had held himself down, hiding away his intellect. On rare occasions, he could sucker a barracks mate into a game of chess. He played a deadly game of poker. But the army didn't want smarty-pants men who read or thought too much. He'd let his education slide to the back of his mind.

Today it came forward. He culled elements from real science, from mythology, and from anthropological studies of primitive beliefs about magic. He drew on the things he'd read in school, and he applied them. "Everything is related to everything else, you see. All things—people, places, ideas, everything—are linked to you by lines of magical force. This is the greatest of all powers."

For six hours, Omicron bought it. For six hours, he let Busk play with him, doing Busk's bidding, performing the peculiar and sometimes humiliating actions that Busk demanded.

Finally he rebelled. "I feel no power!"

"It can't be felt," Busk insisted. He was rather proud of the job he was doing as guru cult master. *Maybe I've got a new calling. . . .*

"I must have power that I can feel!"

Busk stood and faced Omicron. "You can have that if you wish. You can take one of your bombs deep into the lowest caverns and bathe yourself in light and heat." He stepped forward, closer to Omicron than he had ever voluntarily gone before.

"But if you do . . ." He took another step and was inwardly amused when Omicron stepped back. "If you do . . . you'll have thrown away any hope you have of achieving true mastery of the greatest of secret powers." He turned and walked away, then sat by one of the bright-burning oil fires that lit the cavern.

Omicron followed him and stopped just behind him. Busk tried not to flinch. For a long moment, neither of them moved. Busk's heart pounded, leaping frantically within his chest. Omicron was staring at the back of his head; he could feel it. Omicron had guessed; Omicron had realized that Busk was not his ally. . . .

"We will talk again," Omicron grated, his voice low and heavy and infinitely threatening. Then he turned and trod away, headed into the deepest recesses of the network of caverns.

Busk pulled out his belt radio and listened to Omicron's thoughts while a thin sheen of sweat evaporated from his forehead.

I must be strong, Omicron rumbled, gnawing over his never-ending need for power. *Delta comes. I must explode a warhead.*

Oh, hell, Busk thought. He lamented his waste of effort. He didn't know, and had no way of knowing, that the six hours he had delayed Omicron were in themselves a great victory. Omicron would be only partially recharged when Delta arrived, and he could not flee.

From deep below, a rumbling and grinding of great power resounded. Gigantic slabs of rock shivered and fell.

Power, Omicron thought as he fed upon the nuclear flame.

CHAPTER TWENTY-TWO

In the wardroom of the San Antonio police station, Detective Johnstone sat sipping noisily at his coffee. He hunched forward, both elbows on the small, square table. Few other officers were in the room this early in the morning. The room was brightly lit and rich with the scent of coffee and disinfectants. Johnstone tried to wake himself up, alternately sniffing at the aroma of his coffee and drinking small gulps of the scalding liquid.

Two civilian lawyers, appearing without warning, did nothing whatever to lighten the oppression of the bleary, painfully early hour. They strode in, the two of them abreast in an almost military formation. Johnstone looked up, disliking the men from the first instant.

They were tall, slim, dapper, stylish, dressed in sharply pressed business suits, carrying soft leather briefcases. One was clean-shaven; the other sported a small, crisp beard and mustache, which encircled his mouth, hiding that much of his expression. "Detective Johnstone?"

"Pronounced 'Johnson,' " he said and swirled his coffee in the cup. "Silent *t*."

The two men, uninvited, seated themselves at his table. "We represent Carlos Ascendio Cook," one said.

"And Cook Chemical Industries," amplified the other.

Johnstone, for no reason at all, decided that he liked the one with the beard and detested the clean-shaven one. He said nothing.

"You are familiar, are you not, with—" began the clean-shaven one.

Johnstone held up a hand, bluntly forestalling any further introductions. "One Cook Plaza, patrol route seven, private security company, no hazardous chemical violations on record, two off record, burglary two years ago . . . nice place."

The lawyers looked at each other, then back at Johnstone.

"Um, yes," responded the bearded one.

"What would you like?"

"The robot, Detective Johnstone. You are familiar—"

Johnstone gave the man a snort. "You've filed a contempt motion in Municipal Court?"

The bearded lawyer pulled a clipped-together file of papers from his briefcase. "Yes, sir."

"What's this?" Johnstone took the papers and flipped through them, paging one way and then the other.

"These are writs from Department Nineteen, Superior Court, mandating seizure of—"

Johnstone was almost enjoying interrupting the clean-

262   JEFFERSON P. SWYCAFFER

shaven lawyer. He made a mental resolve never to permit
the lad to complete a sentence. "Contempt citation?
Taramasco left town, so you get his robot? You could
have let the court clerk bring the papers over."

"We wanted to see you personally about this. When
can we expect you to obtain—"

"Haven't got her. Haven't any leads. You'll be the
first to know."

"Sir?"

Johnstone looked up at the bearded lawyer.

"Yeah?"

"Are you all right?"

Johnstone cracked a small smile. The man was honestly concerned. It was a refreshing sight to see someone
who gave more than a glance of pity at him in the morning.

"Try this." He pushed his cup of coffee under the
man's face.

Wrinkling his brow in a worried expression, the lawyer
sipped hesitantly at the coffee. "Good god!"

His beardless friend looked at him. "What?"

"It's . . . very strong."

"Six hours of sleep in the last fifty-eight." Johnstone
snapped up his wrist and peered at his watch. "Make
that sixty."

"We can come back—"

Johnstone interrupted him once more. "Sit. Robot's
gone. Legally she's yours. I'll find her, but I'll have to
keep her for a time, get some paperwork specifying public safety measures. Robot's yours, but I'll need assur-
ances. Now git."

The lawyers stood. The clean-shaven man looked back

with anger on his face, but his bearded companion shrugged and pulled him along.

Johnstone hadn't moved from his chair when, an hour later, Detective McStay came in. He looked around, then trudged over to Johnstone.

"You look like hell."

"Same to you."

"What the hell is it?"

"A little of this, some of the other." He looked at Mc-Stay. "Murder in Laurel Heights. Armed robbery in Prospect Hill. Rape . . . How many is that?"

"Three?"

"Try seven. Busy."

"Do you remember our robot?"

Johnstone maimed McStay with a look.

"Well," McStay plowed on, "have a look." He took out a newspaper, popped it open with a snap, and tossed it onto the table.

The headline read "Nevada Test Site Battle." Beneath it was a grainy photograph, clearly many times enlarged, of two figures in melodramatic stances. Flames leaped between them, lending the photograph a harsh, overexposed tone. One figure was dark and shadowy. The other was reflective, her femininity obvious, her silver skin hinted at by highlights. The photo credit read "Department of Defense."

"Some corporal with a telephoto lens took the picture last night," McStay explained. "Our robot and some other robot—man, monster, or who knows what—had a big flame-throwing tussle. Our gal, she chased the other off. Then she went away again."

Johnstone looked at McStay. "Proves something?"

"More. We got a phone call late yesterday. A guy saw the robot and three other people in a red open-top roadster, heading west. He saw them five days ago but didn't know that anybody was looking for them. He gave a full report in Flagstaff."

"All very interesting." Johnstone did not appear interested in the slightest.

"Here's the point. The army thinks that the attacks are by people in some sort of powered armor." McStay jabbed a finger at the newsprint columns. "They don't know that she's a robot."

"You phoned 'em?"

"Well, I've been trying. You know how the army is."

Johnstone had had enough of his drastically overlong day. "So tell it to the marines." He stood up so suddenly that his chair toppled. Draining the last of his supersaturated coffee, he looked at McStay. "Not our robot. Belongs to Carlos Ascendio Cook."

"Cook Chemical Industries?" McStay looked blank.

Johnstone left the wardroom and headed for his office. McStay shrugged and settled down to read the newspaper article.

*   *   *   *   *

Grant led the way over the rocks, pushing past thick stands of spiky desert plants. Sam followed him, his backpack chafing at his shoulders. In the rear, Delta carried Madeline with as gentle a touch as she could manage. They were all together, yet insulated from one another by the darkness of the moonless night.

"I am sorry to have uselessness on this shipment," Madeline muttered. "And I think maybe I could walk now awhile."

Delta set her down carefully. "Please lean on my arm."

"Thank you. *Merci.*"

"Omicron is far beneath us," Delta called ahead to Grant. "He is also four hundred yards behind us. Why are you leading us away from him?"

"Hm?" Grant, quite a distance ahead, stopped and waited for the others to catch up. "You say he's behind and below us?" His brow furrowed. "A mean place to be. I've set many an ambush, and I can tell you with some assurance, behind and below is the place to strike from."

"Why do we not turn and go to him?"

Grant chuckled in the darkness. "Delta, you know where he *is*. But can you tell me where he *was?*"

Delta's mouth opened, but she had nothing to say.

"I'm tracking him. I can read the signs . . . although it's fair to say that it would take a deliberate effort of will to miss them. He rushed through here like a rhinoceros, leaving footprints the size of lunar craters. I think we'll find the entrance to his subterranean hideaway. Perhaps soon."

Sometime before dawn, Grant halted them again. Sam believed that he could barely see a brightening on the eastern horizon, but he wasn't sure.

"Did you feel that?" Grant demanded.

"What?" Sam asked uselessly.

"Yes," Delta said.

"Was no earthquake." Madeline summed it up. "Underground nuclear fusion head, bomb buried. Omicron is make tunnel?" She thought for a moment. "But to make so little a temblor, must be very, very deep."

"He is nearly nine hundred yards below us," Delta reported.

"Let's move on, then."

Following Omicron's path, Grant soon found the entrance to the underground system of chambers. The fissure gaped ominously in the early morning light. It was not the entranceway that the army had used in their assault but was instead one of Omicron's hidden exits.

"Here's our way in."

"Down there?" Sam didn't like the looks of it, not at all.

"I can climb," Madeline insisted. "Better than I can walk, I can climb." She smiled proudly. "I can use hands when climb."

"Very well," Grant muttered. "Let's get to it, then." He pulled the giant rifle across his back and held it ready. "Down we go." Slowly he descended into the cavern.

Sam, close behind him, held a flashlight, aiming the light carefully forward past Grant to illuminate the older man's way. "I hope you reloaded your cartridges," he muttered.

"I saw to that while we walked, lad. I try never to make the same mistake twice."

"There is never a shortage of new mistakes for making," Madeline piped up, her voice more cheerful than usual.

Delta, following the others into the cave, said nothing. She wished that her final battle could have been fought on the surface of the earth, where the beauty of the land could comfort her. She wished that she could see the stars again.

I am following another, she reminded herself and dropped lithely into the darkness.

* * * * *

Sheriff DeSoto was trying not to push the men. He did his best to tone down his natural assertiveness, but his enthusiasm got the better of him. He hadn't intended to become leader of the four-man group, but soon, by simple force of personality, he found himself in command. The task was simply more important to him than it was to the others. He wanted the silver-skinned robot put away. He wanted her dead.

Duncan, Andy, and he were all equally at home in the high mountains. Each of them could have managed well enough in wooded hills or rolling grasslands. The dry, rocky ranges of Nevada were troublesome. Hank, having spent some time in the northern half of Arizona, got along best with the terrain. He led them on, guiding them past deep, dry gullies and through the easiest passes in the razorback ridges. But Hank was the youngest of the men and the least likely to take a position of command. He looked to his cousin, Duncan, to make the decisions for the team.

Andy, loose of discipline and morally lazy, didn't much care for orders and didn't much care who led. Duncan wasn't driven by motives as strong as DeSoto's. DeSoto called the shots.

They hid from the army patrols. They maneuvered through the cold badlands, doing their best to keep out of sight. In their first day and night, they covered nearly thirty miles. The next night, they went another twenty.

Shortly before dawn, Hank thought he felt an earthquake, but none of the others noticed. In the first predawn light of morning, they finally caught up with Delta.

Hank saw her first, far out across one high, wide valley. Far below, to the east, was the Adobe Flats test range, a vast sand-covered dry lake bed, pockmarked with the dimples of old underground nuclear tests. Ahead, just crossing a ridge and coming down into view, Hank saw a tiny glinting figure.

He hushed the others and made them drop to the ground. DeSoto squirmed up beside Hank and peered through narrowed eyes.

They were three miles away, perhaps a little less. DeSoto wished he had binoculars, then grinned. Binoculars never did anything for a man but make him dependent on them. They were like a scope on a rifle; they gave a man too much confidence. What mattered more was the skill to get in close.

"C'mon." He darted out into the rocks and clay of the jagged hills. New energy surged through him. The others scurried to keep up.

Half an hour later, they stopped again. They spent several long minutes looking carefully out over the distance, waiting to be sure of what they saw.

"Three of 'em . . . the robot and two guys."

"The robot's carrying something. A third guy, looks like."

"Hold the chatter." DeSoto scowled. Squinting carefully, he looked for a long, long time. "Duncan, what do you see?"

"I see the robot, a little guy, a big guy, and the guy the

robot's carrying."

"Andy?"

"I can't see that far."

DeSoto grimaced. He reminded himself afresh not to depend on Andy for anything. "Hank?"

"I guess the same as Duncan says."

"Okay." DeSoto stood and marched on. "That's three of us."

He followed an interception course that would give them cover until they were within perhaps a quarter-mile of the party of men and the robot. The others followed him, yawning occasionally in the growing light. Duncan paused once to check his rifle. Then, slinging it over his back again, he hurried to catch up. DeSoto never took notice.

Hour by hour they crept closer. They were faster than the robot and her party, but they didn't want to risk being seen. They kept low, behind rocks, and closed the distance gradually. After three hours of careful stalking, they were ready to spring their ambush. Duncan pushed his forehead over a sharp rise, then ducked down again. He scrambled carefully down over the rocks and joined the others. "All four of them. Right below us."

"Let's do it," DeSoto murmured.

The four men climbed back up over the rocks and stood up, their rifles aimed.

No one was below them. The rocky gully was empty! The four men ducked back down, suddenly afraid that they'd walked into a trap themselves, but nothing happened. There was no hail, no challenge, and certainly no sound of gunshots. Slowly, with exaggerated caution, they crept forward again. They split up, spreading out, trying to spot their quarry anew.

Hank, with the sharpest eyes, was the first one to see where the robot and its companions had gone. He nearly shouted, then gulped and waved for the others to come to him. When DeSoto came up beside Hank, he could only stand and point.

"Where did they go?" DeSoto asked, his voice more puzzled than angry.

"There's a cave . . ." Hank looked up at the others and swallowed. "There's a cave there, and their footprints drop right down into it."

The four men looked at each other.

"Cave?"

They looked back at the rough, craggy landscape. A dark fissure was barely visible, a thin crevice leading down into the earth.

CHAPTER TWENTY-THREE

Grant insisted on staying in the lead, waving his handflash about to illuminate the twisted walls of the tunnel. Beneath his boots, the footing was rough but not difficult to traverse. Delta and Madeline came next. Sam, unhappy in the darkness, found himself in the rear. His friends were only a tangle of silhouettes ahead of him, below him, bobbing along in the path of the wavering blob of light that was the flashlight beam.

So . . . we go to war. Sam shrugged his shoulders, feeling the weight of his equipment pack. He had very little in the way of weapons. Instead, he had packed some electronic gear, a laptop computer, a bagful of random components. He sighed to himself, shuffling down into the deep recesses of the earth behind his friends. *The most deadly weapon I have is a soldering iron.*

Madeline, as fatigued as she was, kept up with Grant's lead. Delta, by her side, steadied her when she stumbled. There was a dogged determination in Madeline's insistent pace.

Equally determined was Delta. Her foe had stopped, at last, and stood to fight. She was aware of him now more than ever. She felt his position, almost as if she could reach out with her hands and touch him. She felt his power; she felt his hunger, now temporarily sated. She felt his fear and his rage.

"Eight hundred yards below us," she whispered to Grant. "Ahead and to the right."

"Very well," Grant responded tersely. A hint of humor remained in his voice, however. "This tunnel may turn right or left as it chooses, but it had best continue down."

Delta didn't understand. "Why?"

"The terrain above us slopes down also. The surface is only thirty feet or so above us."

"You took such accurate bearings?" Madeline asked, sporting with Grant.

"Well, yes . . . I tried to." Grant's harrumph of wounded dignity was a secret admission of optimism. As long as he and Madeline could work together, what foe could withstand them?

They walked down the trail, paying little attention to the sharp-shorn edges of the rock that had been gouged away to make the tunnel. Grant remarked on it once. "The beast leaves an undressed tunnel. It reminds me of the tunnel we drove through Mount Kandrishari during the drought of 'forty-nine. The Old Kraut, Colonel Schwarngerner, made us smooth the stone with fine chisels, working in the path of the drilling team. We took him for a repressed sculptor. You could have slid down that tunnel, slipping the length of it on skates. Now, that's how a tunnel ought to be driven."

Sam, in the rear, listening to Grant's reminiscences, smiled. His smile deepened when Madeline, as always, took the pride away from Grant's accomplishment.

"These was tunnel to relieve drought, bring water from lake to plain, yes?"

"Yes," Grant said, his voice a bit strained.

"Was same lake, this, as dried up month after tunnel, he was finish?"

"Ahem. Yes." Grant was silent for a time. "We'd made the channel a bit too wide, you see, and the lake was more shallow than we had anticipated."

Sam, following along, shook his head. Grant's misadventures in India, were they all true, would go a long way to explaining the loss of British prestige in the years following the war.

Absorbed as he was in the muttered dialogue ahead, he failed to notice the soft sounds of the men who followed.

*   *   *   *   *

They arrived in the first chamber and saw the burning pools of oil. The cave, a bubble of air inside the solid stone, was floored with a tumble of large rocks. A streak of soot darkened one wall, above the burning oil. A stack of oil drums against another wall explained the source of the flames. Grant picked his way unsteadily over the rough floor until he stood in the cavern's center.

More slowly, Madeline, Delta, and Sam moved to join him.

Sam hunched close to Madeline, partly out of fear.

The red, flickering light of the open flame reflected off the reddish rock. Shadows, high overhead, which might have been bats lairing, seemed to twitch.

Even Delta's voice was hushed. "Omicron is still beneath us, five hundred yards down and that direction." She pointed a bright silver arm ahead and to the right.

"I think I see a tunnel mouth," Grant muttered. He moved ahead, working his way from rock to rock. The others followed, loath to leave the light but buoyed along by Grant's energy. He, at least, was not afraid of the dark. Sam, again in the rear, wondered what Grant was, in fact, afraid of.

The next cavern reeked. Sam had no idea what could cause such a blatant, foul odor. Grant and Madeline, from long experience, recognized it as the stench of a slaughterhouse. It took Grant only a moment to spot the bones, skin, entrails, and other leavings of a butchered horse.

"Someone," he said, his voice carrying a powerful disdain, "hasn't the slightest idea of how properly to dismember a horse."

Madeline and Delta looked also, with various degrees of disinterest. "*Oui*, has ripped up, ripped down. Knife work of the impecunious."

" 'Impecunious'?" Grant asked, turning to Madeline and placing his hands on his hips.

Madeline returned his gaze without guile. "Is not word? Means extravagant wastrel, improvident, and profligate."

"Well, it doesn't mean quite that. . . ." Grant rubbed his jaw.

Sam, in an agony of nausea and agitation, lacked the

initiative even to interrupt their banter. Ordinarily he would have been comforted by their byplay, but today, in this deep, red-flaming tunnel of hell, he wanted only to get out, to get away.

Before long, Grant turned away and paced on again. Another tunnel led on to the next cavern and the next.

Down they went, through the nightmare realm that Omicron had carved from the stone. Delta read off the soundings. Omicron was three hundred yards below them, then two hundred, then one hundred.

At times the tortuous path widened, and the four could walk abreast. At times it narrowed, and fear of being buried alive tightened Sam's chest. These catacombs seemed a totally appropriate place to be buried.

Horror came shortly after the thought. Grant pushed ahead around a bend in the tunnel, followed by the others. All halted. The bones and bodies here were human, and there were several of them.

Sam choked and looked away. Grant and Madeline moved ahead to get a closer look. Delta paused, then joined Sam.

The bodies had been soldiers, killed in various ways. Grant recognized the gas masks that some of the men had been wearing. Slowly, reflectively, he picked up an abandoned rifle and manipulated the action.

Delta laid a hand across Sam's quaking shoulder. He looked up at her, his face tear-slicked.

"Sam?"

He turned to her and grabbed her, hugging her with a strength born of misery and terror. "I don't want to be here!" he sobbed.

She held him tightly, having no words with which to

comfort him. She held him in a strong, protective embrace. Little by little his fear left him, until the two of them held each other in a hug of warmth and love, like brother and sister more than like mother and son. Sam's heart swelled. He loved her. How could anyone not?

At last he stood back and wiped his face on his shirt. "I'm okay now." He looked around and saw Grant and Madeline. The two, aware of the intimate moment shared by their friends, were pretending to study the corpses rather than intrude by staring. Their voices were low, their expressions neutral. It was as if they had spent their whole lives surrounded by the strewn bodies of dead men.

Sam shuddered and forced a brave smile to bolster his courage. Grant and Madeline *had* spent their lives among the dead; two great wars and numerous small ones had formed their characters. Grant was a man of war, and Madeline was a soldier as much as a scholar.

"Well, let's go," Sam muttered.

Grant took up the lead once more and guided the team onward.

*   *   *   *   *

They hadn't gone very far before Delta, always aware of Omicron's location, halted Grant with a quick touch on his shoulder.

"He comes," she whispered.

Grant nodded and ducked behind her, giving her the priority of her quest as well as acknowledging the primacy of her power. Tossing the flash to Madeline, he slid the massive rifle from his back and flopped roughly to the sloping stone tunnel.

Madeline shooed Sam back. Together they ducked behind a corner of the twisting path and crouched low. Madeline held the light steady to give Grant enough illumination to aim by.

"Twenty yards," Delta said. Two or three seconds passed by. Sam, in a sudden hurry, ducked back, shucked his backpack, and flipped it open. His electronic equipment had once detected Omicron's signal. Now perhaps he could learn something new about the enemy. He snapped parts together in frantic haste.

Omicron appeared, lumbering up the steep slope, climbing with long, untiring paces.

"Halt, foe!" Delta called out suddenly. She stood forward to meet him.

Omicron braced himself and lifted both arms, his wrists bent, his palms facing up the tunnel. A tight, sharply focused beam of blinding light glanced out, a spear of blazing energy, a razor's edge of blue-white energy. It struck Delta in the breast and bounced away, sparkling in a dozen subtle shades of refracted blue. Where the points of light struck the tunnel walls, rock smoked and glowed.

Then Grant was allowed his say. The concussion that rocked the tunnel was like nothing any of the humans present had ever heard before. The sound had a physical impact, a shock that staggered Delta, knocked Madeline to her knees, and whipped Sam's face around like a sudden slap. The tunnel magnified the explosion. Madeline, who had been bombarded at close range by the large howitzers of the First World War, had never heard such a noise; Grant, who had worked alongside the large cannons at the siege of Singapore, was reminded afresh of what a truly loud noise can do.

He had, in his bravado, discharged both barrels of the .750 Nitro Express rifle at the same time. He paid for this indiscretion.

Grant's shoulder was dislocated, wrenched back and around. His clavicle was shattered, broken into eight small pieces. His shoulder blade had been wrenched aside as the impact shot completely through him. Two ribs had been snapped, but had not separated. The rifle, which he had held low, had been wrenched up, nearly climbing out of his hands with the recoil.

Omicron fared better. The massive lead slugs spun away into the dark, ricocheting away from where they had impacted against his shoulder and forehead. He had been knocked back, very slightly, by the sheer momentum of the bullets, but he was not damaged.

Grant lay where the shock had thrown him. Delta regained her footing, and took a menacing step toward Omicron. Omicron, still unable to destroy his pursuer and tormenter, turned and fled once more.

No one moved for a time, until everyone had had time to look about and see who was still left standing. All of the party was thoroughly deafened, save only Delta. She watched Madeline bend down to tend to Grant's injuries; she watched Sam shaking his head in stunned grogginess; she saw Grant gritting his teeth in pain and in self-chastisement.

Omicron had not been injured. Delta knew where he had gone—down, deeper into the trap he had dug for himself. But there seemed less and less purpose to her pursuit of him.

Perhaps he was like she was, incapable of being injured. That left her with an odd feeling of dismay, until she thought of her own injured foot. She paused, trying to reason it out. She had been damaged in the swiftwater stream in the high mountains. She hadn't known how to harden her surface, how to armor herself. In that weakness and ignorance, she'd been hurt. Perhaps Omicron had a weakness also.

She stood a moment longer, then bent to help Madeline. It seemed odd to her that everyone spoke at once, and yet no one listened.

*   *   *   *   *

The shock reached other ears. Duncan Cantrell stood in the chamber of dead soldiers, looking down in numb shock. Sheriff DeSoto paced ahead, as if more eager than ever to reach the deadly silver robot who could wreak such destruction. Hank Cantrell looked away, focusing on the walls, trying to maintain his sanity. Andy Welty was talking, as he often did, saying something unimportant, something meaningless.

They heard the roar of the gun. Each of the men leaped to his feet.

The sound peaked, then died away. Spread out in the tunnel, echoing in the cavern, the sound could have been one shot, two, or a dozen. There was no way to tell. The men stood in frozen, shocked attitudes.

"Hell," Andy said at last, after the sound had died away completely.

"Dynamite?" Hank wondered aloud.

"I don't think so," Duncan said. He lifted his rifle,

then let it down again.

DeSoto said nothing. Instead, he walked forward, toward the tunnel mouth from which the sound had come rushing. His eyes were narrowed, but his stance was straight.

"Well, come along, men. Let's . . ." He stopped and grinned, showing his teeth in a mirthless smile that none of the others saw. He had been about to say, "Let's get to the bottom of this," when suddenly he'd realized that these pits might have no end. He considered his circumstances and wanted to laugh. A sheriff, he'd broken more laws than most of the petty criminals he'd ever had to deal with. A lawman, he was circumventing the law in favor of independent enforcement. What was most amusing to him, however, was that he, a nominally sane man, stood now in a fiery pit, following a silvery robot on a mission of vengeance.

"Well?" he said over his shoulder. "You coming or not?"

Reluctantly the others fell in behind him.

*   *   *   *   *

Deep below, in a cavern lit, like the others, by burning oil, Private Busk waited, hunched up near the flame, not quite asleep, not quite awake. Startled to full awareness by the rolling thunderclap of the gunshot, he pushed himself to his feet to wait for whatever horror Omicron would bring him next.

The horror was nothing new. Omicron had been attacked and had repulsed the onslaught. Busk looked at his approaching captor and wondered how many soldiers had died this time. Omicron seemed unaffected at first. Then, as he neared, Busk saw the fear that possessed the strange creature's mind. It wasn't in his expression. Omicron's face had never been expressive. It showed in little hints in his stance, in his movements, which were, as always, stiff and ungentle, but which now signaled fear.

"She comes," Omicron said, his voice echoing, as always, through Busk's radio.

"Who?" Busk asked, his voice quiet.

"My enemy."

Your enemy? Then the time comes for me to betray you. Strangely, however, Busk's hatred for the creature was mixed with a softer emotion. It was pity, perhaps, mingled with an ironic admiration for Omicron's strength and determination. *If only he had come peacefully, mankind might have given him an honest, if suspicious, welcome. And,* Busk thought sourly, *if Omicron had come and openly declared himself an enemy, instead of sneaking around belowground, he might have come closer to success.*

He might yet succeed. Busk was resolved to stop that from happening.

"Okay, we've got to prepare. Are you hurt?"

Omicron looked at him without expression. Busk held his radio to his ear to hear Omicron's thoughts.

Busk speaks of my hurt. I could show him how it feels.

Busk looked at Omicron's slightly bent, slightly weary stance and shivered. He was alarmed for yet another reason, however: For the first time, Omicron had reasoned in the *hypothetical case.* The monstrous brute had learned the secret of thinking an action over before undertaking it. He was also thinking about punishing his human servant.

"Well, never mind that," Busk went on airily, masking his worry. "We'll—"

Omicron stepped forward and pushed past Busk. "I will defeat my enemy. I will defeat Delta."

Busk pushed his luck. "Just who is this Delta?"

Omicron went on down into his tunnels without another word. Busk, however, was secretly amused. Omicron had gone down into the blind-end tunnel, where he had spent his time when he was healing. He suspected Busk, but he still did what he had been told.

* * * * *

Once everything had been relatively settled for some time, Sam went back to his electronics equipment to try to make some sense of what his instruments had recorded. He was glad he'd brought along a pocket oscilloscope with memory; he was glad he'd known, in advance, that Omicron broadcast a strange but regular pulse on a known spot in the middle of the AM band of the radio spectrum.

He'd learned something. The jagged trace on the scope showed several unexpected peaks. Two were sharp, with rapid attack and rapid decay. Others were less crisp but lasted longer.

They had something to do with Omicron's defenses, Sam knew. The two sharp peaks came at the time when Grant's bullets had bounced off the monster. They seemed to be associated with the hardening of Omicron's skin.

Sam had seen something of how Delta worked in the

past few days since first sighting her in San Antonio. He'd seen how she could turn her skin crisp, hard, and frictionless. Omicron, it seemed, could do the same thing. When he did, it was marked by the emission of a specific radio signal.

Sam was still quite deaf and assumed that all the others were, too. Besides, his findings were surely too preliminary to be shared. He began to think, however, of how the effect might be harnessed. . . .

CHAPTER TWENTY-FOUR

Madeline fixed Grant's shoulder up in a tight sling, with his ribs bandaged snugly with strips of cloth ripped from his shirt. She worked on him by the light of the handflash, which Delta held for her. Grant's bare chest, with its grizzled mat of white hair, was still that of a strong man, with a deep, proud swell. Grant had gone quite pale from the shock of his injuries, and yet his natural stamina lent him enough strength to sit up, propped against the rough wall of the tunnel.

Sam watched as he and Madeline argued, evidently disagreeing over how best to proceed. Sam couldn't hear a word they said and doubted that either of them could hear the other.

Their argument had one subject: Should Grant continue, or should he back away from the advance down the tunnel? Grant, thumping his chest and braying, sought to demonstrate his health. Madeline, canting her head sardonically to one side and waving her hands in lurid Gallic gestures, ridiculed the idea.

Delta hadn't been deafened, but that was of scant benefit to the group. Sam knew that, deafened or not, she would never permit Omicron to sneak up on them. She knew where he was; in fact, she could never *not* know, she'd told her friends. Sam wondered what kind of a feeling it would give him to know, every minute of every hour of every day, exactly where his worst enemy was.

No one, however, gave any thought to an attack from behind.

*   *   *   *   *

Hank Cantrell was in the lead when he heard voices. He paused and signaled DeSoto to extinguish the flashlight. The four men trooped ahead single file in the sudden darkness.

Before long, they spied the faint glow of reflected light from the tunnel ahead. Hank grew wary and paced ahead more slowly, more delicately. Now each of the four men could see the glimmer of faint light, ahead and below.

There was no way to alter the marching order. DeSoto instructed Hank to proceed cautiously. Hank skulked forward as silently as he could go, his hunting rifle held loosely in his hand. The others strung out in single file behind him, walking slowly, careful not to make any sudden noise.

The voices grew louder as the men approached. There was an argument going on, a strange thing to hear in

such a solemn locale. A woman used fiery words to exco-
riate the foolishness of a man, who, without paying any
attention to what she said, shouted back at her, insisting
on his fitness to travel and to fight.

Hank wondered what it could mean. He stalked on,
moving silently. Approaching the bend around from
which the light came, he took one step too far and knew
it immediately. He had meant to stop just out of sight
and peer around the corner, but his downward momentum in the steeply falling tunnel, even walking slowly,
carried him a bit past the turn, so that his body and his
rifle showed in the lit section of the tunnel.

Swearing, he stepped out around the corner, raised his
rifle, shot the bolt, and stood, his heart pounding, scanning the situation.

He saw an old man, bandages wrapped about his bare
chest, sitting against the stone wall of the tunnel. An old
woman waved her arms at him, reviling him vocifer-
ously. A young man sat on the floor, occasionally glancing down the tunnel at the others but expending most of
his energy on some sort of electronic gear strewn on the
rough tunnel floor.

And the silver robot, the thing that called itself Delta,
the murderer of the eleven men and women of Ramshorn, stood just beyond the three, facing up the tunnel.
She couldn't fail to see Hank. Hank whipped up his rifle
and fired two quick shots into her midsection.

DeSoto pushed up from behind then, his own rifle at
the ready. Duncan and Andy filled the corridor, with
room to aim although no room to pass.

Hank's first shot knocked Delta down. Delta was able
to effect the now-familiar change in her metal surface

before the second shot hit her; that bullet slid over her superhardened skin and sang a high, buzzing note as it ricocheted away down the tunnel.

Grant lunged for his own rifle, then stopped. It was empty, and the four hard-eyed men had the drop on him.

Sam scrambled quickly to his feet, a wild look of rage on his young face. He leaped forward, then stopped when Duncan shifted his aim directly at him. Sam was young and inexperienced, but he knew from one look at Duncan that the man would kill him if he took another step.

The youngest of the four men, the one who had fired the two shots, spoke. Sam shook his head and grimaced. The shots had been barely audible, but his abused ears were still almost totally deafened from the earlier explosions.

Madeline came up to the front of the small, steeply sloping chamber, brushing her hands on her dress. She held up her hands to the newcomers and spoke in a loud voice, as people will when they cannot hear. "Don't shoot any more guns! You have impaled the wrong foe."

DeSoto looked at Duncan, who gestured for him to do the talking. DeSoto crowded past Hank, who held his rifle trained on the fallen, still figure of the silver robot. Sam backed away and joined Grant in looking at Delta.

"Who are you people, ma'am?"

Madeline held a hand to her ear in an unmistakable gesture.

"Who are you people?" DeSoto bellowed, stepping forward and shouting directly into her ear.

"Am Madeline Schenk, of Corey Museum. You have

done wrong thing."

"What wrong thing have I done?" DeSoto shouted.

"Have shoot wrong robot." Madeline's simple answer, coming in a voice much too loud, set DeSoto back a step.

He raised his voice. "Wrong robot?"

"Delta is not Omicron. Is self-evident, *non?*"

While the four men pondered this, Grant and Sam helped Delta rise to her feet. The first bullet had torn a hole in her side, below her breast, where a human's ribs would be. She had been a second late increasing the hardness of her skin. Below the surface, within the bent-back metal, Sam saw a tightly packed cluster of shining silver bands, crossing at sharp angles. It looked a little like the string wrapping inside a baseball, or the lattice-work of a wicker basket. The bands slid, the interstices expanding and contracting, as Delta moved. There was a smooth, mechanical beauty to the arrangement. Sam gazed in rapt fascination at Delta's inner works, at these complex, sliding bands that substituted in her for human muscles and ligaments. He almost reached out to touch it, then drew his hand back. It would have been rude . . . and the bands looked razor sharp.

"Are you . . . okay?" he asked, consciously struggling to keep his voice down to a normal volume.

Delta smiled, her face as blank as ever, and nodded her head.

Grant, moving slowly because of his injuries, turned to face the four men, regarding them with a fierce expression. "Scoundrels!" he snorted, his mustache bristling. He lumbered up the slope, ignoring their guns. "Rogues! You call yourselves Americans?"

Hank fell back a bit from the old man's rage. Andy re

sponded wrathfully, "Damn right we're Americans!"

Grant stopped, cupped his hand to his ear, and said in an utterly ludicrous fashion, "Repeat, please?" The sudden loss of dignity made him human, comic. None of the four men could see him as a threat any longer. Even Duncan relaxed.

Slowly, over the next half an hour, their stories were told. Delta did most of her own explaining, being the only member of her party who still had her full sense of hearing. Interjections from Sam, Grant, and especially Madeline didn't seem to help much, coming most often as interruptions on digressive topics.

Sheriff DeSoto finally lowered himself to the tunnel floor and sat in a relaxed, almost comfortable posture. He shook his head in amazement and chagrin. One by one, the other members of his party slumped down as well.

"I have never killed any human or any living thing," Delta concluded softly.

"It was your enemy who destroyed the town of Ramshorn, then?" DeSoto looked at Delta. "Why?"

"I don't think he knew what he was doing." She smiled, an effect that DeSoto found to be quite eerie. "I understood very little of your world when I first met you. I had no way of knowing that you were not my enemy." She turned her head away. "You tried to contain me, and I dared not permit it."

"Contain you?"

"Imprison me. You tried to close me within a room that had no exit."

"My jail cell . . ." DeSoto nodded. "I should have guessed that was what set you off."

"I was following another. I still am."

"Tell me about the enemy."

Delta explained everything to Sheriff DeSoto as Hank listened avidly, his eyes wide. Duncan and Andy listened with more suspicion, but they allowed Delta to have her say. She made sense. Even Andy, supercilious and sly, couldn't object. The television news of the havoc wrought by the unknown invader didn't fit well with a party of three people and one shining robot sneaking through these tunnels.

"So what do we do about it?" Andy wanted to know.

Delta answered him, turning her faceless face to him and speaking softly. "Omicron is one hundred yards below us, still ahead of us but very near. We must go to him."

The united troupe moved off, the hard men from Wyoming and Colorado in the lead with their hunting rifles held at the ready, then Delta, then Sam, with Madeline and Grant assisting one another at the very rear.

Sam, juggling his electronic equipment in his hands, tried to make sense of the radio-spectrum readings he'd taken. Omicron leaked radio waves on a dozen different frequencies. But he'd already found the most interesting emission signature. He tinkered with components, assembling them awkwardly as he walked. He thought he had an idea of how to utilize this information.

*   *   *   *   *

Omicron sat, squatting low, in his dead-end tunnel. So many other of Busk's bits of advice to him had been faulty, and yet it never occurred to him that he should question this one as well. He hunkered low, resting his palms on the stone, kneading the rock with his fingers.

Busk watched him for several minutes, then stood and, moving with as much nonchalance as he could muster, strode off into the caverns. He knew that now was his best opportunity to escape. He wanted more than anything to dash off up the tunnels, to achieve freedom up on the desert floor. But he had one more vital mission to accomplish.

He went down farther, into the deepest pit of Omicron's hell. He knew how radioactive it had to be down there. He wouldn't delude himself; what he was doing was suicide. He rigged a strip of his torn-up undershirt over his mouth and nose to filter the air. He hoped that would keep the worst of the radioactive dust from lodging in his lungs. And since the deepest caverns were totally dark, he blindfolded himself to force him to keep his eyes closed. That might make a difference. Or it might not.

The walls of the tunnel were cool. Omicron's last nuclear-fire bath had been twenty hours ago. The pit where the detonation had actually taken place, deeper below, would still be furnace hot, glowing with an orange ovenlike glow. Busk had only one hope.

The air was only slightly warm when he stumbled onto the niche where Omicron had stored his arsenal. Busk had kept a careful count of the number of warheads coming in, and he knew exactly how many had been detonated. There were five left. In this small hollow, a rounded and smoothed cup within the rock, he found them all.

They were still within their casings, roughly pyramidical, half a man's height, and quite heavy. It took most of Busk's strength to lift one. Lifting two would be impossible.

Destroying them was difficult. Busk's only weapons were shards and flakes of stone. He set to his work with a will, smiling inwardly at the irony. The human race's oldest weapons were enough to defeat its newest ones. He cracked open the cases, working blind, feeling his way through the internal structures of the warheads. He cracked the firing triggers; he ripped up the bundles of wires; he banged on the metal structures within, battering the delicate mechanisms into lumps of useless metal and plastic.

He wondered, after a time, if he had ever touched bare plutonium with his hands. He wondered how much radioactivity he had exposed himself to, both the ambient radiation from the tunnels and caverns and the intense local exposure from breaking open a bomb.

Finally he had to admit that he could do no more. The bombs were denied to Omicron.

Busk started up the tunnel. It was still dark, still cramped, when he heard Omicron coming down to meet him.

He tore off his blindfold and breathing mask. He wanted to look as normal as possible to Omicron, who could see perfectly well in the darkness. He walked onward, feigning normalcy.

He stopped when Omicron stopped. The two faced one another in the unlighted tunnel.

"I was measuring your tunnels," Busk said, his voice tight with emotions he was unable to hide.

"Why?"

"Because I wanted to know, and because curiosity is a kind of power."

Omicron remained silent.

Busk, mustering all of his stubborn courage, closed with Omicron and pushed past him. He was afraid for a minute that the monster would halt him, but after a moment's hesitation, Omicron stepped quietly to one side and allowed Busk to pass.

Busk walked on steadily. Omicron was not following him. As soon as he reached the first lighted cavern, Busk whipped up his radio and listened. He picked up his pace, jogging up the next tunnel.

My power! Omicron's thoughts came through finally, unmistakable anguish in his voice. *What has Busk done to my power?*

Busk started to run.

He heard two sounds then, both of which spurred him to even greater speed. Behind him, deep in the lowest caverns, he heard Omicron roaring, a howl of icy rage that echoed horribly from the radio. The second noise was the soft chatter of humans engaged in debate, coming from ahead of him in the upward-sloping tunnel.

Soon he saw their light; soon he saw them.

Four men with rifles, obviously not army rangers but cattlemen, ranchers, with hunting rifles. Behind them was a young man, short, his hair long, his posture sloppy. In the rear were two old people, a man and a woman.

But in their midst, a gleaming silver woman came, a robot as totally unlike Omicron as the desert sky was unlike these cramped tunnels.

Busk had no way of knowing who they were or how they had gotten here. He could see one thing instantly, and it was all he needed to know. These were people, and they were no friends of Omicron.

They saw him as soon as he saw them, but he was the first to speak. "He's in the lowest cavern. I've sabotaged his nuclear weapons." His breath husked; it was hard to speak. "He's—he's hurt, but he's mad."

"Who are you?" asked the man in the lead, a tall red-bearded and mustached man with hard eyes.

"Private First Class Edward Busk." Busk smiled wearily. "I recommend retreat, sir. Fast."

"We've got to finish him off!" said the man directly behind him. Busk had respect for the determination on these men's faces. He could even see that they didn't like him, because he was a soldier with a serial number and they were individuals. He shrugged and moved aside to let them pass.

"He's down there," he called after them as they moved along, descending the steep tunnel. Busk paused and looked closely at the silver robot as she walked by. He saw the way she limped, favoring her right foot. He saw the gaping wound in her torso. He looked at her smooth, blank face and her humanlike mouth.

Perhaps these were Omicron's final nemeses. He turned about and joined the cavalcade, walking beside the young man, who reminded him a bit of himself, in his days before enlisting in the army.

Impulsively he held out his hand. "I'm Buster Busk. Who're you?"

After a brief pause, the other took his hand and gripped it. "Sam Taramasco. This is Delta."

"You're here to destroy the enemy?"

"Yes." Sam shook his head. "I'm not completely sure

why, though."

Delta turned around and spoke gently. "Because he is our foe and we must defeat him."

"Good enough reason for me," Busk said and began to tell these people everything he knew.

CHAPTER TWENTY-FIVE

Sam Taramasco and Edward "Buster" Busk hit it off well from the start. Busk explained the way Omicron's thoughts were broadcast over his radio.

Together they listened to Omicron's rage. *Human power must die. Busk must die.*

Sam, hearing the cold, inhuman voice for the first time, shuddered, and the hairs at the back of his neck bristled.

"He's not exactly happy, is he?"

"No." Busk shook his head. "He isn't happy at all."

"He puts out a lot of radio noise; that's how we knew where to find him."

"Eh?" Busk asked. "You traced him with a radio direction-finder?"

"Sort of." Sam explained how Delta was sensitive to the constant signal emanating from Omicron, the high-pitched chirruping sound in the AM spectrum.

"How is it we can hear what he thinks?"

"Band spreading explains some of it," Sam said, excited by the idea. "Military radios listen in on wide spreads of frequencies. I've already narrowed down two of his signals: his constant signature, and this one. . . ." As they walked, Sam pulled out radio components and plugged them together in peculiar ways. He showed Busk the trace on the oscilloscope and the marks indicating what had happened when Grant's bullets had impacted the robot.

"What does it mean, do you think?" Busk wondered.

"I don't know . . ." Sam sighed. "We know he leaks a lot of radio noise, though, and we know what he thinks. We should be able to use that somehow, right?"

Madeline, who had been listening with half an ear, came forward to talk to the two young men. "You hear his thoughts?"

"Yes, ma'am."

"Can you talk to him?"

"Over the radio?" Busk had never tried that.

"Let's give it a shot," Sam said cheerfully and reached for the radio.

"Wait a minute, please," Busk muttered. "I've lived with this guy for two weeks . . . or maybe it's been longer. I'm not sure it's such a good idea to provoke him."

"Phoo!" Madeline dismissed his worries effortlessly. "We are here to fight him, *non?* Grant has placed bullets along him, hurt him perhaps. You destroy his bomb heads, escape. He is already provoke. We merely kill him."

Busk looked at her sidelong. The woman was clearly

insane. But after two weeks or more in Omicron's captivity, Busk had to admit himself less than wholly sane. "Go ahead, then." He handed the radio over to Sam.

"Omicron?" Sam pushed the send button several times. "Omicron?"

Who calls me? The voice was harsh and raw.

Sam looked at Busk in surprised joy. Busk, more familiar with the monster's evil rages, only shuddered.

"He comes," Delta said then, her voice soft. "He will be here in only a minute."

At that, Duncan turned about to look at the others, who lagged behind. "What's this? What the hell have you done?" He stamped back up the tunnel and slapped the radio out of Sam's hands, like a man knocking a toy away from a naughty child. "Damn fool stunt, that was!"

This was too much for Grant. Bandaged, sore, and more tired than he remembered being since his days of war, he swaggered down the tunnel to face Duncan.

"You would be well advised to show some respect for the lad, Mister Cantrell." He spoke too loudly, still partially deafened from discharging his gun. "Sam Taramasco has proven himself in my eyes, and to date, you have not."

Duncan looked at him in amazement. "Get off it, grampaw." He started to turn around in disgust, but Grant caught him by the elbow.

DeSoto, Hank, and Andy all started to move to join what looked like a fray in the making, then stopped.

Grant, injured, nearly twice Duncan's age, had stopped the younger man cold. Grant's fingers bit into Duncan's elbow. The two men stared at each other, the emotions of each man clearly visible as they moved across his face. Grant was not backing down. Duncan gave ground, losing one step, and then another. Then Grant bore down with more strength. Duncan winced and dropped to one knee.

"Save it for real enemy!" Madeline chastised, her own voice also too loud. "Omicron flows up the tunnel, and you fight yourselves!" She tossed her head artfully, revealing for a moment the coquette in her that age had never completely driven away. "Men will be boys . . . a fine thing for them to be. La, and I admire you all. But aim your rifles elsewards. A monster, a black bear, is about to appear."

"She's right," DeSoto said, and his voice carried a ring of authority.

Grant released his grip, then reversed his hand and offered to help Duncan to his feet. Duncan accepted the boost.

"How'd you do that, anyway?"

Grant's eyes twinkled. "Got you in a nerve pinch. Learned that in Mandalay, where I worked for a time with a team of Burmese ninja."

Duncan blinked. It was too peculiar, too *foreign*, for his tastes. He joined the others in the first rank. Grant stood beside him, readying his rifle. Andy, nearby, watched, wide-eyed with amazement, as he saw Grant's extraordinary preparations.

* * * * *

Sam and Busk, bringing up the back of the parade, murmured together softly. "You see Grant's rifle?" Sam asked, with a shrug of his shoulders.

"It's huge!" Busk glanced back at it. "Sixty caliber?"

"Seven-fifty."

"Brutal!" The phrase, condemnatory on its face, was more reverent than disapproving.

"But the rounds bounced right off Omicron."

"Remember," Busk pointed out logically, "he's sat in the center of thirty-seven kiloton test blasts. That's some armor."

Sam couldn't help but disagree. "Look, Delta has armor, too, but only sometimes. She has to harden her surface. When she doesn't do that, bullets just cut into her. I think Omicron works the same way." He and Busk looked once more at the oscilloscope traces and thought about how they related to the impact of the bullets. Busk thought about it a bit longer. "You want to try to jam his works?"

"Yes," Sam said and began fishing out electronics parts. Busk, happy to have something to contribute, helped with the subassemblies. The parts flew together and apart again, recombining in their fingers.

It didn't take them long to put together a transmitter, with its power boosted, designed to interfere with the exact frequencies that accompanied Omicron's invulnerability.

*   *   *   *   *

"He is here," Delta said finally as they neared the very end of Omicron's dead-end tunnel. She sprinted forward, jumped lithely past the four men, and stood, proud and final, guarding the blind passageway.

"Madeline," Grant said, his voice unusually deep, "would you please hold the flashlight for us?"

With that last word of gentility began the third battle of the tunnel.

Omicron came on in a rush, an angry, headlong charge unlike his previous probe. The four men in the front began to pour fire into him, working their hunting rifles swiftly and with deadly accuracy. The slugs merely bounced off the onrushing foe; the men could see their bullets scattering.

Then Sam and Busk decided to trigger their makeshift jammer.

The sound of the bullets striking against Omicron's skin changed noticeably; it was now a deeper, flatter noise, sounding like pebbles thrown hard into soft mud. Small wounds appeared over Omicron's front, tiny black spots, compact and neat.

He was shocked to a jarring halt some ten yards beneath where Delta stood. He looked like a man trying to walk into a strong, rain-laden wind; the continuous sleet of bullets blasted at him, chipping bits of him away, driving into him, damaging him. Finally he stopped struggling, unable to continue uphill.

That was when Delta stepped down the slope to meet him.

Omicron unleashed his deadly beams at her: rays of heat, which she threw off; narrow cutting beams of sharp light, which she reflected; hammering, jarring pulses of energy, which had no effect whatsoever upon her.

Some of the attacks got past her. DeSoto fell, knocked senseless by a ray that grazed his forehead. Busk darted forward to try to extinguish the small flame that burned in the man's hair. He beat at it more and more frantically, gritting his teeth when it wouldn't go out. DeSoto's flesh itself was burning. Busk smothered the small, hot flame with DeSoto's hat, until the hat itself began to smolder.

Hank Cantrell was blown backward by a concussive blast. He scrambled back to his feet, only to be knocked down again. This time it took him some time to regain his footing. His cousin, Duncan, had better luck. Delta had shielded him from the effects of the attack. He, too, was out of the fight for a moment, however. His rifle was empty. With cold, careful precision, he levered shells into the loading slot.

Andy, having emptied his rifle also, simply switched to his revolver and kept up the fire. He didn't seem to be aware of the soft, liquid, jellylike mass that was all that was left of his left leg below the knee. One of Omicron's protein-dissolving rays had struck him. He reloaded his pistol in four quick motions and continued to fire.

Delta continued to advance.

Omicron stood his ground until Delta was within two yards of him. Then slowly he began to give ground.

Behind the others, Sam ripped open Busk's radio, pulled out the batteries, and dumped all the power of his oscilloscope's storage power cells through the broadcast circuit. He was lost in concentration as he watched the circuits begin to smoke from the overload he was shoving through the system.

Grant Alexander, determined to get his own licks in, moved forward, past the two wounded men and the others who were still firing. He couldn't hear a lot. The rattle of four 30.06 rifles in the narrow tunnel had deafened him again. He hefted his .750 Express and aimed it, holding it low in his left hand.

Omicron saw him and gaped, his mouth horribly, impossibly wide in a soundless scream. Grant couldn't hear the monster's words, but reading his lips, it seemed to him as if he were saying, "You fool! You fool!"

Grant smiled. "This fool has had time to reload," he said softly.

He detonated both barrels. The concussion was indescribable, a jarring, roaring impact that could be felt like a fist to the midsection. The rifle's barrels split open, flinging hot fragments of sharp steel through the air. Grant's left arm was whipped backward and up, and the rifle stock was torn from his hand, breaking three of his fingers and several bones in his wrist.

Grant had opened up the shells while the two parties had joined into one and had packed the cartridges with extra powder. One massive slug missed Omicron entirely, slicing into the bare rock and causing an avalanche of stone to fall, half-choking the tunnel. The second hit Omicron and tore his leg off, shearing it away between knee and hip.

Delta took a final step forward and grasped Omicron's wrists in her hands.

Silence descended upon the tunnel—true silence, which the deafened people could feel if not hear. There was little to see. Between the clouds of dust the battle had kicked up and the pall of smoke from Grant's blown-open gun, visibility was severely limited.

Slowly the living humans in the corridor began to stir. Madeline shoved her flashlight into Hank's hands and pushed unsteadily to the aid of Andy, who was only beginning to understand what had happened to his leg. His mouth opened wide, and it was a mercy that no one could hear his scream. Madeline wrestled him down. He would have fought her, but she made it clear, with a gesture, that any more hysteria from him would bring a stinging slap from her. He subsided, and she began the grisly work of amputating his melted leg.

Sam joined Busk in smothering the stubborn fire that burned on DeSoto's temple. Both Sam and Busk knew that the heat, transferred through the man's skull, was doing irreparable harm to his brain, but they also knew that the damage was localized. If they could get the fire out, the man would live.

Grant, with both hands now immobilized, shook his head in amazement and staggered back to the wall, where he slumped down to a seated position. He figured he'd earned the right to a bit of a rest.

Duncan made his way forward, his feet unsteady, and looked at Delta.

Delta stood immobile, in a firm stance, her feet spread wide. She held each of Omicron's wrists in a tight, unbreakable grip. She was braced against his struggles. As Duncan watched, Omicron lunged, trying to escape from her grasp, Delta never moved, not so much as a millimeter.

"Delta?" Duncan said, his voice awkward because of his deafness.

Delta made no response.

Duncan went back to the others and did what he could to help.

It looked to Duncan as if the war were over and the good guys had won. There were injuries, though; there were always injuries. Omicron was contained at last, however. Delta had won.

* * * * *

A long, surprisingly peaceful hour passed in the tunnel. Andy lapsed into merciful unconsciousness and lay still. DeSoto rested less easily, now and then thrashing about in his sleep. Madeline stayed with the two injured men, nursing them as best as she could. The two men could not be carried; the transport would be far more hazardous to them than the wait. Hank, the strongest and fastest of the men still unhurt, set off up the slope to fetch an army medical team.

One by one, the rest of the party who were able went forward down the slope to see Delta, who stood motionless, holding Omicron captive. The two stood at the termination of the dead-end tunnel, in the very place that Omicron had thought would be his sanctuary. Busk, coming down to have a look, shied back when Omicron made an effort to free himself, but stayed to watch. Omicron, for all his strength, could not budge Delta. She stood, a statue now, unmoving and unmovable. Omicron continued to struggle in silence.

Sam came up to stand beside Busk. He looked at the scene and was astonished. Just as Grant had forced Duncan to his knees, so Delta had subdued Omicron.

He touched her. He had never felt her skin before when it was hardened, totally frictionless. It was like touching oil-slicked metal, although it felt like no metal he'd ever handled before. He reached for her arm and blinked as his hand slid away.

"Oh, my god . . ." Sam cried.

"She's got him," Busk said, astonished.

"But he's got her, too!" Sam looked at Busk, then back at Delta and Omicron. "Don't you see? She can't let go of him!"

"Wait . . ."

Sam would not wait. He put his arms around Delta and pulled, but his hands merely slipped free. His strength was not enough to move her.

"Delta!" he shouted.

Very slowly, very patiently, Delta turned her head toward him. He looked in vain for some sign of expression on her blank face.

"Delta . . ."

"I have contained my enemy." Her voice was neutral; she was resigned. "Now I wait."

"Wait?" Sam tried to touch her again and watched in frustration as his hand slid from her metal. He stepped back slowly. "Wait for what?"

"For the ages to pass. For the light to go out, the tunnel to fall in, the earth to bury us."

"No!" Sam ran to her and buried his head under her arm. She was impossible to hold, almost impossible to grip. He hugged her nevertheless. "No! You can't mean that. You've defeated him. You're free now!"

She smiled then, a thin, unhappy smile. "No. I have never been free." Her mouth stiffened. "Go now. I will never move nor speak again."

Busk stood back, then turned and joined the others, leaving Sam to weep in privacy. The former captive explained to the others what Delta had done and how she was doomed to her eternal guardianship of Omicron.

Grant and Madeline looked at one another, mutual understanding and resolve in their eyes.

"It isn't over yet, lad." Grant stood and gestured helplessly with his elbows. Madeline's bandages left him without the use of either hand. "It isn't over quite yet."

"An idea has captured Grant," Madeline sighed. "There is no escape for any of us."

CHAPTER TWENTY-SIX

Duncan and Madeline worked to Grant's directions. Soon Sam, the tears still pooling in his eyes, rejoined the others and began to work apathetically on the project Grant supervised.

First Madeline reached into Grant's trousers and pulled out the long Khyber knife he kept hidden, strapped against one leg.

"Your hammer, would you please?" she asked Duncan. He brought out his hammer-headed fenceman's tool and held it out for her.

"Oh, *non*," Madeline said cheerfully. "You are the best to know the workings of your own tool."

"I suppose," Duncan said. He didn't quite know what she was up to, but he felt reassured a little. It was good to be able to hear again, good to be with someone who at least thought she knew what to do.

"Sam?" Grant nudged the youth with his boot. "Can

you and Private Busk get that electronic counterforce operating once more? I saw you use it to good effect during the skirmish."

"Yes, sir." Sam, sharing a bemused expression with Busk, reset the circuitry. He didn't quite understand what was about to happen; a deep soul weariness hung over him.

Madeline felt expertly with her thumb at the edge of the long blade. To Duncan, it looked more like a small machete than a personal knife. He watched sharply, not quite suspiciously.

"She'll never come back," Sam said softly. Busk went to stand by him. "She's lost. The continents will crack, the land heave up, the desert will rise . . . and she'll still be here. The engines of the earth will claim her at last." He looked at Busk, then looked away. "I . . . I think I loved her."

Busk looked at the floor.

"I don't think it's going to happen that way," Duncan said softly. He looked at Madeline. "Ma'am, with all due respect, mightn't it be a bit better if I do the work with that knife?"

"*Oui*, you are too kind." Madeline passed the knife, hilt forward, to Duncan. He lifted it, admiring its heft and balance.

He glanced at Busk. Busk, after a moment of surprise, nodded. Duncan handed Busk the fenceman's tool.

The two men stepped forward and began cutting Omicron apart.

Omicron struggled and fought, but Busk and Duncan didn't pay him the least heed. With Sam electronically circumventing his defenses, Omicron was helpless to resist. The rancher and the soldier bent back the deep, stiff layers of Omicron's flesh. They kept at it, exposing the dark, gristly matter that formed Omicron's interior. From the gaping, ghastly wounds, a dark, tarry liquid began to seep, steaming as it met the air. In half an hour, Duncan had off half the top of Omicron's head, from the crown to below the ear on one side, cutting through the resilient workings of his face near his eye. From this incision, also, a thick black gel dripped slowly, a hot, strong-odored exudation.

Once Omicron shrieked, a vast, soulless sound, as one might expect from a machine that was being dismembered. He also continued, fruitlessly, to struggle in Delta's unfeeling grip.

Headless, he continued to struggle. Lacking both legs, he struggled. Taken completely into parts, fragmented, an Osiris in pieces, he struggled.

Soon Delta held only two wrists, short sections of arm that connected to no forearms, no hands. Omicron's inner workings were exposed, a system of sliding gray metal plates and bands lubricated with the pungent black fluid. No central control unit was evident, nor were any storage packs for the power he had once wielded.

"Delta?" Grant said. He came closer. "Delta? Your frozen pose lends grace to the tunnels in which we are entombed. Come forth, and let blaze upon us the light of your agility."

Everyone looked at him, stunned by his use of poetry. Madeline made a face, a little expression of purse-lipped disdain. Duncan swallowed. Sam and Busk blinked.

Delta turned her head.

"Grant." She looked beyond him. "Sam?"

"Delta?"

Slowly she straightened. "I . . . I had resigned myself to eternity." Her mouth twitched, then a smile blossomed. "Where is my duty? Where is my charge?"

"You mean Omicron?"

"Yes." She looked about, clearly failing to recognize her foe in the stack of limbs and body parts strewn about the room. "Where is he?"

"You can't sense him anymore?" Sam was astonished.

"No." Delta tilted her head and sought Omicron's signal, using the odd sense that had always linked her to her quarry. "He is no more."

"Oh, Grant," Sam sobbed, hugging the old man roughly. Then he took Delta in his arms. "Oh, Delta."

A lovers' embrace may, to the lovers, seem to be eternal. But Sam pulled back, gazed raptly at Delta, then leaned forward again and kissed her.

*   *   *   *   *

Not long thereafter, an army medical squad arrived, along with several platoons of heavily armed infantrymen. There was nothing left to fight. The soldiers stared at the ruins, then took over from Madeline, giving the wounded men the best care they could arrange on the spot. They carried the men out on stretchers—even Grant, who would have preferred to walk. Slowly the group returned to the surface.

It was night, and the hostile stars glittered across the sky.

EPILOGUE

The army accepted the story told them by the strange assortment of adventurers who came out of the ground. No charges were filed. PFC Edward "Buster" Busk was given a constellation of awards, as well as immediate hospitalization for severe radiation poisoning.

Sheriff DeSoto recovered from his injuries, although he bore a large wrinkled red scar on his temple for the rest of his life. Andy Welty grew used to having only one leg. He and Busk would look at each other when they were in the hospital together, the one with scars from bone marrow transplants and weak from chemotherapy, the other lacking a limb, and each swore that he was happier with his own injuries.

In San Antonio, Sam was served with a writ demanding the surrender of Delta to Carlos Ascendio Cook, who claimed legal title to the robot.

"Carlos Cook is a god-damned, good-for-nothing,

low-down, two-bit horse's ass," Sam responded on the courthouse steps.

Grant and Madeline looked sorrowfully at the lad.

The court awarded Delta her freedom, which she accepted, choosing to stay with Sam.

The court also awarded Carlos Ascendio Cook another hundred thousand dollars in damages stemming from Sam's public slander.

FANTASY ADVENTURE

EMPIRES TRILOGY

HORSELORDS
David Cook

Between the western Realms and Kara-Tur lies a vast, unexplored domain. The "civilized" people of the Realms have given little notice to these nomadic barbarians. Now, a mighty leader has united these wild horsemen into an army powerful enough to challenge the world. First, they turn to Kara-Tur. Available in May.

DRAGONWALL
Troy Denning

The barbarian horsemen have breached the Dragonwall and now threaten the oriental lands of Kara-Tur. Shou Lung's only hope lies with a general descended from the barbarians, and whose wife must fight the imperial court if her husband is to retain his command. Available in August.

CRUSADE
James Lowder

The barbarian army has turned its sights on the western Realms. Only King Azoun has the strength to forge an army to challenge the horsemen. But Azoun had not reckoned that the price of saving the west might be the life of his beloved daughter. Available in January 1991.

FORGOTTEN REALMS
FANTASY ADVENTURE

THE MAZTICA TRILOGY
Douglas Niles

IRONHELM

A slave girl learns of a great destiny laid upon her by the gods themselves. And across the sea, a legion of skilled mercenaries sails west to discover a land of primitive savagery mixed with high culture. Under the banner of their vigilant god the legion claims these lands for itself. And only as Erix sees her land invaded is her destiny revealed. Available in April.

VIPERHAND

The God of War feasts upon chaos while the desperate lovers, Erix and Halloran, strive to escape the waves of catastrophe sweeping Maztica. Each is forced into a choice of historical proportion and deeply personal emotion. The destruction of the fabulously wealthy continent of Maztica looms on the horizon. Available in October.

COMING IN EARLY 1991!
FEATHERED DRAGON
The conclusion!

DragonLance Saga

PRELUDES II

RIVERWIND, THE PLAINSMAN
Paul B. Thompson & Tonya R. Carter

To prove himself worthy of Goldmoon, Riverwind is sent on an impossible quest: Find evidence of the true gods. With an eccentric soothsayer Riverwind falls down a magical shaft--and alights in a world of slavery and rebellion. Available in March 1990.

FLINT, THE KING
Mary Kirchoff & Douglas Niles

Flint returns to his boyhood village and finds it a boomtown. He learns that the prosperity comes from a false alliance and is pushed to his death. Saved by gully dwarves and made their reluctant monarch, Flint unites them as his only chance to stop the agents of the Dark Queen. Available in July 1990.

TANIS, THE SHADOW YEARS
Barbara Siegel & Scott Siegel

Tanis Half-Elven once disappeared in the mountains near Solace. He returned changed, ennobled--and with a secret. Tanis becomes a traveler in a dying mage's memory, journeying into the past to fight a battle against time itself. Available in November 1990.

DragonLance® Saga

HEROES II TRILOGY

KAZ, THE MINOTAUR
Richard A. Knaak

Sequel to *The Legend of Huma*. Stalked by enemies after Huma's death, Kaz hears rumors of evil incidents. When he warns the Knights of Solamnia, he is plunged into a nightmare of magic, danger, and *deja vu*. Available June 1990.

THE GATES OF THORBARDIN
Dan Parkinson

Beneath Skullcap is a path to the gates of Thorbardin, and the magical helm of Grallen. The finder of Grallen's helm will be rewarded by a united Thorbardin, but he will also open the realm to new horror. Available September 1990.

GALEN BEKNIGHTED
Michael Williams

Sequel to *Weasel's Luck*. Galen Pathwarden is still out to save his own skin. But when his brother vanishes, Galen foresakes his better judgment and embarks on a quest that leads into a conspiracy of darkness, and to the end of his courage. Available December 1990.

FANTASY ADVENTURE

1990 Novels by
R. A. Salvatore

THE HALFLING'S GEM
Icewind Dale Trilogy: Book Three

Assassin Artemis Entreri whisks Regis south to Calimport and into Pasha Pook's vengeful hands. If Pook can control the magical panther Guenhwyvar, Regis will die in a real game of cat-and-mouse. Available February 1990.

NEW SERIES!

HOMELAND
Dark Elf Trilogy: Book One

Exotic Menzoberranzan is the vast city of the dark elf, where families battle families. Possessing honor beyond his unprincipled kinsmen, young Drizzt asks himself: Can I live in an honorless society? Available September 1990.

EXILE
Dark Elf Trilogy: Book Two

Exiled from Menzoberranzan, Drizzt must live among races normally at war with his kind. And all the while, the hero must look over his shoulder--his people are not a forgiving race. Available December 1990.

Dark Horse

Mary H. Herbert

After her entire clan is massacred, a young woman assumes her brother's identity and joins her uncle's tribe as a warrior--all to exact revenge upon the chieftain who ordered her family slain.

But the chieftain, Lord Medb, has resurrected the forbidden art of sorcery and plans to destroy all who oppose him in this dark ages fantasy world.

With the help of an intelligent, magical horse, the young warrior-woman goes against tradition and law to learn sorcery, all in the hope of thwarting Medb's evil plans of conquest.

Mary Herbert has studied medieval literature and history at the University of Montana, the University of Wyoming, and the Center for Medieval and Renaissance Studies in Oxford, England.

B·O·O·K·S

**Available in
February 1990.**